RULEBREAKER

RULEBREAKER

Kat Bastion
with Stone Bastion

Cover Design by ©Sarah Hansen, Okay Creations
Image provided by Love N. Books
Photographer: Made by MK
Model: Jase Dean
Interior Book Design by:

E.M.
TIPPETTS
BOOK DESIGNS
emtippettsbookdesigns.com

First Printing, November 2016
ISBN-13: 978-0998232904
ISBN-10: 0998232904

Racial Tensions Flare as Hot as the Passion in
RULE BREAKER, a Modern-day Romeo and Juliet Story

Leilani Kealoha wants to be set free. Of family expectations. Of generations of prejudice.

Chafing at rules made by the proud Hawaiian men in her family, she yearns to discover herself and hungers to explore the world. Her adventuresome heart? Longs for something even greater, deeper.

The last thing she expects is an East Coast *haole* surfer to hold the key to everything.

Mason Price is done walking his parents' path. Done with social acceptance—with cold politics.

On a surfing quest to reinvent himself, Mase finds an exotic beauty standing on his towel. But it's her feisty bargaining that catches him off guard. When he challenges her with a "Truth or Shots" drinking game, she unwittingly reveals more than she'd intended about herself…and him.

The raw truth stuns him: She's suffered like he has, is lost like he is—keeps secrets like he does.

But will young love and shared situations be enough to conquer racial and cultural divides?

Lines in the sand…were meant to be crossed.

Praise for
HEARTBREAKER

"This book has definitely earned its five stars and I am just floored right now. The passion is explosive, the story itself is beautiful, and the emotions are so real my heart is ready to burst. Beautiful book. Absolutely breathtaking."

~ One Page at a Time

"Heartrending, passionate, and captivating! *Heartbreaker* is a riveting page-turner that will leave you breathless with raw emotions, and the need to hold tight to the ones you love!"

~ Beneath the Covers Blog

"This book is all about flawless writing, exemplary storytelling, f*#king insane character development. The right does of sexy hotness..."

~ Love N. Books

"The Bastions are at it again with this beautiful and heartbreaking story. You will absolutely fall in love with Kiki and Darren's love."

~ Under the Covers Book Blog

"Heartbreaker is a phenomenal story."

~ *That's What I'm Talking About*

"I loved it...wonderfully compelling, a story that touched my heart in so many ways and characters I will remember for a long time to come."

~ *Girl Who Reads*

Praise for the
NO WEDDINGS SERIES

"One of the best romantic comedies of the year!"

~ *Agents of Romance*

"The No Weddings series is one of the best I have read that follows one couple. Cade and Hannah are both lovable characters, the storyline is real and entertaining, and the banter is fun and witty."

~ *Lives & Breathes Book Blog*

"I loved it, and I mean REALLY loved it!"

~ *Orchard Book Club*

"This is an exceptional series...You find yourself fully engrossed in their world and can't put the book down."

~ *Books -n- Kisses*

"The No Weddings series has a group of such amazing characters; you can't help but relate to them and feel the emotion in every situation they encounter. It has been a long time since a story has made me feel that way let alone an entire series!"

"The story of Cade & Hannah's relationship is realistic, heart-warming, and filled with real-world connections that shook me in a way that few titles I've read this year have managed...I have loved every minute of the No Weddings series."

OTHER BOOKS BY

Kat Bastion
with Stone Bastion

Standalone Novel
The Espionage Effect

Unbreakable Series
Heartbreaker
Rule Breaker
Lawbreaker
(future release)

No Weddings Series
No Weddings
One Funeral
Two Bar Mitzvahs
Three Christmases
For Valentine's
(a steamy nightcap novella)

BOOKS BY
Kat Bastion

Highland Legends Series
Forged in Dreams and Magick
Bound by Wish and Mistletoe
Born of Mist and Legend
(future release)
Found in Flame and Moonlight
(future release)

Romantic Poetry for Charity
Utterly Loved
Foreword by Sylvain Reynard

To the human race…
May we find peace with one another.

We wish everyone aloha.

1
TRUE NATURE

Mase...

The wave can kill...or save.

  Its staggering force humbled—kicked my ass often.

  But when I pointed toward the curling crest, shot up from its thundering energy, then caught perfect air...the rest of the world faded.

  Breath.

  Pulse.

  Wind.

  Spray.

  Gravity...ruler of all.

  I dropped in on a one-eighty spin. Tail skimmed down the face of the wave. The collapsing barrel roared with fury behind me. And through a salty cloud of mist, I glided out, riding the exhilarating power of nature.

But once I hit sand, the peace I'd sought ended. A lone girl stood by my gear.

I heaved out a sigh and tucked my board under my arm, preparing to face yet another one.

"Are you Mason Price?"

"Mase." I dropped my board, then grabbed my towel. Had to tug the corner out from under her bare foot.

"Mase, for sure." She gave a nod.

Pretty thing, but then they all were. Want to bait the fish? Need a tempting lure.

"I'm Leilani Kealo—"

"*I'm* not interested," I grumped. My stomach growled; even my body hated her intrusion.

Her expression darkened. "You don't even know what I want."

"Not interested in a sponsorship." I did my best to ignore her exotic beauty and enticing curves when I uttered the rest with a poker face, "Not interested in a beach-bunny fuck."

Her eyes narrowed, gaze locked to mine. Unlike all the others, she didn't notice my body. They'd always swept hungry gazes over me like I was a mouthwatering cut of steak. But not her.

"*I'm* not interested in *either*."

I snorted. "On an isolated beach that took me days to find, on a tiny island in the middle of the South Pacific, you show up with your very *Hawaiian* sounding name" —I arched my brows on a questioning pause— "standing by my stuff. What do you want, then?"

Fists clenching tight, she rose to her full height—all five-foot-nothing of her—pulled back her slim shoulders, and lifted her chin. "*Not* a *damn* thing."

She scowled then stormed off in a huff.

I grinned, entertained by the drama.

But a frown pulled at my mouth as I watched her.

She plucked a stubbed-antenna satellite phone from a front pocket of her short flowery dress and crossed the single-lane dirt road. A horn blared from the one moving car on the roadway as she stepped in front of its bumper without looking up. Hand still on her phone, she held the other up and gave a slight apologetic headshake to the driver. After jogging out of harm's way, she stopped a short distance down an alley beside the only restaurant on our windward side of the island, then dropped her head, talking into the phone.

Curious, I grabbed my gear and followed.

"…don't know why. Yeah, probably every other idiot after a money grab. No, I know that's not what we're—" She paused, as if cut off. "I'm here aren't I? N'kay, fine. I will. *I will try.* Yeah, Makani, 'ohana. I know. How can I forget? You keep reminding me."

"Trouble in paradise?"

"Gotta go," she murmured into the phone before dropping it back into her pocket.

Coffee-brown eyes pegged me with a penetrating gaze. On a slow breath, her expression softened and she gave me an assessing once-over. "Could we—"

"Look I was—" I ran a hand through my hair.

"—start over? I didn't mean to stomp off…"

"—rude back there…" We paused, processing what we'd

3

said while talking over each other.

She let out a defeated sigh. "Could I buy you lunch?"

"Now *that* I'm interested in." I leaned my board against the faded red wall beside the door.

When I gestured an arm ahead for her to take the lead, she paused in the doorway and stared at my beat-up surfboard. "Not windsurfing?"

"Not always." *Obviously.*

"But you do windsurf…competitively?"

"Plan to."

Also obvious? Her line of questioning. It smacked of sponsorship.

I held up two fingers to my man Rico behind the bar and he nodded. By the time I glanced back, she'd already grabbed a table by the window, one apparently she'd claimed before; green sandals hung from a corner of her wood chair, and a Tommy Bahama beach bag slumped on another chair nearest the cement wall, right under a framed and signed black-and-white picture of surfing icon Kelly Slater.

"But…" The furrow between her brows deepened. "I thought you won two competitions."

"Did you see them?" Didn't deny it, but wanted to know how devoted she was to her cause.

"No, but—"

My stomach growled again. Matched my mood. "What do you want to eat?"

"What do you recommend?" She cut a glance toward the menu-board over the bar.

Rico slid two beers between us, then dropped an

appraising look at her before arching a brow at me while he answered her question, "Fish tacos."

"Done." I gave a short nod. "Five. I'm starved."

She spread a paper napkin over her lap with an outward sweep of her hands. "Two, please."

Please. The proper way she said the word struck a chord. So did the poised manner in which she held herself and the way she'd schooled her expression after the phone call. Her overall demeanor, including how she controlled her breaths and her practiced smile, pinged an alert with me—an undercurrent rumbled beneath her carefully polished surface.

Impressed with the flair in which she hid her true nature, I crossed my arms and leaned back in my chair. I studied her with an unwavering stare.

"Why are you here?" Direct. I was all about getting to the bottom of her mission.

"Your sailboard."

I blinked. "My equipment brought you here?"

"And my brother." Almost imperceptibly, she let her perfect posture slump on a short sigh.

"Your brother." The word flattened with my growing confusion.

"Makani." She gave a nod, as if his name explained everything. After taking a healthy swallow of her beer, she stared at the amber bottle for several long seconds.

Then the most amazing thing happened: She smiled.

And the exotic girl who'd been merely pretty…became stunning.

I watched with fascination as a spark of wild defiance transformed her expression. Her honey-bronze skin flushed pink up her slender neck to her defined cheekbones. Long dark lashes blinked heavily an instant before greater amusement lit up her eyes.

And then it died. Gone in a flash.

Hmmm. "Gonna need more info."

"Those two competitions." She waved a hand toward the breaking waves outside the open window. "You won them on *his* sailboard. And *he* wants to sponsor you for windsurfing competitions."

Finally. The nuts and bolts of it. "Don't need a sponsor."

"He'll pay you well."

"So will all the others." Half a dozen big names so far. "Don't need money."

Without skipping a beat, her head tilted a fraction. "What *do* you need?"

Damn good question.

I stared long and hard at a girl vastly different than me… and yet entirely familiar.

She held herself with a certain grace I'd seen play out my whole life. You can't fake that. Refined. Well-mannered.

Yet I saw right through her mirror-calm surface no matter how expertly she masked it.

Because a similar rebellion railed deep within me.

"Not a damn thing." *Total truth.*

Because all anyone needed was food, water, shelter, and sex.

And…the size of my trust fund would cover that for

small nations ten times over. But I'd abandoned civilized life to wander the world uncharted.

She frowned, and her lower lip pouted out into something almost as amazing as her smile.

"But there is something I want."

Her expression brightened. "What's that?"

"You live in Hawai'i?" Educated guess with her name and accent, but had to be sure.

"Yeah, Maui."

"Perfect." *Actually,* fucking *perfect.* Windsurfing mecca. But I kept calm: the art of negotiation. Cade, my friend and former roommate, would be proud. "I need a place to live."

"To live?"

"Your place?"

"*Nooo.*" She crossed her arms, shaking her head. "Definitely not."

"Nearby, then. You'll hook me up with something."

The headshake thing happened again. Her lips parted, her hardening expression broadcasting loud and clear that a fierce protest was coming.

Unwilling to hear her argument on an empty stomach, I cut her off with a piercing look. Then I added to my list of demands, "Waves to windsurf."

Her features softened as she nodded. "Almost all year round at Ho'okipa Beach."

An electric thrill charged through me as I pictured endless surfing—one thing I'd never gone after before.

"And a personal guide."

"Guide?"

"Assistant. PR rep. Whatever you want to call yourself."

"*Me*?"

"You."

"No way."

"*Only way* it's happening."

Her eyes narrowed, breaths shallowing as she struggled to maintain that cool composure. "Why?"

Yeah…why?

Pretty sure I hadn't knocked my head on coral in the surf today.

Damn sure wasn't looking for a relationship—just got out of one.

But when an adventure-bound guy, who could have anything, sits in front of a girl with enough fire in her to make every step of the journey ahead a glorious fight?

She becomes the only thing he wants.

2

THE UNANSWERED QUESTION

Leilani...

Mase was the *last* thing I needed: a cocky guy who thought he knew everything and could conquer the world—conquer me. Been there. Done them.

But...

Something different about him fascinated me. And his chilled posture hid a quiet excitement just under his skin. I got that—had lived it all my life.

Scraggly blond hair surrounded a pretty-boy face. Pretty *white* boy. Even so, those crystal-blue eyes mesmerized me. Drew me in. Calmed me. Yet when he tore his glance back from the bar and stared at me with a piercing gaze, my breath caught.

Damn. Did I want him?

No! How *did I get dragged into this?*

Oh. That's right. Stupid decisions? Suck-ass consequences. *Not* the way I'd pictured traveling the world.

But I hadn't chosen the punishment for my crime. Law hadn't caught me. My brother had. So the price for him to keep my secrets? Was a total bitch.

With a heavy sigh, I stared at the surfer I'd been tasked with. Concentrating on calming my breaths, I willed myself to chill.

As we continued our staring match, my pointed "why" question dissipated into the tropical breeze flowing in.

There was an indescribable peace about him. To the remote place around us. To the unusual slice of time-out I'd been forced to take. And a part of me that I'd buried long ago made me want to drag my feet in the blissful feeling, tumble down, roll around, and bask in the dreamy warmth of it.

Three uncles with leathered skin and salt-and-pepper hair strolled in as the bartender slid our food onto the table; my plate held two tacos and a ceramic cup overflowing with mango salsa, his had a taco mountain with a big salsa bowl cradled on its peak. The newcomers claimed a corner table, setting up a board game with polished white and black stones as their rich laughter rumbled out, the undertones filled with lazy contentment; the atmosphere was polar opposite to the vibrant pulse of my island community.

The magic of the moment sank further into my bones on a slow exhale.

And as we began to munch on fish tacos on a remote island nestled deep in the vast South Pacific, I let the earlier tension of expectations fade away.

Yet when my mind relaxed into nothingness, his name floated to the surface: *Mase.*

I chewed with care to savor the fresh flavors rolling over my tongue and considered the short masculine name. He'd been firm about using it, not his full given name. And he'd delivered the correction with a clipped bite to his tone and inscrutable flash in his eyes, like a deeper story lay hidden in their icy depths.

By the time I swallowed down the last bite of my first taco, my need to know more about him shattered the quiet in my mind.

So I threw the last topic back out between us, ending the silence on our side of the room. "You still haven't answered my question." The "why" about his asinine terms, about me being an assistant of some kind to him.

He held my gaze as he took long gulps of beer. Then without giving any reply, he began devouring his third taco. But he watched me with steady curiosity, head slightly tilted, like he'd been doing from the moment we'd sat down—as if I'd become a new puzzle he wanted to solve.

Yeah, good luck with that.

Used to testosterone-pumped males and their bravado, I held his intense gaze until amusement sparked in those startling pale eyes. But then his expression clouded over and he broke our staring match, his attention shifting to the last two tacos on his plate.

The bartender waved at us, then pointed a large black phone at me. "Miss Kealoha?"

"Yes." I straightened in my seat. I'd been waiting for an

update from their small airport, news about the delay of my charter back to Tahiti to catch a connecting flight to Maui.

Mase remained silent as I took the phone, though he continued to watch me with mild interest.

Nothing but island music streamed through the receiver, so I settled back in my chair, waiting.

I tried to ignore the man across from me—the one whose presence overpowered the room even as he slouched in his chair. Easily six-foot-two, his body had been leanly built of muscle honed by surfing. When he reached to the left to put our empty plates on the table beside us, a shaft of sunlight hit his shoulder, making the grains of sand and salt glitter over his bronzed skin.

Yet even with the deep tan, he stood out among the half dozen people in the room: light golden skin to darker shades, dark-blond hair in a sea of jet black, crystalline blue eyes amid varying shades of brown.

The differences between us—between him and me— were like day and night.

The haole *won't survive a week on my island.*

A crackling static broke through the music. "Miss Leilani Kealoha?" a friendly female voice asked.

"Yes, I'm Leilani."

Finally. I needed to go home. Hadn't wanted to come in the first place.

"I'm very sorry, but the pilot cannot fly until tomorrow morning at 9:00 a.m."

"Why?" I sighed. Not that it helped. Did nothing to rescue me out of a sucky situation.

"I'm not sure, miss. The pilot...all he said was engine repair."

"N'kay. Thanks." I blew out a frustrated breath, disconnected, and put the phone down onto the table.

"Bad news?" Mase quirked up a thick blond brow.

"Flight delay."

"Till when?" He tilted his head a fraction, doing that stare-thing again.

The world pressed in on me under his focused attention, my pulse speeding up, breaths quickening. A sudden intimacy grew between us though neither one had moved a muscle.

I drew in a slow breath, forcing my attention on all things *not* Mase, anything not directly related to my reason for being there. My gaze scanned toward a wide-open window on the side wall, to a picturesque view: a green beater car parked in front of a silvery stretch of sand topped by turquoise crashing waves. Breaths calming, I noticed more locals had arrived, talking story in a couple of different conversations, one about their day's catch, another about aching joints and a coming storm.

Chilled out to somewhere close to normal again, I finally answered when I'd be leaving, "Tomorrow morning."

"Stay with me."

I blinked. "What?"

"Spend the night with me."

My heart kicked up again. He'd tossed out the statement with the same blatant cockiness that he'd suggested living with me in Maui.

"No."

"You like that word."

"It applies to everything you spit out."

"And yet, your eyes say something else."

I rolled them toward the ceiling, then shot a glare at him. "What do my eyes say?"

"They're saying yes with a capital *Y* and three exclamation points."

I snorted, amused by his analysis. "Three?"

"Three."

"Not one or two?"

"Girls put three when they're excited."

"I'm *not* excited." I crossed my arms.

The corners of his lips twitched. "Yes, you are."

I narrowed my eyes at him. "What do you know?"

"I know you want more than you're leading on to. You *are* more than how you're acting. Which tells me plenty." Voice and expression softening as he spoke, he watched me with clear interest.

Rattled, I settled back in my chair, reassessing him. I'd underestimated him. And completely misjudged him.

Maybe more sat across from me than just a pretty surfer boy.

I tightened my jaw. "You haven't answered my question." Wasn't budging till he did.

Surprise flashed in his eyes at my challenge.

Thick tension crackled in the air between us again at the reminder of his last ridiculous condition. But the only unknowns *I* jumped toward? Wild pools at the base of waterfalls—not wild surfers with pipe dreams.

And so I repeated what I needed to know before our conversation went any further, before I abandoned the stupid attempt to help my brother, to fulfill my obligation. "Why?" *Why can't you just accept the sponsorship and leave me out of it?*

His unrelenting gaze hardened. Infinite pale blue eyes stared deep into mine. For several seconds, he didn't twitch one sun-bronzed muscle from his relaxed position.

Then his jaw tightened. He swallowed. A slow, deep breath expanded his chest. "You'll see."

I will? Clouds will part, the sun will shine, and I'll magically see why you threw down an inflexible condition to my brother sponsoring you: Me?

A beat passed in the silence between us. Then another.

A seagull cried.

Ocean waves crashed.

Bar glasses clinked.

I blinked, heavily. His vague answer had thrown me, and like a total idiot, no flippant response came. Other than the *no* which seemed so amusing to him.

"C'mon." In a graceful sweep of his leanly muscled body, he stood.

My restraint snapped on a quick inhale. I'd had enough. Of my responsible brother. Of confident Mase. Of cocky guys.

I couldn't stop the defiance raging through me. Or the word... "No."

"Suit yourself." He shrugged, then gave a nod to the

restaurant owner. "Thanks, Rico."

And then I was alone. With six strangers.

In a foreign land.

Defeated.

Seconds raced by as my anxiety swelled into a towering tsunami.

"Shit," I bit out under my breath as I swiped up my bag and shoes.

When I rushed out the door, a gust of fresh salty air hit my face.

Mase stood to the right, shoulder leaning against the corner of the building, other arm hanging casually from a loose grip on the top edge of his board.

"Took you long enough." The corners of his lush mouth twitched.

Whatever. I let out a dramatic sigh. "Where are we going?"

"Where else is there to go?"

Your hotel room? I scowled. My lips parted, another *no* hovering on the tip of my tongue. Even though a vital part of me buried deep down, screamed *yes* with that capital *Y* and a million exclamation points.

He shot me an amused look. "Breaking waves."

"Oh." Of course. The only thing riders wanted during daylight hours when the surf's up.

I snorted, then shrugged. Nothing else to do for the rest of the day. And he hadn't kicked me to the curb. Not yet. Not with my unanswered "why" dangling out there between us.

Curiosity. That's all it was. The only thing that had me

sticking with him longer versus camping out at the airport.

He grabbed his board then headed down a side street… away from the ocean.

I paused, confused.

After several more long strides, he stopped and turned. "You coming?"

An open-top Jeep had been backed against a banana patch a couple dozen yards beyond him. I'd been dropped off at the restaurant by a cab. What choice did I have? Unless I relished hanging out at a humid airport in a rigid plastic chair…with nothing to show for dragging my foolish ass all the way down to some tiny dot on the globe. "Yeah."

Almost twenty minutes later, after a bumpy silent ride through sparse jungle, we approached a desolate crescent bay. I would've pressed for an answer, an explanation of his smartass "you'll see," but the roar of the sickly engine made me bite my tongue.

And the unspoiled landscape was too beautiful to taint with talk about business.

The road ended at a sand dune as high as the hood. He got out, pulled his board from the back, then paused by my door, leaning against the Jeep.

He held my gaze, his blue eyes shimmering liquid silver in the bright late-afternoon sun. "Wanna ride?"

His low tone purred into my ears, warming my body as its weight flowed downward.

I swallowed hard, then drew in a deep breath, trying to find a brain cell to use as I stared up at him.

He'd meant the board. But my leashed thoughts broke

free, latching on to the blatant innuendo of his words, of the sizzling heat that hovered in the scant inches between us.

Then I licked my lips, finally being honest with myself. My gaze drifted down that body, landed on those clinging board shorts, then rose back up to the long fingers that gripped the edge of his surfboard.

Yeah, I do.

But with years of practice ignoring my wants, I tamped down gut instinct. I stared at the board, considering his true offer. Would be great to catch a few waves, work out frustration, just throw on my suit and let the ocean soothe me like it always did.

Only if I went out there, he'd have nothing to do but watch me. While I let my guard down. And I'd rather be the one studying him.

"No thanks."

He gave a half-shrug. "Suit yourself. Water and snacks in the back if you want 'em."

Then he turned without another word and crossed the shallow strip of sand to the foaming surf. With quick strokes, he paddled out to a sizable reef break.

And for the next two hours, I watched him carve out waves.

Damn, he's good. The decent lefthander had a slow build to crest, then a quick and heavy drop, but his moves were masterful. Makani had said Mase was from some big city on the East Coast. But the way he handled the challenging waves told another story.

He didn't surf like islanders. An element of difference I

couldn't quite pinpoint made his technique different. And effective.

Mesmerized, I watched him dance with the ocean until the coral sun turned pink as it kissed the horizon.

By the time he returned to the Jeep, I'd already rummaged his snacks, eating a handful of trail mix and one of two apples. I held up a piece of the loot. "Protein bar?"

"Sure." He took it, then reached into the small cooler and grabbed a banana too.

He ate the *grindz* like a starving man, then washed it all down with a bottle of Gatorade. The second he took his last swallow, I crossed my arms. "*Sooo*...why?"

Fingers pinching the key in the ignition, he paused, then glanced at me over his shoulder. Those blue eyes darkened in the shadows. "Why what?"

I waved an arm out toward the waves, as if they'd help with the explanation. "You know."

"So will you."

Confused, but beginning to get used to the feeling, I shook my head. "This how city boys catch girls? Riddles and comebacks?"

"You're intrigued."

No. Yes. Neither word fit. And infuriatingly, both did. But the more I talked with him, the more tangled my thoughts became. Instead of answering, I huffed out a frustrated sigh.

"Patience, padawan." Instead of starting the Jeep, his fingers abandoned the key and he leaned an arm behind my seat.

Then suddenly his body invaded my space. Salty, sweaty,

heated male, golden skin inches from mine. I gripped my knees, forcing my hands to keep away. Because I wanted to touch, taste. The untamed part of me needed to connect with the wildness of him.

His hot breath feathered over the corner of my mouth, then trailed along my jaw until it reached my ear. One slow hot exhale, then a pause. "You know why."

Did I?

My breaths shallowed. My throat locked up. I closed my eyes as warmth ebbed from the spot where his lips nearly touched my skin. That heat pulsed lower, grew hotter.

"I don't." The words were whispered, all I could manage.

His deep chuckle rustled the hair above my ear. "You'll figure it out."

A current of cool air whipped between us as he pulled back. An instant later, the engine growled to life.

My head still spun. My body tingled, a delicious heat still aching between my legs.

Sex? He couldn't be just after sex. Didn't want a "beach-bunny fuck"—what he'd said.

Nothing had changed. He still had something we wanted.

And we had something he wanted. I just needed to get him to see that.

And that the *something* wasn't me.

Definitely not me.

3
ENTICING NEGOTIATIONS

Mase…

Wow. Only word that formed between my ears.

Couldn't think through the buzzing in my head.

Through a rush of adrenaline, a realization sparked.

All I knew? I'd stumbled onto it. The path. The road I'd been seeking all my life.

And somehow, today, it revealed itself to me all at once.

Ideal surf.

Perfect girl.

The whole expectant world had faded away—leaving me be.

"You *must* want something." Her soft, hesitant words broke into the silent space.

*Annnd…*peace shattered.

Still, couldn't help the smile tugging my lips. "I stated my terms."

"Ridiculous ones." With a cute huff of breath, she struggled to fasten her seatbelt until it clicked.

I braced my hand on her headrest and twisted, backing the Jeep down the road. *Damn*, I enjoyed sparring with her. And throwing her. So I did it again. "How much?"

She visibly startled, partially turning toward me.

At her speechless long pause, I gave her a slow grin.

She schooled her expression and faced forward again, settling back into her seat. "Thirty thousand."

I choked down a laugh while I shifted into drive. "Do you have a job?" I turned left to begin traversing the stretch of dirt road on the southern side of the Pacific speck we floated on.

More silence. When I glanced her way, her delicate features had drooped into a cute frown.

A tiny wrinkle formed between her brows. "What does that have to do with anything?"

"You'd know *thirty thousand* isn't anything." When she didn't reply, I prodded, "Do you?"

"Have a job? No."

"Why not?"

"Just went grad."

I winced, her slang sinking in: graduated high school. *Young.* "Eighteen?"

"Nineteen."

Good. Old enough. I gave a sharp nod. "Make a better offer."

"Forty thousand." She rattled the bold number off without hesitation. Like she'd been given specific instructions: what to start off with, what increments to climb—how high her brother, Makani, was willing to go.

A gut feeling screamed we hadn't hit it yet. "Higher."

She dropped an adorable deadpan look at me. "Thought you didn't need the money."

"You arguing or offering?" My knee-jerk sarcasm hid sudden anxiety. At wanting to shed my old skin. Try on a new one. And, oddly, with every second that stretched by, getting her to agree grew more and more important.

She let out a heavy sigh. "Forty-five."

Better. But I couldn't cave. Wouldn't. Not yet. I waited. Felt the tension rise. Saw her leg bounce, as if the tightrope we'd toed out across did the same to her as it did to me: thrilled, even as it terrified. Breathing out on a slow exhale, I pushed the envelope. For her. For the unreal thing that had begun to unfold between us. "Fifty."

Another long pause followed. Then she gave a slow nod. "Done."

"Good, that's your salary."

She blinked, face whipping toward me as it wrinkled in wonderful confusion. "What?"

"Your salary. As my assistant and PR person."

"But..." I could almost hear the gears in her brain stick. For a fresh high school graduate, it was an obscene amount of money out of the gate, without degree or experience. She knew it. I knew it.

"Fine." She crossed her arms with a heavy drop at the

end—doing dangerous things to her cleavage. "Surfer's assistant? How hard could it be?" she grumbled.

"Fine?" I glanced at her, arching my brows, totally amused by her stubbornness.

Her jaw hardened, eyes narrowing. "I'll take the job."

"Good. And I'd have paid sixty."

"I'd have taken forty." She shook her head, staring out the windshield with a faraway look. "And you have *no* idea what you've gotten yourself into."

I tipped my head back against my headrest with a smug smile. "Oh, I have some idea." Especially if the sharp tongue and quick wit was any indication. "And it's gonna be a blast."

"You're just trying to get into my pants."

Not entirely a lie. Not the whole truth, either. Not even close. I glanced down at a silky expanse of bared upper thigh, most of it brightened by a shaft of sunlight into a golden caramel. *Fucking delicious.* "You're not wearing any pants."

"Up my dress, then."

Oh, damn. *You're making this too easy.* "Bet it looks *really* nice up there."

"No. No looking up there."

I fought a smirk. "Can't stop me from thinking about it."

"*No…thinking…about…it.*" Each word gritted out from her, enunciated.

Then silence.

The instant I glanced at her, we hit a nasty pothole.

She jostled, but refused to unwind those tense arms folded tightly over her chest. *Way* too angry for our lighthearted banter.

Hmmm...Maybe I'm not doing it right. "We should just get it over with and have sex."

Laughter burst out of her and she broke apart those folded arms to brace her weight on her thighs. "No."

I liked the sound of her laugh. Raw. Uninhibited. Teasing her brought out the wonderful things she wanted to keep bottled inside. "There's that word again."

"Yeah." She shot me a wary glance. "It's only spelled the usual way. *N* period, *O* period."

"Why?" Yep. I asked it.

Her mouth dropped open with a shocked sound. "*Excellent* question."

It boomeranged around full circle back at me. *Why I wanted her?* Right. Excellent question. But something deeper hummed under the surface between us. Her overreaction meant more lay behind the mask she wore so valiantly. There were things she hid from me, maybe even from herself. "Does it have an answer?"

"I have a rule: I don't date guys I work for."

Slick. Sure. *Poof*...she suddenly had the perfect rule. I didn't bother to point out that I said nothing about *dating*, only *sexing*.

Then sudden alarm crept up my spine. "How many guys have you worked for?"

"Only the one."

Relief slumped my shoulders even as I shook my head. "Then it's not a rule."

"Yeah, it is. Just made it."

Knew it. "Well, unmake it."

"No."

Another smile plastered onto my face. "I'm beginning to love that word." From her. It shielded all the secrets she kept. Became a challenge to me…to discover them.

I hooked a left past a sea-rock cairn, its graduated seven-stone pillar my only marker to the nondescript shoreline turnoff.

She twisted in her seat toward me. The weight of her stare filled the seconds of silence. Without glancing over, I felt her trying to figure me out—a mystery trying to unravel an enigma.

Her head moved slightly left, but she never took her gaze from me. "You don't like rules."

"Nope." Never had.

Her unasked "why" hung in the air right as we pulled up to the crash-pad I'd been staying in, a rustic beach *bure*: steep thatched-bamboo roof in need of repair, outdoor shower obscured by a reed screen, hammock strung between a metal hook on a corner deck post and the trunk of a coconut palm fifteen feet away. The Spartan digs came with a basic toilet, sink, and a small metal stove. A sturdy bed long enough for my feet not to hang over had clean sheets. Worked for me.

But the best part about it?

Location, location, *location*. On the beach, steps from the high tidemark. Not a damn thing else a guy wanting to escape the world could want.

Well, except for a girl who stood loudly beside me without uttering a word.

Twilight faded into darkness by the second, casting the

deep crescent beach into richer blue-black shadows. Waves crashed against a jagged black reef on bracketing points of the bay, but by the time they reached the midpoint dead ahead, they gentled, slowly stretching over the soft sand.

"I need to make call for a morning pickup," she said from somewhere behind me.

"Cool." I nodded, then closed my eyes, soaking in the ocean's rhythm: roaring booms, gentle splashes.

After the muffled one-sided convo ended, a distinct click sounded. I turned to see her grasping a string connected to a now-illuminated lightbulb that dangled from the ceiling. "There's electricity?"

"Solar panels around back." I nodded to the far corner.

She stared at the sink. "Water?"

"Catchment."

"Oh." Her gaze continued to pan the room, then froze on the obvious. "I'm *not* sleeping in that." She pointed at the large bed that took up almost the entire room.

"You're not?"

"No." She gave a firm headshake, arms crossing once again.

"Okay, Lani." My voice lowered, turning raspy as I stepped closer. "No sleeping? Sounds like you're breaking your own rule: got your mind set on wild all-night sex. Gonna make your morning connection and all-day flight home a bitch."

Her expression turned incredulous, eyes narrowing then flashing wide, mouth falling open. "We're *not* having wild all-night sex."

Taking my time, I swept a hungry stare down her body... taunting her. "Slow, then?"

27

"No."

Fighting a smile, I met her gaze. "There's that word again."

"Accurate."

"Premature."

She narrowed her eyes again. "Interesting word from a guy talking about sex."

"I was talking about your opinion of me." Which had become more important with every passing second.

Forcing away any doubt—regarding her overreaction, the secrets she hid, how she felt…about herself and about me—I took a step closer to her. A primal urge vibrated under my skin: to prove to her whatever electric thing was happening between us sparked hotter than something physical, that we were connected on a deeper level.

Only I didn't have any proof. Pure instinct, nothing more.

And the skittish girl in front of me needed time. To realize it for herself.

Hell, even I didn't get why I wasn't sprinting the other direction. Had just bailed out of an all-in with another girl. Had vowed to be single. Uninvolved. Detached.

Had no fucking idea why I felt the sudden, very real, need to attach.

Even so, I took one more step toward her.

Then another.

Her feet stayed planted, shoulders squared, defiant look in her eye as she held my gaze.

But her breathing shallowed.

Her eyes dilated.

She pressed her lips together, then swallowed hard.

Our bodies collided in innocent slow-motion, arms brushing, backs of our hands touching and lingering together at the point of contact. As she softly gasped, I wondered what she saw: my shallow breathing, my dilated eyes, my swallow as my throat grew bone dry?

Do you feel the connection too?

4
TRUTH OR...

Leilani...

Mase invaded my senses as I drew in a deep breath.

Damn, you smell amazing.

His muscular forearm touched my elbow, his index finger curved against my pinky, but the seemingly harmless act showered a riot of crackling sparks through my body, where they settled unnervingly between my legs.

"This isn't happening." *Couldn't be.*

"What isn't?"

"You and me."

"Sure it is." Without warning, he broke contact, turned, then stripped his wet shorts off and walked across the room.

I averted my gaze. But not before I got an eyeful of sculpted buns and well-equipped male. "No. It's not."

He hummed, tone low and disbelieving. "You just don't know it yet."

"Look" —I blew out a controlled breath as I pushed my hair from my face, then stared up at the woven pattern of the bamboo ceiling overhead— "you and I *can't* happen."

A noise sounded, like a refrigerator seal had released. Glass clinked. Metal scraped. The soft release of carbonated pressure hissed out.

Then a chilled beer bottle appeared in my vision. "Keep telling yourself that." He walked out the door, black cotton shorts now hugging his stellar backside.

I touched the cool bottle to my lips, then gulped down one swallow after another, fortifying myself. "Where are you going?"

"Outside."

"Why?"

"To watch the stars." He disappeared toward the right. "They're incredible out here."

"For sure." No denying it. Even Maui's night sky from any beach didn't compare with total darkness in the middle of the South Pacific.

Curious, I followed him out. He grabbed folded beach towels from a wicker stand beside the outdoor shower, handed me one, then unfurled his onto the ground in front of the small deck. Intrigued by his childlike love of nature, I did the same, keeping mine a good foot away from his.

Tucking an arm under my head, I gazed up at the diamond-encrusted black velvet sky. Iridescent pinholes glittered back at us, most in hues of white, but some sparkled green, blue, or pink.

31

The silence lasted only until his long legs settled. "Let's play a game."

Haven't we been *playing?* I pressed my lips together to stop a smile. "What kind of game?"

"A drinking game." He popped back up, then spun around, stepping back into the *bure.*

I leaned up on an elbow, then glanced over my shoulder. He went straight to the nightstand, then wrapped a hand around the neck of a squat pyramid-shaped bottle. When he returned, he balanced the bottom on his other palm, twisting it; clear liquid sloshed halfway up its Patrón Silver label. He tipped his head toward the bottle. "Truth or Shot."

"Ah, tequila." I wedged my half-empty beer bottle into the sand and sat upright, crossing my legs as I took the tequila from him. "Shouldn't that be 'Truth or Dare'?"

He dropped back onto his towel, two shot glasses clinking between the fingers of one hand. A mischievous expression lit up his face, then he slowly pressed the palm of his free hand into his towel and leaned forward, face tilting downward as he stared hard at me. "You want dares?" His voice grew huskier with every word, his finger brushing the skin above my knee before traveling in a lazy trail up my thigh. "Then, I get to start."

"Shots." I blurted, knocking his hand away. I blew out a shaky breath. "I'm good with shots."

His deep chuckle followed, the kind filled with sin and hidden promises. And though I'd broken his intentional contact, the side of his dropped hand still touched my thigh.

I stared at the warm connection. Innocent. And not.

On a slow inhale, I tried to clear my head. "I'm not telling you anything. I could drink half that bottle." Sort of. Well, probably more than likely. But he didn't need to know that.

"What's the matter? Scared of a little truth?"

"No." *Yes...* "But why should I tell you anything about me?"

"We *are* going to be working together." He uncorked the bottle.

"So?"

"Sooo…think of it like a job interview."

"Oh." Totally confused, I furrowed my brow. "So the questions won't be personal."

"They most definitely *will* be personal." He took the bottle back and filled one shot glass halfway.

I warily eyed the sad amount of alcohol. "Right. Then, I'll just drink."

"Nope. Doesn't work that way. Question first. Then you decide."

I huffed out a laugh. "How's that even a game? I don't have to answer any question I don't want to."

"Which tells me a lot about you."

I narrowed my eyes at him. "Fine. But it goes both ways, surfer boy. And I go first."

"Do your worst."

"You're from Philadelphia."

"Truth. But not a question." His brows raised. "Do I need to draw a diagram of how this works?"

"No. I'm not a *keiki*." Not a *grom*. Not a kid. Suddenly, I sat straighter, pulling my shoulders back, sticking my chest

33

out. *Not a girl either.* "Speaking of: What's with the baby shot?" With a determined swipe, I grabbed the bottle and half-filled glass from him, then poured to the brim.

His attention drifted toward my breasts. But then his gaze lifted to meet mine, the corners of his lips twitching with amusement, and he explained anyway, talking slowly. "You ask a question. I either answer truthfully, or I drink."

Ignoring him with a wave of my hand, I began my interrogation. "How in the world did an East Coaster become so skilled on the waves?"

"Ah. Good question."

"See?" I gave a solid nod. "I got this."

"Well, my parents traveled a lot when I was a kid, every year from before I was born. Always near a glamourous beach. Learned how to ride days after I took my first steps."

"And you've been surfing ever since?" I hadn't heard of him. Not that I was the expert on wave riders, but something that unusual got around.

"That's a follow-up question."

"What fun is this if I don't get follow-up questions?"

He tapped a thumb on his bent knee. "Gotta put those in the rules."

"I was never very good at following rules."

"Me either."

Tension pulsed between us. Like something had been said…that hadn't been said.

"Fine." I slammed back my waiting shot, then hissed in a breath at its stout burn. "New rule: Wanna tack on a follow-up? Gotta take a shot."

"My turn." He grabbed the bottle. When I pulled my shot glass close to my chest, he shook his head and grabbed the empty he'd planted in the sand.

"You didn't answer my follow-up."

"Chill, young padawan." He dropped me a hard look. "I'm about to."

"Padawan?"

"Student...apprentice." He narrowed his eyes, then scowled. "Didn't you watch any Star Wars movies?"

"Yeah, I've seen them all once. Doesn't mean I have to commit the geeky terms to memory."

His gaze held mine for long seconds. Then his lips curved into a lazy smile. "Nope."

"Nope what?"

"Nope is the answer to your question."

He hasn't *been surfing ever since.*

"So you took a break? For how long? When did you start again?"

He raised the bottle. "He who has the tequila asks the questions."

"You're making up the rules as we go."

"You made one? I made one."

I tapped a finger on my empty glass. "I'm *way* too sober for this."

"Wait your turn. Then you can drink away."

Seconds ticked by as he watched me.

I stared at him the entire silent time.

My brows slowly rose. "Well?"

"I'm asking the question."

35

"So *ask* the question."

"Tell me about your family."

"You suck at this. That's not a question. And you need to be more specific."

"All right. What did you mean when you told your brother 'ohana?"

My heart plummeted to my stomach. Figures, he'd zero in on the one thing I didn't want to talk about. But no way was I drinking to let Mase know that. " 'Ohana means family."

"I know what the word means; I saw *Lilo and Stitch* as a kid. But what did *you* mean? You made it sound like an obligation on the phone, like you were irritated—about having to come talk to me."

"I was." *Still am. Don't like to pay for stupid mistakes.* "I owed him a favor."

"Big favor."

"Yep." I grabbed the bottle, contemplating what I wanted to know about him. If he hadn't been surfing all this time… "What have you been doing the last few years?"

He dropped a put-out look at me. "Did you want a day-by-day account?"

"Right. Specific." I studied him a minute with narrowed eyes. Even though he was fit, he seemed smart. And for some reason, he didn't need the money Makani had offered him. Which made me want to phrase my question carefully, to get the most information from him.

"Clarification rules" —I tapped my lip with a finger, thinking— "our question can be multipronged, like an if-then situation."

His lips scrunched a little, then an eyebrow raised and he gave a slight nod. "I'll allow it."

"If you worked, what did you do? But, if you went to school or college, what did you study? And if you did neither, then..." I reconsidered his lean muscular form. Definitely not football, but maybe an athlete of some kind. "Did you play sports?"

"Clarification question."

I fought a smile as I repeated his phrase. "I'll allow it."

"And if I did all three?"

"Then you have to answer all three."

"Okay." He stared up at the star-studded sky a moment. "I did work some, when I wanted and time allowed. Odd construction jobs mostly, an addition to someone's house was the last."

He paused. Neither of us moved. After a few seconds, I turned toward him, watching the slow rise and fall of his chest then the peacefulness on his face as he stared up into the darkness.

On a slow sigh, my body relaxed into the extended silence. Odd that I'd feel so comfortable with a complete stranger, yet we shared kindred blood, a love for the sea, and that alone forged a connection of sorts. Thirsty after a dry swallow, I untwisted my beer from the sand and lifted it to my lips, guzzling down a good quarter of its contents before coming up for air.

Finally, he shifted, tucking a bent arm under his head. "Went to school, too."

No further explanation came, seconds ticking by again.

"Need I remind you of the rules? Don't answer? Drink." And, as he'd so readily pointed out for me, drinking was an answer unto itself.

The lapping of the waves a few dozen yards from our feet filled the space between our quiet breaths. I took another healthy swallow of beer, waiting.

"I studied pre-med."

I gasped, then sprayed out beer from tightened lips, followed by coughing and sputtering to clear what had slipped into my lungs. After a convulsive jolt upright, I bent my head down between my knees, taking stuttering breaths and a few lung-clearing deeper coughs.

"You okay?" He hit me hard on the back. "Didn't think it would be that shocking."

But it was. I rasped out, "To be...*a doctor*?" Couldn't wrap my mind around it. If I'd had to guess a vocation the furthest from his laidback surfer demeanor it would've been that—well, or an accountant, maybe a lawyer.

"Usually why it's done." He gave another hard thwack between my shoulder blades, jarring my teeth.

"Easy." I drew in my first solid lungful of air. "Trying to catch my breath, not dislodge stuck food."

Sifting my hands through the cool sand beside my feet while I steadied my breathing, my mind started clicking. "Wait. So you're not going to school anymore? Why?"

He stared at the tequila bottle expectantly. "I heard two questions; but we'll count it as only one follow-up. The first was rhetorical."

I poured the obligatory shot, then tossed it back with

a hiss, feeling more of the burn down my throat after the coughing fit.

"Why?" I repeated, the question of the night.

Why *me*? Why *not pre-med*? Only for some inexplicable reason, the first "why" had lost its interest for me. Maybe it was the alcohol beginning to warm my veins and buzz my head. But the more I sat there, at peace and enjoying myself in his company, the less I wanted to question the "why *me*" of it. And the last seemed like the most important of the night to him, so far.

On a deep breath, he stared at me, chest expanding as he filled his lungs. Then he held motionless for a second before letting it all out in a hard whoosh. He gave a slight headshake. "Didn't fit me."

That's all he said. Except his tone, his demeanor, the dark hooded look of his eyes shouted there was more to the story than him simply righting a wrong direction.

And I knew plenty about wrong directions. Why I'd struggled so much. I'd been placed on a path in my life, no matter what I wanted, no matter how wrong it felt. But out of duty for family, and fierce love for a brother who protected me all he could, I remained on the path—even if I strayed from time to time.

The silence grew tense.

Like we needed to move on, only he'd gotten stuck.

And I'd put him there.

"Here, take a shot." I shoved the bottle against his side.

"Uh…"

I pressed it harder into his ribs, shaking my head at his

hesitation. Offering him an out felt like it gave both of us a break. "You need another drink. You don't have to answer the sports thing."

"Yeah, I do. No biggie." He took a shot anyway. "And yeah, did the sports thing too but only when I could. Didn't entirely give up surfing, just didn't do it much. And typically only at Poverty Beach and Harvey Cedars with the Jersey surfers in the winter."

He sighed, settling back as he stared out into the darkness. "Snow covered the beach."

"Snow?" I couldn't imagine surfing in that kind of cold.

"Yep. Full wetsuit. Gloved hands. Booted feet. But the waves…" His voice turned breathless with reverence. "They're thick and heavy. One right after the other, full of power. Humbling. Terrifying. It's *fucking* amazing."

"*Niiice.*" I'd been there before, riding the fear and thrill all at once.

"Okay. Ready for another one?"

"Sure."

"I did my story on school, work, and play." He leaned in, raising his brows. "What about you? I toss your multipronged question back at you."

"Oh." No clue why I hadn't expected turnabout, but it threw me. Curious as I'd been about his story, I didn't want to reveal much about mine. With good reason. But how to play along?

"I went grad at Seabury Hall." Simple enough. "You know I don't work. Why you hired me. And I surf a little. There. Questions answered."

"*Nooo*…not quite." His finger tapped the bottle. "You're hiding something." His gaze intensified, eyes widening then narrowing as he tipped his head to one side, like maybe he could unlock my secrets with telepathy. "What did you study? And if you can't answer, or don't want to, then what did you want to do after graduation? Can't imagine you've longed to be my assistant all this time."

"Hardly." I snorted.

When the silence dragged out, he continued tapping the bottle with his nail. The rhythmic clinking served as a countdown.

"I dunno."

"Lie."

I let out a heavy sigh. "I want to travel. See the world. Study marine biology maybe. Or archeology. There are some cool ruins on the islands that have always interested me." There. Not the whole truth, but close enough and more than he'd shared.

"But…"

"Nope. Nothing more. I answered the question." Minimally. The only way I was willing to.

More silence followed. A comfortable safe stretch of nothingness. No expectations. No rules. But the longer I hung suspended in the temporary place of solitude we'd found on a starry night in the middle of nowhere…the more important the moment became. Like I'd found myself— somewhere.

Lost in a hazy buzz I didn't want to cut short, I poured another shot, then tossed it back. Leaving my head tilted back

41

for a few seconds, I stared out into the glittering vastness above us. "Mind if I ask you a question?"

"Isn't that what we're doing?"

"No. A real one. Deep. Off the record." *More important.* One I'd never been able to ask anyone.

"Sure. Shoot."

"Ever feel like you're living someone else's life? Like what everyone wants for you, expects for you...*isn't* for you?"

A soft snort sounded out as he glanced at me. "Story of my life." He leaned up on one elbow, stared out over the dark ocean, then scrubbed a hand over the stubble around his lips and down his chin. "Well, up until a couple of weeks ago."

"What happened a couple of weeks ago?"

He swung a heavy gaze at me. "Decided to live for me."

"That simple?" His life must've been different. Less complicated. Mine was anything but.

He gave a halfhearted shrug. A few beats passed while he stared hard at me, as if considering how worthy I was of the answer. "We gotta be true to ourselves. Gotta do what makes us the most happy. If we don't search out our best selves, how can we expect to give that to anyone else?"

His profound words hung between us like a shining beacon. Far away, yet urging me to follow. If only it was so easy; see what I want—what I most need for me to be whole—and go after it.

Not in my family.

Not in my world.

But I didn't want to think about my world. Not when I'd escaped to a beach a million miles away. Not on a remote rock with a stranger who'd quickly wiggled his way into my heart as an almost-friend.

All that existed—all I wanted to think about for the next twelve hours—was Mase and me.

A comfort settled between us after the depth of my question and his insightful response. We let it linger there for a while as the waves lapped at the shoreline in the darkness beyond our feet. The breeze scratched palm fronds over the thatched roof of his *bure* behind us.

After we polished off our beers, high on the silent bonding that had unfolded between us, I decided to continue the game. "My turn."

Mind still lulled by the heavier detour, my thoughts blanked out. But since he'd asked about my family, and he'd mentioned his parents, 'ohana seemed a safe place to stay. "What about you?" I shifted to face him, then stared into eyes that sparkled from the glow of the light behind us. "Got any brothers or sisters?"

His eyes widened, but only for an instant. Then his lips parted and he let out a long exhale.

Instead of answering, he poured a to-the-brim shot and slammed it back before planting both bottle and glass into the sand. "I need some air."

"What?" I stared at the lean muscles of his back as he strode toward the surf lapping in. "Game over?" I shouted.

No reply came. Instead, his shorts dropped. Could hardly see a thing with the darkness of a new moon at play, but dude was definitely buck naked.

"Game over, then," I grumbled as I stood. I dusted my hands off, then followed him.

Game or not, one last question shimmered to the surface, murmured slowly from my lips. "What spooked you, Mase?"

The man who was sensitive about his name—maybe who didn't want to be known as a "Price"—clearly had family issues.

Perhaps we had more in common than I'd thought.

Which could be good. And a whole lot of bad.

5
WHAT LURKS BELOW

Mase...

Blood hammered through my veins.

Choppy breaths sucked down into my lungs.

Water swirled around me, and I pinched my eyes shut, drowning in raw memories that refused to stay away.

The tropical current was warm. But all of a sudden, an odd coolness washed over my legs, swept up and through my chest. In a flash, the sensation vanished.

But as a familiar calmness lingered, I let out a heavy breath.

"Deke?" *My brother.* Whispered from my lips, I hadn't spoken his name in years. I stared at the enormous darkness overhead. A million stars sparkled through the black canvas. "The Milky Way," I murmured. What he'd taught me long ago on a darkened beach in our youth.

After another couple of measured breaths, awareness of my surroundings sharpened back into focus.

And then I turned around.

My breath caught.

Leilani.

Even from the pitch black of the moonless night, I had a clear view of her. Naked. Soft light glowing from the beach *bure* behind her silhouetted her curves. And *holy fuck*, what curves.

Uninhibited, and probably totally unaware I could see her so clearly, she glided into the water right in front of me. Chest-high on me, the gentle waves skimmed her shoulders as they rolled by.

From the *bure's* distant glow, a low shine reflected off her cheek, which plumped a little when she smiled. "Hey."

"Hey." I huffed out a breath. *Get your shit together, Mase.*

"You okay?"

No. But I would be—what traveling to the ends of the earth with no roadmap was all about: facing fears, chasing dreams. Even if I didn't have a clear view on either. Not yet, anyway.

"Yeah." My gut clenched at my habitual lie; it tasted bitter with her. "No." *Honest. Real.* For some undefinable reason, I needed to cleanse my soul with an unexpected beautiful stranger who'd I'd met only hours ago.

Concern wrinkled her brow. The soft lapping of water on her shoulders grew louder as she closed the distance between us to within a couple of feet.

"But getting better the closer you are." Didn't know how

or why, but being near her calmed me on a visceral level. Instantly addicted to the feeling, I wanted more.

The wrinkle over her nose softened as she raised her brows. "Can I help?"

"No." Honest again. Even though the night had become something totally remarkable—and still continued to evolve—I wasn't ready to deal with my demons.

On an abrupt squeal, she launched a good foot out of the water and landed in a curled position against my chest, legs dangling over my forearm. As I instinctively braced an arm around her back, wrapping her up tight so she wouldn't dunk below the surface, she clung to my shoulders, breaths coming in fast gulps.

Shocked, but not hating her sudden one-eighty, I gave her a smug smile. "*Well*, look at the lucky guy who doesn't have to look up your skirt."

Her gaze darted to our left as she smacked my chest. "Shut it. Something brushed against my leg…a shark."

"Uh-huh." I gripped her hips, holding her tighter against me, then made a dramatic show of scanning the water—made certain no fins circled us for real. "Says the naked girl in my arms."

"It's a shark," she insisted.

"It's *not* a shark."

"Do *not* let go of me." The water wasn't cold, but her entire body began to tremble with terror.

My smile faded. So did my amusement. With a gentle squeeze, I tucked her closer against my chest. "I've got you. If it was a shark, he's gonna have to take a good bite of me

47

before he'll ever make it to you."

"Do you think it's a shark?" Her words were whispered.

I tried not to smile. Her fear wasn't funny. At all. But her knee-jerk reaction to it? Adorable. "No. Pretty sure it isn't a shark."

"What, then? Some enormous creature with serious power bumped into me."

"Probably just a sand ray."

"*Big* sand ray." She continued to search the scant few feet of calm surface visible in the dark.

"Sure. Mantas can be twenty-plus feet across the fin, tip to tip."

"Manta is not a sand ray. Sand ray sounds like a puppy. Manta is a wolf."

"Better than anything else that could've bumped you. And far more likely." Probably. Mantas went shallow during the day, but I thought deeper at night. Not a chance in hell I'd share my doubts, though.

"Okay." She slowly nodded as the rigid muscles in her arms and legs began to relax. "Just a ray."

"You surf some, right?"

A long pause stretched out. Then she pulled slightly away from my chest. "Yeah." Her warm breath fogged over my lips. The tart scent of tequila reminded me of how drunk she was. "I surf some."

I had a good buzz going myself, but the faint warning bell firing in my head did nothing to stop me. I tightened my hold, quieting my voice. "Don't you have sharks in Hawai'i?"

Things were getting real. Fast. The volatile girl who'd

dropped from the sky and stood so independently on my towel earlier today clung to me. Soft, yet strong. Sexy.

And my body began to harden for her.

"Yeah, we do. Tigers, mostly. They're the ones that attack the…"

Her pause then soft gasp told me she'd felt the pulse of my growing erection against her hip. Yet she made no move to pull away.

And I refused to loosen my grip. Instead, I softened my voice further, like I'd found a young doe in the forest and didn't want to startle her into bounding off. "The ones that attack *what*?"

Our bodies rocked up and down with a larger wave, unusual for the protected bay.

When the action pulled us apart, she settled back against me, as if comfortable there. "The tourists."

Her comment, though funny, came out matter-of-fact. Like it was perfectly acceptable that residents there looked at their prime source of income as shark bait.

But I didn't laugh. Because the conversation had turned surreal. Paramount in my head—the one above my shoulders with brain cells quickly being deprived of oxygen-rich blood flow—was the incredible creature nestled in my arms. And still, I didn't want to stop talking with her, I wanted to stay with the true Leilani, the one under all those earlier posturing layers. She'd stripped herself literally and figuratively. Naked. Real.

"Why tourists?" I had to ask.

"Tan lines. Slapping the water." She gave a half-shrug.

Then she shifted, adjusting her body higher.

I closed my eyes and gritted my teeth from the friction of her movement; every nerve ending at the tip of my cock throbbed.

"Do you?" The question whispered over my ear.

Totally confused, I dipped my head toward her and rested my chin on her head. "Do I what?"

"Slap."

Her voice had gotten a whole lot throatier. Like she wasn't talking about water.

"No." I ran my hand over her hip, then stopped it to rest on the tantalizing curve of her ass. "Slapping is for sissies and cowards. So is smacking." I pulled my hand away from her skin, letting water rush in under my hand. "Spanking?" Her gasp wisped over my neck as I shoved my palm back through the water, then cupped it over her flesh, barely touching her skin, taunting her. "*Entirely* different issue."

"Spanking." Her question came out flat, on a breathy exhalation.

"Yes."

"How so?"

So many words, *totally* wrong timing to thoroughly explain. "You'll see."

She turned her head, facing me in the darkness. "I will?"

"Yeah." Our lips almost touched, the barest sliver of air between them.

Somewhere in the far reaches of my brain, that warning bell pinged again, and I huffed out a frustrated breath. It would be so easy to let go, pull her down into a wild session of carnal sex.

I felt her body relax, then tighten. Like indecision warred within her too.

"Not now."

"No spanking now?" Disappointment tinged her tone.

Fuck. "No."

Softness brushed over my lips. "What about a kiss?"

Innocent. One small taste. *So fucking tempting.*

My brain fuzzed. Every beat of my heart throbbed heat to my cock.

But I'd never stop with a single kiss. Never. Not with her.

"No." I pulled away, dropped my forehead to hers. "Neither of us is thinking straight now."

"What about getting up my skirt?" Her words softened, slurring. Body settling further, she pulled her head away from mine and rested it into the crook of my shoulder with a sigh.

Yeah. What about that? What my body rioted about. "That was before."

"Before?" Her voice lowered as her grip on my upper arms loosened.

I didn't answer her. Didn't really know the reason for the change myself. "No more questions tonight."

"Because the game is over," she murmured.

"Yeah." Long before the drinking had ended.

The gentle push and pull of the ocean, the late hour, the drinking…all had lulled her. I lifted her higher, cradling her to my chest as silence fell between us. But all around, the night played a soothing song: distant crashing waves, rustling palm fronds, the occasional splash of a jumping fish—*probably our night-bump culprit.*

Tired from a long day myself, I made for shore. As I lifted her out of the water, she stirred, lifting her head, drowsy eyes blinking open. After a dozen steps, she wrapped her arms around my neck and leaned to the side, glancing over my shoulder. "What about our clothes?"

"We won't be needing them for what we're doing."

"We won't?"

"No."

"What will we be doing?"

"Sleeping."

A soft laugh. "Oh."

Assuming I could sleep.

"But my dress…"

"I'll get it after we get you get tucked in."

"Oh."

Curving a wide path toward the doorway, I stretched out my fingers and grabbed a towel off the stack. With care, I perched her on the edge of the bed, wrapped the towel around her, and gently dried her off. Then I guided her down and pulled the thin sheet over her body, but its threadbare fabric hid nothing of the tempting curves beneath it.

"What about you?"

"I can sleep in the hammock."

"You don't have to." She patted the tiny space between her body and the edge. "Sleep with me."

"No fucking way."

"Why not?" Her eyelids drifted closed again, head nestling into the pillow. Her breathing grew deep and regular.

I pressed my lips to her forehead, brushing a gentle kiss to her skin. "Because we won't fit in that bed. Not without you on top of me." *And me inside of you.*

Later.

As promised, I picked up her dress, shook out the sand, then hung it over a roped end of the hammock outside to let the wind air it out overnight. Then I grabbed a dry towel and a square pillow from a wicker chair and went outside to catch a few *z*'s before sunup.

On an exhausted twisting lunge, I dropped into the fraying hammock, tucking the pillow under my head as I fell back. A couple of creaky swings followed. Then the only sounds became the soothing lap of waves in the bay and occasional booms of larger surf in the distance.

Tequila still buzzed in my head.

But nothing quieted thoughts of her, the girl who slept a few short steps away. Not a girl, *a woman*, who wrestled with finding her own path too.

And as I drifted off, memories of Leilani's soft laughter wove together with the best moments of my past with my brother—deeper belly laughs among two other young souls who sought their way on a deserted beach too long ago.

6
SOBERING REALITY

Leilani…

A forced swallow finally made it past my sandpaper throat.

Needle-sharp agony pierced my temples with every punishing heartbeat.

My stomach growled, empty and clearly angry about it.

After a deep inhale of stale putrid air, I crinkled my nose and held my breath. Then I cracked my eyelids open.

Shadowy darkness greeted me, the only traces of light glimmering down through slits in a thatched roof. An unfamiliar coolness seeped into my bare legs, the side of my shin, knee, thigh resting on…*hard concrete?*

Disoriented, I slid a hand along its dusty surface, leaning toward my left.

A solid wall of warm bare skin stopped my shoulder. *Mase.*

Images from last night flashed into my head: surfing, game-playing, *tequila*—explained the fuzzy memories of hugging the porcelain bowl a couple of feet in front of me. *Annnd* my naked state.

I glanced left to confirm his *also naked* state.

What happened last night?

Fragments of dreamlike moments drifted in, then faded away. But other than my throbbing head and an aching hipbone from the hard floor, I felt no other soreness. And I vaguely remembered him ditchin' on the kissin'.

He slumbered peacefully, the slow but steady rise and fall of his chest evidence of how deeply he'd fallen under.

Exhausted from all the hangover thinking, I settled back against his warmth, tucking neatly under his shoulder. Not in any hurry—my phone would've trilled up a storm if I'd been a no-show with the chartered pilot—I soaked in my last minutes of freedom.

Mase had no clue how precious a gift he'd given me last night.

To offer him the temptation of sex...and for him to clearly want me but turn me down? A first.

Yet I didn't feel rejected. Strangely, the interesting turn of events empowered me.

Without much thought, I skated a flattened palm down his forearm, then threaded my fingers together with his, my tiny hand to his larger one. His long fingers stretched, curled tightly around mine for a beat, then relaxed.

On a long sigh, I soaked it all in for the last bit of time I had left, so far away from real life. Right here in the palm of my hand, existed something different, sacred. To be wanted. Cared for—for me. Not for who I was…or wasn't. Just that girl from last night on a beach.

A chime sounded, muffled but distinct above the ocean waves and rustling palm fronds. Seconds later, another chime prodded: the phone alarm, my ten-minute warning before the pickup I'd arranged for my flight. My time away— my escape from life—had ended.

Reluctant to leave, I stayed motionless for two more chimes…as long as I dared.

Finally, I released his hand and turned toward him, watching his peaceful expression. Then I leaned forward and brushed a kiss over his cheek.

He stirred and his eyes fluttered opened. "Hey. You feeling better?" The murmured words were barely audible. His eyelids drooped half-closed waiting for my answer.

"Yeah." I brushed his messy bangs out of his eyes. "Go back to sleep."

And he did. My phone chimed once more, but he didn't stir.

With only a few minutes left, I got up, dug out my phone, then swiped the alarm off. Outside, I found my dress tangled around the end of the hammock, the one Mase had said he would sleep in. Only he hadn't. While I pulled the gauzy fabric over my head, I eyed a folded pillow on one end of the hammock and a towel crumpled into a ball in the middle. Back inside, the bed had no further story to tell, its top sheet tossed aside to reveal a slight impression from my body.

A horn honked. I ran outside to the corner of the hut

and saw a beat-up blue pickup truck with its back fender crunched in. I waved to the same driver who'd dropped me off at the beach café yesterday, held up a finger, then dashed back in to gather my bag and shoes.

I paused, halfway to the open doorway. No time for a note. Nothing to write it with or on anyway. I settled for checking his phone by the bed. Tracking farther backward, I leaned sideways to see him one more time.

All the incredible moments of the past sixteen hours fluttered through my mind. An unexpected obligation had turned into an adventure—a surprising gift.

"Good-bye, surfer boy."

All he could ever be to me. A surfer boy I'd once met.

Because once he came to my home?

Everything would be different.

A turbulent bump jerked me up so hard the plane's lap belt dug into my thighs.

"Should've slammed the rest of Mase's tequila," I muttered.

My second tin-can plane ride in two days. Not much better than the previous flight which had taken me from Tahiti to the tiny island.

Same pilot, for sure. Except then, I'd been heavily buzzin', thanks to the Hawai'i -to-Tahiti business-class seat Makani had bribed me with and Air Tahiti Nui's complimentary mixed drinks. But the puddle-jumper flight on the flip side with a nails-on-chalkboard hangover? I'd rather have sunburned nipples barbed by jellyfish.

Trying to distract myself, I grabbed my phone. Without getting too stuck in my head about reaching out to Mase, I ignored the airplane-mode rule—not even knowing if a message would go through till we landed—and sent him a text:

Can you make it by Memorial Day?

The timeframe Makani had requested.

Of course, no reply happened during the rest of the short flight. Nothing came during the hour I waited in a red plastic chair near the gate at Tahiti's airport. Bored as hell, I got up and stalked the gift shop filled with tacky tourist items and snacks.

For some reason, restless energy tingled under my skin. I blew out a slow breath, trying to calm my thumping heart. *It's just a place, Lani. He's just a guy.*

Then why did I feel like the plane leaving in about an hour was taking me farther away from everything I'd been aching for? Freedom. Foreign lands. New people. And a very sexy new *person*—with a smile that made my heart skip a beat and eyes the color of the clearest wave right as it crests toward the sky.

A shoulder-bump knocked me back into the present when a male customer reached beyond me for a bag of David's Pumpkin Seeds.

Damn, Lani. Focus on where you can *go…not where you can't.*

A half an hour later, after I'd looped through the open-air walkways twice, my phone vibrated. A text appeared from Mase:

Uh...who is this?

I smiled.

Too many girlfriends to count, surfer boy?

The clock at the departure board showed I had about twenty minutes left before my flight.

Ohhh...smartass. You must be the cute Hawaiian chick.

Shaking my head, I typed:

Not cute.

An immediate reply:

Pretty?

I scoffed.

You're not sure? *points lost*

When more than a few seconds went by, I glanced at the clock again. Finally, my phone vibrated again.

**Not texting you how beautiful I think you are.
Need to see you blush in person.**

"*Damn*, surfer boy," I muttered as I typed.

blushes

Seconds later, he volleyed back.

Fucking hell. {takes it back}

"Uh-uhhh…" Not even.

You can't take it back.

A loudspeaker blared a boarding announcement for my flight when he replied.

How did you get my number, anyway?

After slinging my bag over my shoulder, I typed as I walked to the back of the forming line.

Bumped phones with yours.

The attendants were moving faster than our messages. Another reply made it through.

Lucky phones.

One passenger remained ahead of me as I furiously typed.

Memorial Day?

No reply came as I entered the gangway. During the next fifteen minutes, all the passengers boarded, and then the doors were closed. After the tenth time of checking my phone reception with no message, I sighed, angry at myself for getting worked up about something...*someone*...I couldn't even have. By the time the plane pushed back from the gate, I stopped wishing for the impossible and finally shut off my phone.

A hard bump woke me up from a dead sleep: We had landed. I shifted back against my seat while the plane quickly slowed then taxied toward its gate. Back home. Where make-believe fun had to come to an end. Where responsibilities and generations of attitude existed. *Aloha*, but only so far.

To keep my emotions under control, I deliberately kept my phone turned off in the airport. Didn't reach for it once on the drive home. Refused to grab it from my bag when I remembered—all three times. *Well, actually thirty, if I was being honest with myself.*

On the thirty-first time, I growled in frustration and

retrieved the damn thing, grumbling out, "You're making too big of a deal over a stupid text."

When I turned it on, his reply flashed brightly on the screen.

I can do better than that. How's next Friday?

A thrill ran through me, imagining him saying the words aloud while his blue eyes sparked with playfulness. Then I scowled at myself, tamping down my foolish excitement, and replied:

Sure.

Good. Basic. Unemotional.

To my surprise, he instantly fired back another reply.

Pick me up at the airport?

Great. No excitement came with his last reply. Only dread. That I would want too much. Hope too much. *Better to kill it now.*

Sure.

7
NUTTIN' BUT TROUBLE

Mase...

Excitement buzzed through my body.

And shockingly, it wasn't from the thrill of a wave.

A beautiful island girl with a fierce gaze, sharp tongue, and secrets in her heart had promised to pick me up at the airport.

After grabbing my bags, I scanned the faces in the crowd. But no one looked familiar.

Instead, beyond baggage claim in the middle of an open-air walkway leading to the curb, an older Hawaiian man in a red tropical shirt with salt-and-pepper hair held a placard below his double chin with one word on it: PRICE.

Thrown by the change in plans, I made my way over to him.

As soon as I made eye contact, he broke into a wide

smile and held out an arm, reaching for one of my bags. "You Price?"

"Yeah, but call me Mase."

"Aloha, Mase. I'm Kevin, Makani sent me."

Makani: Leilani's brother. "What about Lei—"

The blaring airport paging system drowned out my question while Kevin grabbed my other duffel and turned toward the parking lot.

I retrieved my two loaded board and sail bags—ten feet apiece and stuffed to the seams—then followed him out to the parking lot, gear in tow. When we arrived at an older but well-maintained Ford SUV, I helped him load my smaller bags into the back then strap the board bags to the roof rack.

Irritation still chafed at me about the unexpected airport switch. But the warm midday sun and cool steady breeze began to wash away the negative vibe. Arriving at any new destination by the ocean had that calming effect on me. I sucked in a lungful of salty air, then sighed, a step more content on a spiritual level.

"Evah been ta Maui?" Kevin asked as he backed out of the parking space.

"No." Not because I hadn't wanted to, but while growing up, my country-club parents traveled to glitzier locales. If there wasn't upper echelon networking potential in his political world? My parents didn't bother.

Blowing out a hard breath to clear out the bitter taste in my mouth for the seconds I'd wasted thinking about my parents, I stared out the window as our SUV rumbled out of the parking lot and took in my first glimpses of Maui.

"Costco?" I craned my neck out the open window, shocked to see the familiar red-and-blue sign. The place looked brand new, glass walls separating a large indoor/ outdoor eating area.

"Yeah. An' a Target. Home Depot. Lowes is buildin' a biggah store. Even got one a dem fancy Whole Foods. Don' got no Victoria Secret, but dey suppos' ta be workin' on it."

I choked out a laugh. "It's okay. I'm not into buying lingerie."

"Me eidah. But my wife an' her friends talk story 'bout it, on an' on."

Not that I was opposed to lingerie. Women needed bras and panties. I got that. But lace and ribbons. Uh...no. *I'm a simple man. Naked works.*

Silence filled the cab as my thoughts drifted to Leilani. And the two of us days ago on our isolated stretch of beach. Her...naked.

The earlier calm I'd felt dissipated. Restlessness flooded into its place. Too many days had passed since the night she and I had spent together. A night filled with unspoken hope. And unfinished business.

The stoplight turned green, but Kevin waited.

"*Makai* or *mauka*?"

I blinked at his foreign words, shaking off my guttered thoughts and agitation. "Uh...what?"

"Toward da ocean or toward da mountain? *Makai* or *mauka*. Where to?"

"Where's Leilani?" I didn't explain that she was supposed to pick me up. The slight was between her and me.

"Not sure. Makani said she said she had t'ings ta do. Would meet up wit' choo latah."

But no text. No word from her. Just her clear message of wanting distance by sending a stranger without warning. Uneasy about where she and I stood, I sucked in a tight breath. Then a horn blared from a car behind us as the traffic light turned yellow.

"Hoʻokipa Beach," I finally replied, looking to settle my nerves. Firing waves were the only consistent thing that ever did—my form of therapy. "How's the surf?" At least the trade winds had the good sense to be reliable.

"*Sick.*"

"Awesome." I'd only seen video footage of windsurfing there. Looked forward to the real thing.

For a short distance down Hana Highway, the ocean spanned to the left. But my attention kept drawing right, across open fields, up green foothills, climbing further to a massive mountain whose peak disappeared into the clouds.

"Dat's Haleakala." When I glanced toward Kevin, he continued, nodding toward the mountain. "Dormant volcano. Got an observatory up der."

My thoughts flashed to the stars, gazing up at them with Leilani...*with Deke*...

We passed a polished silver-sided food truck, where the rich, salty scent of cooking meat made my mouth water. Approaching a second one, my stomach growled. "Those food trucks any goo—"

Before I got the word fully out, he swerved onto the dirt shoulder. Pings of gravel peppered the wheel wells and a small cloud of dust rose into the air, only to dissipate seconds later in a gust of wind. "Want tacos? JoJo's got da best road *grindz* dis side of da island."

My stomach growled again in answer. "Sold."

Knowing I'd be surfing in a few minutes, I only ordered one of the fish tacos on special. After our food came up, we leaned against the side of the truck, staring at the ocean as we ate. "So if food trucks aren't around, what are good places to eat?"

"Mama's Fish House. Spendy. But worth it. 'Specially if ya wanna impress a lady."

After polishing off the taco in a few bites, I crumpled up the paper wrapper, then tossed it into a trash can beside the truck.

"Wait." Pausing as I turned, I narrowed my eyes at a group of five Hawaiian girls in bikinis across the street; a couple of them held colorful shave ices.

"Ai'ight. You wase no time checkin' out da beach hunnies."

"No." I shook my head, pulse suddenly jackhammering. "Not all of them. *One* of them."

I'd recognize her anywhere. Those luscious curves. Her silken hair. But even from behind, it was the way her slight frame defined her attitude when she jutted her left hip out and dropped a hand on it.

"Leilani." The moment her name left my lips, she turned, bright smile on her face, hair whipped back by the wind. But she didn't see me, only nodded to something one of her friends said, then laughed.

Kevin snorted, then slapped me on the back. "Nuttin' but trouble fo' you der, *haole*."

Exactly.

"Yeah, I know," I mumbled under my breath.

Every bone in my body hummed with how perfect trouble sounded.

I'd done the straight and narrow. Chased *their* dream. Followed society's wishes. Been the good son. Dated the accepted, pedigreed girl.

Wasn't my path. Wasn't living. Not even close.

And as I stared at a girl filled with wildness vibrating just under the surface, I saw myself a few months ago. Someone wanting to break free, but not quite knowing how.

Hell, even I didn't have a roadmap. There wasn't any guidebook to follow when you're being true to yourself— when you're only just discovering what makes you tick deep inside.

When she finally turned my way, the easy smile on her beautiful face fell. Then her eyes narrowed. Her shoulders pulled back.

Oh, *fuck yeah*. I'd definitely strayed *far* from the safe path. Leilani Kealoha? Made wandering into an untamed jungle worth every dangerous step.

"Surfing can wait. Give me a minute, will you?"

Kevin gave me a smirking nod before I crossed the street.

Leilani said something to her friends as she cautiously watched me, and they turned my way. A couple of them smiled. One girl laughed and shouted something. An instant scowl lined Leilani's face before she whirled around to face the girl, raising her hands toward her with a jerk, fingers flaring wide in agitation. Then she stormed away from the group and tossed her barely eaten treat into the trash.

Veering toward a picnic table, she grabbed a dress and pulled it on over her head.

An additional layer of attitude rolled over every tense muscle in her body by the time she reached the side of the road.

"What are you doing here, stalking me?"

"Good question. I have a better one: Why didn't you pick me up at the airport?"

"I did. Had Makani send Kevin."

"We agreed *you'd* be my assistant. Tour guide."

"I delegated." She waved a hand toward Kevin. "He wanted to meet you. I didn't argue."

"Why did he want to meet me? He a fan?" I glanced back at Kevin, who handed over a few bills and grabbed another sizable taco from the vender.

"Sure." The corners of her lips twitched in amusement. "You could say that."

More riddles and secrets. *Fine.* She wanted to be vague, I could play. I wrote the book.

"Well, I didn't agree to delegation. I hired you. And I expect you."

"Fine."

Exactly.

"Where to? Find any houses to show me or am I staying with you tonight." I weighted the last word, dropping the question right out of it.

"Like hell you are. C'mon." She turned and started across the road, toward Kevin's SUV.

I remained where I stood, staring at her back while I marveled at the one-eighties in her demeanor. She'd reverted back the irritated girl standing on my towel in the South Pacific, as if she'd been forced to go and recruit me against her will. Back then, all it had taken was a few tequila shots to ply out the real Leilani, the one she hid under all the layers of pretense…or protection.

When she reached the back bumper, she turned to face me from across the road. Her shoulders shrugged up, brows lowered, and upturned hands raised while she mouthed something toward me with an irate questioning expression.

I read her lips, interpreting her unmistakable words: *What the fuck?*

"My thoughts exactly," I muttered.

Then I shook my head and crossed the road, suppressing a grin—pleased as fuck at how interesting an entire day with her promised to be.

8
TOO CLOSE...

Leilani...

R aw anger grated under my skin.

From my stifling circumstances.

And with my intolerant family.

But most recently—about the infuriating man sitting beside me.

It felt weird thinking about Mase as a man—same age as Makani, as most of the *kanaks* I hung out with. But no other word fit.

Arms crossed, body crammed to my side of a bench seat in the back of the real estate agent's car, I stole a glance over at him. He had the nerve to look my way. And smile.

I sighed, mad at him. But more at myself. For landing my rebellious ass into this mess.

"You two lookin' for a place to settle down in?" Evelyn,

71

the Realtor at the wheel, asked.

"No!" I cringed at my screeched word. And its violent exclamation point.

"No," I repeated lower, tone *way* calmer. Why the sudden outburst? Had to be the unexpected question, nothing more. *Not nerves.* But denial didn't change the clear evidence: I clenched my shaking hands together, stressed out. What I got for choosing a real estate agent who didn't know me.

At first, I'd thought finding a stranger would be impossible to do. Turned out, every other person living on the island, especially "retirees" who lived here year-round, had their real estate license, dabbling in selling or leasing houses between sets of waves. "Or rounds of golf…" I muttered.

"What?" Mase nudged my shoulder. When had he closed the two-foot distance between us?

I shoved him back, making him shoot an arm out to keep from crashing against the far door. Then I forced my body over into the couple of inches of space he'd lost and stayed in the center of my seat, claiming my territory back.

You can do this, Leilani.

I could do anything. Had fooled my family for years. And I had no intention of them getting un-fooled. I wouldn't let them find out; their acceptance was too important to me.

Focusing on the back of Evelyn's shiny black hair, how the blunt cut fell perfectly above her shoulders without a strand out of place, I answered her question, "He's only here to surf."

"To live." He glanced at me with an arched brow.

My ass. "Temporarily."

"Permanently."

Doubt it. "We'll see."

"You think I can't plant roots?"

I dropped him an exhausted look. "Why should I? Most people don't."

"It's true." Evelyn glanced over her shoulder at him. "Average stay is less than two years."

"Island fever," he added with an understanding nod.

Evelyn slowed as we approached our first stop, someone's one bedroom 'ohana behind a main house. "Seems only those who have a love for the island never want to leave."

"Right." The person I was supposed to be. Only...

"Except for adventurers at heart," he murmured loud enough for only me to hear as the warmth of his hand covered my thigh. He gave a gentle squeeze, then left his hand there.

Intimate.

And...not.

Under the solid, continued pressure, sizzling tingles formed beneath my skin. A deeper heat gradually spread up my thigh, until it settled into a low throbbing ache, right between my legs. But it didn't stop there. A heavier warmth drifted upward, into my gut, then higher, surrounding my thumping heart.

I gasped at the realization—that he affected me so much, so quickly. Not just physically. Deeper. Stronger. And that... he *got* me—understood what I wanted, remembered what I'd longed to do with my life from one drunken night where we'd poured our hearts out with no fear or judgement.

Then I drew in several deep breaths, until my head spun with dizziness.

"Ready, kids?" Evelyn had already opened her car door, stood outside looking in toward the two of us.

We'd been sitting there. Me breathing. Him touching.

Snapping the rest of the way out of my brain-fuzz, I pulled my gaze from her, stared at the back of the headrest straight ahead for a beat, then glanced at him.

He stared at me. Had probably been watching me the whole time.

Lifting his brows ever so slightly, the corners of his lips twitched into a small knowing smile. "Ready?"

"Sure." *Not even close.*

But I'd ridden the unknown before, had dropped into fearsome waves blinded with where to carve my line until the last second. If I could do that with the deadly power of the ocean nipping at my heels? *I can do anything.* I repeated the mantra.

And maybe…

I opened the door, slipped out from under the sensual weight of his hand, and planted my feet on solid ground. He got out and shut the door while I blew out a steadying breath. Gaze locking with mine, he rested a hand on the roof of the polished black Lexus sedan. I didn't look away from him—didn't flinch. I stared down what I feared most at that moment in time.

Just maybe…

I get off on the danger.

"…and this is your place to park," Evelyn droned on, as if Mase and I hadn't been on our own planet until seconds ago, as if we'd been listening.

"No." He opened the door and began to get back into the car.

The emphatic word from him surprised me. "Not even gonna look?" The place needed a coat of paint. The metal roof had rust in a ton of places, but it didn't look like it would leak. Much.

"Nope. Not big enough."

"The land or the house?" Evelyn asked while rifling through a handful of pages she'd tucked under her arm.

"Both." He narrowed his eyes in thought, staring at the older buildings as we got back in. "Not some shack behind another house."

"You willing to go rougher for it?" She paused on one of the pages, scanned down its length. Then she started the car and backed out of the driveway. "Maybe a fixer upper?"

"Prefer it, actually."

"There's a couple of places that might work."

"Where at?" I asked, suddenly needing to know where he might live.

"Haiku." She drove to the end of the neighborhood street, then turned left.

Oh. Close. "Where else?"

"Kula." Her eyes met mine in the mirror.

Better. Farther from my place. From the beach, too. Which was a whole lot safer for me. Wasn't about to point it out to Mase, though.

Minutes later, Evelyn slowed, then turned onto dual concrete strips with grass growing in the middle. "This is a ribbon driveway. Center needs to be mowed," she added as the long uncut blades brushed the underside of her car.

We'd passed the historic sugar mill but hadn't yet hit downtown Haiku, its sleepy town center reclaiming new life with retail and restaurants occupying the renovated pineapple cannery.

The tires hadn't even rolled to a stop before Mase opened his door and got out. The plantation-style house was small, but bigger than the last one. He walked along the line of plants that marked the edge of the yard as he scanned the surrounding properties. "Neighbors are close."

I blinked. Never having shopped for a house to live in before, I grew more and more fascinated by what was important to him.

Curiosity rippled under my skin. "You need faraway neighbors?"

He walked toward me with slow steps, expression growing intense. My breath caught at the mischievous spark in his eyes. The world fell away; I had no idea where Evelyn had gone.

I continued to stare at him as he approached, but I didn't move a muscle.

Close.

Closer.

My breathing grew shallow as he gradually pressed into my space. Determined to keep our eye contact, I held my ground, tilting my face upward. Every instinctual sense I had riveted on him: I heard the subtle rasp in his deep breaths, noticed his pupils widen in those ice-blue eyes, almost felt the pulse beating at the base of his neck.

He broke our eye contact, lowering his head. Breath feathered over my ear, ruffled through my hair. "Sounds tend to carry at night." Gruffness edged his tone, along with a heavy dose of innuendo.

Riiight…

I swallowed hard, mind reeling with the sordid images. Because I didn't get the impression he was a screamer—which meant he *caused* said sounds.

No awesome smartass reply came. My brain got stuck on all the things he might do to make a woman scream loud enough for neighbors to hear.

And my body responded, aching with heat in all kinds of intimate places.

Blowing out a hard breath, I stepped away from him and glanced up into eyes blazing with fire. With firm resolve, I gave him a slow headshake, then turned away.

I said *no* to him.

No to me.

Even though every cell in my body was already screaming *nothing remotely close to a no*.

"Yeah," I muttered, taking one solid step after another to increase the space between us. When I reached the front corner of a small overgrown garden beside the house, I turned to see him still standing there, in the same spot where he'd teased me with clear intent. Then I drew in a breath that in no way calmed me. "*Dangerous.*"

And so off limits.

Not only because he was different—was *haole*. I warily eyed him from the good fifteen-foot distance I'd made with every step away from him. Most of all, because I sensed something more powerful rumbled under his pale tanned skin than he exposed on his player surface.

Something more *same* to me than anyone I'd ever met.

9
A TOUCH ROUGH

Mase...

She's flustered.

Leilani narrowed her eyes at me.

I held her gaze and stifled a smile.

She seemed to be realizing the truth: I got to her.

She pulled in slow, deep breaths. Had physically moved out of reach. Wrinkled her brow in concentration, probably trying to ignore her body...and shove thoughts I'd intentionally planted out of her mind.

None of it would help.

I'd already gotten under her skin. Burrowed down nice and deep to the point goose bumps broke out right before my eyes. Not from the warm day. Not from the balmy wind. From me.

Yeah, my chest swelled with pride. Not gonna lie.

But was it enough? Would she be true to her nature…or continue with her own denial?

Only one way to find out—continue paddling forward. And I couldn't wait to keep pushing her buttons, testing her limits.

Did doubt still rub at me? Sure. It had spiked with the instant icy treatment on her home turf. But no risk? No reward. And even though she'd built up an impressive wall to hide behind, I was gambling she'd be brave enough to let me drop in past her defenses.

Never breaking our gaze, I slipped my hands into my pockets and walked after her, taking my time in our slow-motion chase. She held her ground once more—while taking those deep inhalations that did incredible things to her enticing breasts.

When I got close enough to touch her again, her chin raised. Simply to keep hold of my gaze? Not with that defiant look sparking in her eyes.

All of a sudden, something lightning fast skittered in my peripheral vision.

"Whoa, shit!" I launched backward a good couple of feet.

Low laughter rasped from her lips as she quickly stepped between me and the monster. "It's just a cane spider, surfer boy."

"That fucker isn't *just* anything." I leaned to the side, trying to get a better look around her. "It's as big as my hand."

"*Nooo…*" She turned, then slowly reached her spread hand a good ten feet away from the spider but in a direct line over its body. The ginormous arachnid quivered on long, hairy spindle legs. "Only as big as *my* hand."

Between one blink and the next, the damn thing scurried away from her, a shadowed blur. "Fuck!" My entire skin crawled from the image stuck in my head, and I shook my body from head to toe like a wet animal, trying to rid myself of the creeps. "*Nope.* It's the size of my dog."

She turned toward me, surprise registering on her face. Then her luscious lips curved into the most incredible smile: corners half-lifted with the center kept pressed together, like she hid a juicy secret behind them; even though cold logic told me she tamped down hysterical amusement.

Her head tilted a little. "You have a dog," she murmured.

Then her lips quirked, her enjoyment at my freak-out flashing back. "*My* hand size," she insisted. Then she lifted her arm and held it out from her body, facing an open palm toward me as she spread her fingers.

Stunned with her sudden one-eighty openness, I mirrored her action, raising my arm, spreading my hand open to connect our palms. My hand dwarfed hers, my fingers stretching a good inch-and-a-half longer.

We didn't move.

Barely breathed.

We both simply stared at our joined hands.

I got pulled under, tumbling fully into the moment, feeling like a little kid.

And just like that, any remaining doubt I had ebbed from my mind.

Momentarily stunned by the power of the simple act— her seeking to be nearer to me, even to prove a point, while my entire being drew closer, craving the same connection—I sucked in a shaky breath. Then I replied to her comment while we stayed joined in our hand-size comparison. "Not *my* dog, exactly. Ava. She belongs officially to my ex-roommate and his wife, Cade and Hannah."

Her smile softened, her sparkling gaze holding mine as her voice lowered, "They're good luck…cane spiders. You should always try to save them."

"From what?" Couldn't imagine.

"Don't hurt 'em. Catch 'em and—"

"Catch them?" I laughed at the ridiculous thought, breaking our fragile spell of seriousness. "With what? A drinking glass and piece of paper? Even a giant margarita glass wouldn't cut it."

Her brow firmed as she pulled her hand from mine. "A bowl, then."

I crossed my arms, shaking my head. "Did you *see* how fast that thing moved? Fucker could race a cheetah and win."

Her brow wrinkled further into a scolding look, then her features softened into amusement. "They do move pretty fast, for sure."

"You ever caught one?"

Her expression turned thoughtful as she stared into the garden where the creature disappeared. "No."

"Ever have one in your house?"

"Yeah." She dropped me an exasperated look. "I *did* grow up here."

I shot her a deadpan right back. "And you just left it there?"

"Where?"

"In your house." The whole idea fired another shudder down my spine.

Her lips pressed into a firm line. But the corners of her mouth twitched, as if she fought a smile. "Yeah. They're beneficial hunters. They don't spin webs. They're typically nocturnal, stalk prey at night, kill mostly other pests."

"What kind of other pests?" I wasn't convinced anything could be as bad as that.

"Cockroaches. Scorpions."

"Okay." I exhaled, somewhat relieved. I didn't want any of those bugs around either.

"Bats, I've heard."

"Bats?"

"Hoary bats."

"Hairy bats?" Hairy spider. Hairy bat. Sure. Why not?

"*Hoary.*" Her gaze became thoughtful and unfocused as it lifted to a blue bat-less sky. "They're endangered. And the only indigenous mammal to Hawai'i."

"Uhhh…the spiders don't spin webs—but hunt bats." I held up my hands in surrender and shook my head, shoulders quaking with laughter. "Yeah, I give up. Damn things can take whatever they want. I ain't catchin' jack shit."

She smiled, wide and genuine. Her hip bumped out a little as she crossed her arms and stared. Like she didn't know what to do with me.

I'd have come up with a dozen suggestions under normal circumstances…but my mind got stuck on one very important thing. The girl so intent on hiding her true self from me had let her mask slip. She had a soft spot. For dogs. And ickier creatures.

Maybe…*maybe*…she'd grow to have a soft spot for a long lost white boy who she herself had lured into her world.

There's hope for you yet, Mase.

Evelyn stepped out the front door. "You two coming inside? I've turned on all the lights and opened all the windows to let the trade winds flow through."

Leilani and I held each other's gaze, neither flinching. The smiles faded, but something positive remained in the aftermath. Quiet seconds ticked by, heavy with unspoken meaning.

"No," I finally replied, staring into bottomless dark-brown eyes filled with emotion. "Neighbors are too close."

Leilani's eyes widened. Her breath caught.

Yep. I'd pushed one more of her fantastic buttons again. Worth the risk.

Evelyn stepped between us, breaking the tender emotional spell. "Then, I think the last one might be perfect. Touch rough on the surface, but worth the effort…if you have an open mind."

Evelyn went back inside to resecure the house. As we waited, Leilani tried to hunt down more cane spiders with a mischievous grin—while I resolutely kept a good ten-foot distance from her at all times.

When we got back on the road, Leilani kept to her side of the car, staring out her window, away from me. She needed space. To process everything. Process me. And I respected what she needed.

Along both sides of the road, countless acres of pastureland rolled by. Around the next lazy bend, we encountered a herd of cattle and a couple of ranch hands on horseback right as they finished crossing the paved roadway.

"Those are *Paniolos*," Evelyn tipped her head toward them. "Hawaiian cowboys."

Leilani nodded her head, but said nothing.

Done with her silent treatment, figuring Leilani had gotten plenty of space for now, I nudged her knee. "Not the tour-guide type?"

"Was tour guide in my job description?"

"Huh. I'm thinkin' we should talk job description."

"Nah, I'm good."

Ha. Not even. "Tour guide? A definite."

She snorted. Seconds later, she glanced my way for the first time since we'd gotten back in the car. Amusement sparked in her eyes. "I could do tour guide." She stared out the window beyond me. "Coming up on your right? Goats." She pointed at hundreds of the floppy-eared critters; a few munched on tall grasses near the fence line.

"Very funny, master of the obvious."

"Those goats belong to Surfing Goat Dairy," Evelyn supplied. "Lower part of Kula is where they have their main operation. They've won a bunch awards for their goat cheese. They even have a children's petting zoo."

Chaotic images of a bunch of kids running around flooded in—both knee-high screaming humans and bleating goats. But the *kids* pun wasn't funny enough to comment on. "Uh, yeah. I'll skip that."

"Not into kids?" Leilani glanced at me.

Little humans, she meant, not baby goats. "They're not bad, once they're old enough to take care of themselves. It's all the squealing and sticky hands on everything."

She said nothing. Only stared at me with an inscrutable expression. She didn't look pissed. Only curious. Which fired up questions in my head. Did she not care for kids either? Or did something more devious unfold behind those expressive dark eyes? Like arranging for delightful tour-guide activities, such as a goat-farm adventure...or a kiddie-surfing camp.

"We're heading *mauka*, farther up into Kula," Evelyn announced as we turned left.

Toward the mountain, I thought to myself, doing my best to remember Hawaiian words.

We began to drive up a steep switchback road through a tighter residential neighborhood. But the higher we climbed, the more rural and spread apart the properties became. After a last long uphill, Evelyn turned onto a graveled driveway.

"Here we are." She got out and we hiked uphill with her to a dilapidated square structure. "Not much, I know." She crossed her arms and squinted at the small house. "But imagination is key here."

When she opened the front door, I scanned above us, taking note of the massive amount of wood rot, the sagging roofline. Inside, stains marked several spots on a low popcorn ceiling. Spray-painted graffiti covered every available wall space. Windows were gridded shells without glass. Carpet had been worn threadbare. What remained of the ceramic tile flooring in the kitchen and breakfast nook was cracked or broken apart, but most had gone missing entirely: large gray areas of cement surrounded smaller patches of faded yellow tile.

"*Whoooa*," I whispered under my breath, drawn through the house toward the back deck and out the sliding glass door the moment Evelyn opened it.

The whole island gently unrolled below us before resting at an impressive double coastline; two graceful blue arcs curved between us and the distant majestic West Maui Mountains.

"Right there." The reason the sad shack behind me had any chance to be lived in again—a view unlike any other.

A stronger wind suddenly whipped through, rattling some chimes off to my right. When I went to investigate, I found what used to be a garden. Jungle vines ran through it, wild thorny bushes and gangly trees had sprouted here and there, and even a night-blooming jasmine had claimed a back corner. A weathered wooden bench peeked out from under a mass of green in the center.

One bush toward the front caught my attention. "What are these?" It had odd sizable buds that resembled pinecones. Only they were fuzzy. And pink. One bloom had opened and was huge, almost the size of my face.

"King protea," Leilani, my new tour guide, graciously supplied.

"Yes." The Realtor walked past us, pointing downslope. "This property has rows of different species. The owner leases the land to a neighboring farmer. So you get the beauty of the flowers and he gets an agricultural exemption."

"Who, the farmer?"

"No," Evelyn clarified, "the owner. Makes his property taxes cheaper."

"Oh. What about all this?" I gestured a sweeping arm alongside where we stood, toward the overgrown mass of vegetation.

"A badly neglected garden. That's avocado. Lemon. There's even a protected banana patch toward the back, but they struggle at this higher elevation; it gets colder than bananas like at night. Doesn't look like anyone's caring for the garden, but if you cleaned it up, it'd be a nice producing space."

"Hmmmph." Not really into fruit, I eyed the ground. I hadn't been into gardening…ever. But I had been interested. Never really had the space to explore my ideas. Or the location.

Tabling my thoughts, we continued on to examine the rest of the house. "Not bad."

I inspected the eves around the perimeter more closely. Most were crumbling from dry rot with no protective coat of paint. I grabbed hold of a few sections, knocked a handful of others. Further in, the framework appeared solid. Shingles on the roof had begun to crisp, curling under the baking sun. The covered back deck suffered from neglect, but nothing a few replacement boards, a good sanding, and sealant couldn't repair. "Got good bones."

"It's only a rental." Leilani's sour tone hinted that she didn't approve of me fixing it up. While I'd done my tire-kicking inspection of the property, she'd followed me the entire time, silently and a good half dozen paces back.

A rental in need of a miracle occupant. "Looks like it's sat abandoned for a *long* time."

She cast a doubtful expression at the place. "Needs *a lot* of work."

"Needs an *overhaul.*" My voice raised loud enough for the agent to hear. "I'm thinking seven hundred a month."

Evelyn perked up and headed toward us from the shade of a tree the moment dollars were mentioned. "Places this size easily command two thousand."

"Those places about to collapse?" I grabbed a solid-looking beam beside a dry-rotted section. The entire portion beneath my hand broke away, then crumbled to dust under the crush of my fist.

Evelyn blinked, staring at the gap I'd created.

When I clapped my hands together, a brown cloud puffed up before vanishing into a strong wind gust. "I'll fix it up in exchange for the rent allowance."

Evelyn raised her black manicured brows. "And once it's fixed?"

"Does he want me to keep it in good repair? This level of deferred maintenance tells me the landlord doesn't want to spend money. It's only going to fall apart again once I fix it up if they don't seal the wood, paint the metal, clean off the mold. I'm guessing they'd rather sell this someday with a standing house versus a pile of rubble?"

The Realtor sighed. "Let me make the call." Cell phone pressed to an ear, she turned and walked down the side of the house.

"Make sure to run by a lease of two years with that price. I'll want to keep my fixed-up pad for a while." I'd already completed a generic rental application before I flew out here, so she knew I'd be good for the deposits, the rents, and the improvements.

Evelyn nodded, then disappeared around the front corner.

The second we were alone, I crossed my arms and glanced at my tour guide. "Well, what d'ya think?"

"I think it's a dump."

"But a livable dump."

"Barely." She eyed the back of the house with suspicion.

"What's that?" I nodded toward a smaller structure in the back of the garden that listed toward the right.

She huffed out a laugh. "A chicken coop praying to die?"

"Chickens." The gears in my mind started turning. "As in, daily eggs?"

She gave me a precious look with an arched brow. "Uh, yeah. That's the idea."

"Where do I get chickens around here?" I lived off eggs. But had never had them fresh.

"Kula Hardware. Has 'em in the spring."

"Think they have them still?"

"Maybe. Look, I dunno about this place. Maybe Evelyn can find more to look at."

"It's perfect. I don't need to see anything else."

Her expression hardened into seriousness. She took a deep breath, crossed her arms over her chest, then bumped her hip out a little as she tapped her right toes. As if she struggled with a problem. Her gaze grew unfocused in thought like she weighed out something heavy—*about me?* On a quick nod, as if decision made, she snapped her gaze onto me. "You hired me, right?"

Her sudden decisiveness threw me. Curiosity about all her problem-solving made me bite. "Yep. In fact, you can review the lease for me. I need to go to the hardware store anyway to get estimates on supplies. I'll give you the list of materials and costs and you can make sure with other rents that I'm getting a fair deal."

"But...don't you want my opinion right away?"

"Sure."

"You're twenty minutes from the nearest surf. Twenty-five from Hoʻokipa. Thirty or more from others. Why not get a surf shack or apartment steps from the beach?"

How to explain a lifetime of searching? Then feeling for the first time that I'd found it. Not at all what I'd expected. But the best things in life never were.

"Because *this*" —I took a deep breath, looked around, then pegged her with a serious look— "*feels like home.*"

10

WHEN THE WORLD TILTS...

Leilani...

Mase's last word echoed in my head as I stared at him.
Home.

What Maui meant to me. Deeper than any dot on a two-dimensional map. Stronger than the ancient land beneath my feet. Greater than the vast blue oceans. Her energy sang through me.

And that feeling, the loyalty to something undefinable, was the very reason why I'd been distancing myself from him.

He represented everything *haole—not* of my island.

"You got something to take notes with?"

I blinked, his voice snapping me from my thoughts. "No."

Thick blond eyebrows shot up, then his gaze dropped to the front pocket of my dress. "Don't tell me you can't type something on that phone burning a hole in your pocket."

"In what? A text?"

"No, smartass. There's a Notes app."

I glared at him and pulled out my phone. With an irritated flick of my finger, I animated the screen. I had no idea why I fought against him so hard with every little thing. Maybe I'd been ordered around all my life. Wanted some freedom to make my own decisions.

Scanning the apps on the first page, before sliding to the next, I was vaguely aware of him pacing the back length of the house. A yellow-and-white app tucked into the middle of the third screen caught my eye.

Huh. Notes.

Refusing to admit he was right, I glanced up. Unstoppable, an indignant tone laced my words, "What *note* is so important?"

Walking the side of the house, lips moving with every step as if counting, he held up a finger, signaling me to wait. When he finished, he nodded then looked my way, eyes squinting in the direct sunlight. "Make a list. First item: Get something to taking notes with."

My scowl was met with his smirk.

"Funny. Next?"

"Dimensions of house: twenty by thirty. Materials: carpentry tools, two saw horses, plywood, lumber, toolbox…" He droned on, giving estimated amounts and other details.

My fingers did their best to match his quick words. And the longer he spoke, and the faster I typed, the more I realized I shouldn't have fought him so hard. My typing fumbled as it finally hit me.

I need this. A purpose.

And if I wanted to make my own decisions, then I'd have to figure out what he needed before he knew it. Be the assistant he never expected me to be.

Filled with a greater motivation, I followed him and did my best to look at the house through his eyes, his vision. "It's not so bad."

"Good. You're gonna help me fix it up."

I choked out a laugh. "Definitely not."

He cupped a hand to his ear. "What's that? Is that another 'no' I hear? With that capital *Y* and exclamation points?"

"You're insane."

"Possibly."

I crossed my arms, shaking my head. "Not gonna do it."

"Our lack of details in your job description says you are."

"We should put my responsibilities in writing."

He gave a halfhearted shrug. "Don't need to. We have an oral agreement."

"I'm sure I have a legal-out there," I grumbled.

"I'm sure you don't. You agreed when I said personal guide, PR rep, assistant, whatever I need."

"No, you said 'whatever I want to call myself.'"

"Doesn't change the implied duties. Guide, PR rep, assistant."

"*Office* assistant."

"Didn't say that, but yeah, that too."

I scowled. "And if I don't?"

"Don't what?"

"Agree to your terms?"

"What, you gonna hire a lawyer?"

"Maybe. I know lawyers here."

"No dice. You agreed to our verbal terms—on a remote island where *you* found *me*, in a place where things scrawled on napkins and handshakes are binding contracts. And I'm here—as we agreed per your verbal stipulations—ready, willing, and able to represent your brother's company."

All of a sudden, he moved, stealthy and smooth, but fast. One moment he stood ten feet away, the next he towered over me, the heat of his body almost touching mine. *My ass, he couldn't catch a cane spider.* When I tilted my head up, staring into blue eyes that had darkened, I swallowed hard.

His breath fanned over my face, minty and warm. "I know lawyers too, helped one study for the bar for months. And she aced it. You don't have a legal leg to stand on."

My fists clenched, anger sparking in my gut at hearing about a "she" in his life, even as my body reacted to his, turning hot for an entirely different reason, lower, and achier.

"Or, instead of battling it out in court" —his voice lowered, booming deeper and softer with every next word— "we could battle it out here, see what you're made of."

I took a step back, needing more inches of distance. "I don't need to prove myself to you."

"Didn't say you did."

And still, the challenge hung crystal clear in the tense air between us.

I narrowed my eyes at him. "I'm sure I could swing a hammer."

A lazy grin curved his lips. "That's my girl. We'll start

you off light. How are you with weeds?"

His humor got lost on me. Because, without warning, my heart stuttered at his possessive words. I had no idea why. Not like he was any different than any other guy. Same idiot ideas in their head, like tricking girls into being construction workers and weed pullers. And same thinking with their dicks, getting all up in my space like that.

Evelyn reappeared before I got a chance to respond. "He'll take it. First month's plus a security deposit, and he'll do a two-year lease."

My head spun. He'd be here to stay. For real. For two years, at least.

"Okay." He clapped his hands once, then rubbed them together, oblivious to the fact my entire world had shifted. "Let's check out this board shop of your brother's."

Right. I blew out a hard breath. Makani's. Where Kevin had dropped Mase's bags off after taking us to the real estate office.

The twenty-five minute car ride down seemed surreal. Going up the mountain, everything had remained up in the air. On the drive back, things were settling into place for Mase. Fast. Me? Totally unsettled.

But the conversation in the car seemed lighter than before, mostly Evelyn sharing Maui factoids with Mase and his follow-up questions back at her. Staring out the window, I focused on steadying my breaths, grateful for the reprieve.

Eventually we made it back to the shop. When Mase walked in, his gaze scanned the room and I let him take the lead.

When my brother came through the back workroom doorway into the retail area of the shop, sanding mask still on his face, Mase tipped his head toward him. "You Makani?"

My brother gave a nod. "Mase." Then Makani pulled the dust mask down below his chin, and extended a hand out toward Mase. "*Howzit, brah?*"

"Not bad." Mase gave him a firm handshake. "Found a house to rent."

"Yeah? Where at?"

Mase glanced at me, raising his eyebrows with a questioning expression.

"Kula." Uneasiness rippled through me again the instant I said the place, as if speaking it aloud made it more real. On a deep breath, I tried to shake the feeling. "He grabbed Nelson's old place."

"Wot, dat shack?" He slipped into Pidgin drawl. "Dat t'ing fall down t'morrah aftahnoon."

I laughed, glancing toward Mase. "That's what we always say."

Makani nodded. "Winds kick up to twenty plus miles an hour most days. Batter those crusty walls. Then the rains come. Can't believe the damn place is still standing."

With a nod toward Mase, I folded my arms over my chest. "He's gonna fix it up."

"Yeah?"

"Yeah." Mase scanned the room. "Let's talk boards. And sponsorship."

"You sure you wanna take Leilani on?"

"Kani!" I punched him in the shoulder. "It's a done deal."

"I *dunnooo*…" Mase rolled his eyes toward the ceiling, as if reconsidering it.

"Fine. You wanna ditch me before I even show you what I've got, suit yourself. Not the first time." I stormed out of the suddenly too-small room.

But I hung back within earshot, leaning against the outside wall between the door and the corner of the building, digging my toes into the cool shaded sand as I glared out toward the ocean.

"No, *brah*." Makani's voice drifted through the open door. "Let her chill."

"She always so…?" Mase let the unfinished question hang.

What? Strong…independent?

I nodded, to the world, to Mase. "You bet your city-boy ass, I am," I mumbled.

"Defensive?" Mase filled in the blank as his voice drifted closer. "Stubborn…?"

My breath caught and I froze as his tone dropped to a near whisper. The hairs stood up on the back of my neck. He had to be inches away, hovering just inside the doorway.

"Yeah." My brother's voice had lowered, even as it also grew louder, clearer.

In my mind's eye, we stood lined up at the front of the board shop, me hidden from their view, Mase in the doorway barely out of sight, and my brother just behind and beside him.

Makani, don't say anything*…don't you dare* breathe a word.

Controlling my breaths, I stared far out across the calm blue of the ocean. On a slow exhale, I cast a wish out to the wind—that I'd find my way, discover some kind of peace.

"And...*more*." Mase finished.

The weight of his last word held meaning and wonder—*respect*.

Tears sprang to my eyes. I pinched them shut, willing them away, as a choking cramp seized my throat.

It'd been such a long time since anyone had had *that* kind of belief in me.

11
PARADOX

Mase...

Instinct kept me rooted in place, even when Makani turned and walked deeper into his shop.

Nothing felt good about leaving Leilani hanging after she'd stormed out, clearly upset at me; my gut screamed to go and find her, settle things down between us.

But her brother knew her best.

And even after spending hours looking at houses, I still had no idea what had set her off between the first time I'd met her in the South Pacific, where we'd been real with each other, and today, where we'd been skirting real all day long. *Something on Maui? Me?*

Resigned to the fact that I couldn't do anything for her at the moment, I followed Makani through the front retail area, past long quivers of boards lined up on either side of the shop. He lifted a hand with slightly gnarled fingers to briefly touch the last few, an artist paying reverence to his creations. As we reached a work bay in the back half of the building, I noted his resemblance to Leilani with his lean muscular frame and their similar dark facial features. He even had long black hair, only his was pulled back and fastened with a tie.

When he turned, he stared at me, cocking his head a little.

I furrowed my brow. Had I missed something? "What?"

"Leilani likes you."

"You're high." Even if I suspected it, wouldn't dare flinch about it in front of her brother.

"Nuh-uh." He crossed his arms. "She does."

"You'd have to be—to think she likes me after all the drama back there."

"Means she likes you. A lot. Never seen her that fired up over nuttin' before."

I glanced toward the front of the shop again and caught her profile through the large plate glass window. She leaned against a railing by the walkway. Her arms were rigid, her jaw clenched. Cogs turned in my head, trying to make sense of her irritated demeanor, but nothing clicked into place. "But…she doesn't *want* to like me."

"'Ass *right*. Leilani want nuttin' ta do wit' choo. An' she do."

Confused as fuck about the contradiction, I shook my head.

He picked up a sander from the table between us, then relocated it safely out of the way on a workbench beside other shaping tools. "And you?"

"What about me?" I pushed off the wall, turning my back on the paradox outside to focus on the main reason I'd come in the first place. *Not* the girl. I'd made a vow before meeting Leilani not to live for anyone other than me first. "Why am I here, you mean?"

Makani shrugged. Like that wasn't what he'd meant, but accepted the misunderstanding anyway. "Sure. You like my boards. Gotta be somet'ing redeemable 'bout you."

"I do like them. Especially what you're making them from. Recycled materials, right?" He had one half-shaped on the worktable. Admiring its lines, I ran a hand over one curving rail from tail to nose.

"Yep. Experimenting with new woods and natural resins, too."

"They're light."

He gave a nod, then lifted his work-in-progress, angling it toward me. "Try this one."

"Whoa." The board felt light as a sail, but had great balance. No idea how he achieved a level of art with a structure so simple, but he did—better than any I'd seen. And to be able to make a better board without poisoning the environment? "Pure genius," I whispered.

He crossed his arms and shrugged again, expression remaining humble. "Ain't much to it. I care 'bout 'āina, kai: da land, da water. We live, drink, breathe it all. No dollars or biz should touch that—not for me. Doing and caring? Same thing."

His voice hardened with every word, vocabulary

sharpening, Pidgin almost disappearing. Maybe his family spoke it, maybe he'd grown up around the dialect. But like Leilani, he seemed highly educated, quick-witted, and appeared to have serious business acumen.

Which circled back to the reason why we'd hooked up in business. "And you want me to represent the brand…" And by association, spread a message of conservation, protection of our planet. Until then, I hadn't given the whole thing deeper thought. But standing in his shop, my decision to sign with him—one initially prompted by his spirited sister, not the earth-friendly boards—felt better than ever. "I'm honored."

"Yep. Name on the boards. Mentioned in interviews."

I nodded at a sailboard mounted on the wall. "Windsurfing only?"

"Why, you entering other competitions?"

"Maybe. Gonna feel out what I like."

He dropped an assessing look at me, then narrowed his eyes. "Not surfing for prize money?"

"Nope." A long pause followed. Something he should've questioned never came. Annnd…yet another layer added to the Leilani-paradox. Earlier, he'd teased about me taking her on, but mentioned nothing about his sponsorship money—I wasn't getting a dime of it, Leilani was. However her brother didn't seem to know that yet. *Interesting*. But not my secret to tell.

The primary reason burned in my chest. "Don't want to be governed by money." My whole life had revolved around it. Sickened by the fucked-up world that couldn't see beyond greed and power to value the important things, I'd left to seek a simpler way of life.

With Makani's beliefs, maybe I'd found it.

"It's about the wave." Always had been. Why I'd returned to the water. "Doesn't matter to me whether I'm on a surfboard, sailboard, or kite."

"You prefer short or long?"

"Depends on my mood."

He nodded in understanding. "Trick or chillin'."

"Exactly."

"And the wave. Oahu's got dozens of breaks along her north shore, from Kahuku Point to Ka'ena Point. We've got a decent amount, but from now until fall, it'll depend on the storms. Windsurfing will be your most consistent ride."

A breeze kicked through the place, rustling papers on a table-turned-desk in the back. I caught images of design sketches on the pages as they settled. Curiosity drew me closer. "Mind if I have a look?"

"Go for it. Tell me what you think."

A black lava stone sat as a paperweight on a stack of drawings. I moved it to an open wood surface area on the corner, then began flipping through the loose pages, turning each over as I went, holding them down so they didn't fly away in the crossbreeze.

"Want a beer?"

"Yeah. Thanks." My attention caught on an unusual offset design, a single fin jutting out from the longer side, a pair of fins angled on the other. "These are really great."

"Enough to try out?"

Order boards, he meant. And what the hell, we'd embarked on a business journey together. And I didn't do things half-ass. "Yeah, I'm in."

My gaze shifted up to the cork tiles mounted on the wall. Pictures hung there, some of him on big waves.

A few looked like Jaws. "You ride this winter?"

"Fuck, yeah. El Niño churned up some monsters. Too good to pass up." He handed me a beer, nodding at a couple of photos in the upper corner. "Bone-jarring day. Thirty-footers roarin' down. You rip any big waves?"

"Chased a few winter storms. Didn't have much time to catch—" I blinked hard and leaned forward, focus stuck on another picture in the center—on the girl in it.

"That Leilani?"

"Yep. She can crush it with the best of the guys."

"Damn. And that's Jaws?" The famous unforgiving wave erupted offshore in winter, not far from where we stood.

"Yeah, Pe'ahi." He called the break by its official name. "Crazy girl ordered a quiver of nine-footers. Only broke two of 'em."

Huh. I guzzled down a few swallows, remembering how she'd turned down perfect barrels when we'd met. Even then, instinct had pinged at me that she surfed. But... "Wow. Had no idea she was that good."

"She doesn't like to broadcast it. Only surfs with people she knows, trusts."

Okay. I got that.

After turning through the last of his sketches. I flipped half of them back over, then reassessed a couple of the innovative designs, taking another long pull of beer. The name at the top of one page was "Reef Flyer," the other, "Cobalt Dream."

"Okay." Ideas tumbled in my head as I righted the rest of the stack, then returned the lava rock on top. "Hook me up with two sailboards to start. I like these last two designs here. Only I'm thinkin' for the Reef Flyer" —I grabbed a pencil and a blank sheet of paper from a torn-open ream sitting on a shelf above me, then began sketching— "cut the angle a bit sharper here. Less rocker curve. Wider here."

"Yeah, I could do that." He stared at my sketch, tilted his head, then bit his lip in thought. "What do you think about this…" With quick strokes, he removed an interesting nip in the tail.

"Yeah, cool. And I want a Cobalt Dream, as is."

"Got it." He grabbed a lined notebook, wrote a few comments, then paper-clipped my drawing to the page before flipping to a clean one. "Anything else?"

"What kind of turnaround do you have?"

"I can do three or four a day, depending. Couple of guys help me shape most afternoons."

"Yeah. To start, I want a short and a long. Surprise me with the design, and I'll try them out. After I get a feel for them, we'll collaborate on making more."

"Sounds good."

His laidback demeanor threw me. Doing business his way sounded so…*non*business. "So you got expectations of me?"

"You plan on competing the circuit?"

"Yeah. I'm still finding my legs with everything, though. You okay with that?"

"You ride like you do on *my* boards? We're good." He

stared hard at me. "When I saw you surf? I saw me. Your love of the wave, of everything around you, came through. We're the same in that."

Makani's gaze shifted toward the front window. "So is she. We all respect the same things."

I gave him a nod. That connection happened bone-deep with Leilani and me the moment she'd let go days earlier.

If I could only figure out how to convince her to let go again.

12
SKIRTING REAL

Leilani…

Seconds after my breaths finally began to calm, a sound made my heart race: Mase approaching.

His *slippahs* shuffled along the concrete not far behind me, inside the shop. A high-pitched whir followed when Makani fired up one of his sanders, but the sound muffled with the closing of the wood-and-glass front door.

For the first time since he'd arrived, it felt like were truly alone.

I didn't turn, kept facing toward the ocean. Closing my eyes, I willed my body to chill.

The air stilled to my right as he blocked the sandblasting afternoon wind. But while his action protected me from one element, he introduced one even more dangerous: him.

No big deal, Leilani. Just any other guy. Who happens to be your boss.

He let out a long sigh. "Why are you acting so different here?"

My emotions jumbled, making every breath heavier than the last. *Do not cry.* With determination, I focused on those three words, my own mantra pounded into my head over too many years. When I found my voice, I forced strength into it. "'Cuz things are different here."

"What things?" His voice had softened. His bare arm angled closer until it touched my shoulder.

And still, I struggled to suck air into my lungs, bottled-up anger threatening to explode. I glared at the peaceful crystal-blue sky—didn't dare look at the same color in his eyes or I'd lose it, for sure. The serenity of the outside world seemed like a lie, revealed nothing of the raging storm under my skin.

But eventually my gaze landed on curling surf just beyond the shoreline. Gentle foam licked at its crest before gravity tumbled it over into a vertical burst of spray. Another wave rose, gaining height as hydraulic force met seafloor. As I looked farther out, on and on the swells came, a line of liquid corduroy sailing toward us on the wind. And as the sight of them grounded me, the storm within me gradually began to calm.

"*Every*thing." My gruff word boomed in my head, like crashing surf.

He didn't push. Just nodded slowly, like he knew. Or accepted that I wouldn't explain. Then he stepped forward, leaned down, and braced his forearms on the rusted metal railing.

My attention shifted from the calming waves to him: how the wind ruffled his blond hair over his face, where the sun glinted off specks of windblown sand on his muscled biceps, when his breaths slowed, became more even.

His face angled down, stared at a small pile of sand he toed with the front of his rubber *slippah*, before raising back up to stare toward the horizon. "Anytime. You want to open up? Hell, vent, scream...even cry. Anytime you need it. Just like our first night, I'm here."

When we'd bared our souls. Where it had been safe. Because it had existed a million miles away from reality. "Okay." I blew out a breath, relieved on some level, even though it made no sense.

"No judgment," he added. "I'll even supply the tequila, if it helps."

Against my will, my lips quirked a little. "Okay."

"But I can't promise I won't cop a feel the moment you let your guard down."

Laughter choked out of my throat. And in that instant, my anger dissipated into the wind. Furrowing my brows, I pulled in a hard breath, then sighed. All day I'd been irritated that some guy I didn't want to like—*couldn't* like—had such a potent effect on me.

Standing in front of Makani's shop, stuck in a crisis of identity, amazingly, all I felt by Mase pulling me out of my head was grateful. "Yeah, okay."

"Wait, what?" He glanced at me, genuine confusion in

his adorable frown. "'Yeah, okay' to the talking? Or okay to the feel-up?"

I shot him a look of warning. "Talking. Don't push it." When amusement tugged at the corners of his lips, I let out a steadying breath. "But not now." Couldn't even imagine opening up. Not without that tequila.

"Whatever you need. Whenever you're ready."

"Why are you doing this?" The elusive *why* of it all surfaced once more.

He fully turned toward me, protecting me further from the wind. "Doing what?"

Overwhelmed by a blast of his intoxicating scent and heat, I took a step back, drew in a breath of fresh air, then met his gaze. "All this. The house. Makani's offer. Me."

"That's a lot to cover."

"Not going anywhere." The truth of things. Even though I longed to go…*every*where; however, loyalty ran deep in my family.

"What if we did go somewhere?"

Pulled from thoughts of traveling, I frowned, totally confused. "Like…?"

"Food. Girl, what did they put in that shave ice you ate earlier? Aren't you hungry?"

"A billion calories. And yeah, I could eat."

I opened the front door, and the sound of Makani's sander blared out once more. Under Mase's watchful stare, I leaned in and pressed the buzzer on the narrow counter by the front window. A few seconds later, when the sander wound down, I shouted, "Kani, I'm takin' the Tacoma!"

"Keys are in it!" Makani's shouted reply came without any visual sign of him.

Knew that. Just wanted to give him a heads-up that he'd be without wheels for a while.

"Seriously? You leave keys in your cars?" Mase stared at me with an incredulous expression as we walked alongside the building.

"Truck. And it's a Tacoma. Might as well make it the official vehicle of the island. Someone takes a Tacoma? They're messin' with a Hawaiian or a local. No one would be so stupid."

"Why the truck? No place to eat nearby?"

"You buyin'?"

"Yep."

"N'kay den. We go 'ono *grindz*." When my Pidgin got a blank stare from him, I smirked. "Only the most delicious food. You're feedin' me the best pizza on the island."

"Where's that?"

"Flatbread Company. Gotta drive there."

Not five minutes later, I spun a u-ey and we glided into a spot right across the street. "*Pono*."

As I cut the engine, he gave me a puzzled look.

"*Pono*. Means a ton of things. Righteous. Good. Perfect."

As we stood waiting for a long line of cars to clear up on Hana Highway, Mase's head swiveled back and forth to take in all the shops and restaurants on the *makai* stretch of Pa'ia. "How long will it take me to learn the language?"

"Which one? Hawaiian or Pidgin?" I threw up a *shaka*, the Hawaiian raised-thumb-and-pinky hand signal, thanking a beer-truck driver who stopped and waved us across.

"Both." Mase held up a blocking arm to stop me when two cars sped by going the opposite direction.

Then we strolled across the road in front of a slowing VeeDub that had a surfboard strapped to its roof. "Years."

"Cool." His confident, satisfied tone surprised me.

I huffed out a long, tired breath, shaking my head as we stepped inside the restaurant. "I have another Hawaiian word for you. *Lolo*."

He acted like he had all the time in the world.

I heard a clock ticking down.

"What's *lolo*?"

I pointed at him.

His brows lifted and he smirked. "Sexy?"

I rolled my eyes, staring up toward the ceiling a beat before dropping my gaze back at him. "Crazy. Or stupid. Take your pick."

"Crazy." His tone turned bold, matter-of-fact again.

Fearless.

"Stupid," I muttered, correcting him.

If he heard the last comment, he ignored me and grabbed a couple of menus on the red-painted *Please Wait to be Seated* podium. I scanned the room, nervous about being seen in public with him. Then I got mad at myself for being so shallow and acting like the rest of them. With a strong huff out, I ignored my fears right as a server in a faded gray Led Zeppelin T-shirt walked up. Mase pointed toward the farthest high-top table in the front corner, against the window.

We passed the curving cement bar top crowded with patrons on wood-backed barstools, but Mase stared out the front window the whole time. He read aloud the wooden sign that dangled from two hooks under the sidewalk overhang. "*Flatbread Company. All natural pizza.*" Then he took a far seat against the wall. "Never had all natural pizza. That good, huh?"

I nodded. "*Pono.*"

"So, a parking space can be *pono*. And pizza? What else?"

"Anything. Anyone."

He pointed at me with a shit-eating grin. "*Pono.*"

I lifted my menu to hide my unstoppable smile. Damn *haole*.

Our server returned before a smartass reply hit my brain. After we ordered drinks, Mase lifted his brows with a tipped head at me and gestured an open hand toward my menu. I nodded and ordered an organic salad with their blend of Hawaiian goat cheeses and a Pa'ia Bay Ohana pizza.

Mase scanned the menu, then summarized the pizza I'd ordered, "Wood-fired cauldron tomato sauce, caramelized organic onions, white mushrooms, mozzarella and parmesan, homemade organic olive oil and their custom blend of herbs? *Fucking sold.*" Scooping up the menus and handing them over, he glanced at me. "Mind if we share?"

I gave a halfhearted shrug, then nodded to the server before he left. "As long as you stay on your side of the table."

The look in Mase's eyes flashed molten for an instant, then his gaze dropped to the roughhewn surface. He gripped the edge and pulled down, as if testing it for strength—as if

I'd inadvertently implied something sexual with my rule.

Sensing I needed to close that wide-open loophole, I added, "And *I* stay on *my* side."

Smug expression washing over his face, he almost smiled. As if he knew how to play with me and got points for luring me in.

I glared at him, narrowing my eyes.

His smile finally broke free as he relaxed his shoulders back against the wall, getting as comfortable as a wooden barstool under his cocky ass would allow. The familiar posture—his laidback demeanor matched with an assessing gaze—reminded me of our first meal of fish tacos in a primitive bar on the beach. The few days between then and now seemed like a lifetime ago.

Because so much had happened that night, on levels I hadn't begun to sort out yet.

"*Pono.*" In a low satisfied tone, he repeated the word while staring at me, like he wanted me to know how he saw me.

Uncomfortable under the powerful microscope, I detoured back to our vocabulary lesson. "Kinda like *da kine*. We use it for everything."

"Like whatchamacallit."

"Sure. And anything else. When you can't think of a word."

Silent seconds followed. Then his gaze hardened. "So. Spill it."

"What?"

"Why the change?"

Too many reasons. None I was proud of.

As I struggled to find words to explain the worst of it, he folded his arms over his chest. "I'll take a wild guess. Has something to do with me being *lolo.*"

"Yeah." Total cop-out, but easier than fessing up.

"Why?"

My eyes widened and I almost laughed. "Really? You get to ask that question after not answering me every time *I* ask?"

"Okay." He pegged me with a serious look. "Ask me again."

"You're *lolo.*"

"Maybe. But not the point. Ask."

The questions had rattled in my brain for days. *Why* so adamant about the condition of me working with him? *Why* was he so single-minded about chasing after me? *Why me?* After all the time that had flown by between drunken us being real on a beach in the middle of nowhere and sober us front-and-center and blindingly real in the middle of my everyday somewhere, with *everyone* having eyes on me and talking story about *everything*...I hesitated.

Did I even want to know the answer?

Yeah, I did.

I sighed and braced myself for the worst. "Why?"

He leaned forward, sliding his forearms across the table. "Because you're worth it." The simple words were quiet. The power of his dead-serious stare pierced through the protective front I'd been hiding behind.

My breath stopped. As if buried under a turbulent

three-wave hold down, my lungs stopped operating and all the sounds became muffled. Only my heartbeat remained, thumping louder...harder...

Finally, I drew in a deep breath. Then I swallowed hard.

No one had ever said that to me before. Not in those words. Not with that meaning.

And those ice-blue eyes stared at me, through me, as if they saw the true heart beating in the core of what made me who I was.

My gaze wandered from those eyes to his pale skin, his shaggy blond hair—what he represented...who he was.

Are you *worth it?*

"Why my attitude change?" Anxious about having the heavy focus stay on me, I shifted it back toward him. "You don't know what you're getting yourself into here."

"Never stopped me before."

"Chasing girls?"

"Going after what I want."

Me. He meant me. "Nice sidestep."

"I've never had to chase a girl."

I snorted. "Ego much? And you aren't chasing me."

"Oh? You decide to give chase?" He leaned back on the barstool, shoulders hitting the wall again as an easygoing smile curved his lips. "I'll play along."

Damn. *Lolo* East Coast surfer boy was making me start to like him. More.

My brows furrowed as I fought a smile, but the corners of my lips twitched anyway. Shaking my head—to him and me—I rolled my eyes. "Dream on, surfer boy."

The server brought the pizza as I finished my sentence, then left. And to my embarrassment, my stomach growled loudly as I stared at the *ono* meal I was about to eat.

But when my gaze lifted to connect with bright blue eyes, no humor lay there—only unrelenting confidence. He radiated the feeling so strongly, it blasted right into me and settled deep within my chest.

My spirits lifted, buoyant for the first time in so long… with the tiniest bit of hope.

13
SEEKING THE HARD

Mase...

Leilani likes you.

Her brother's words echoed in my head. They rang true when she finally relaxed enough to let a genuine smile break free.

When I exhaled, tension left my shoulders; I'd been on edge all day.

Because I *more* than liked her.

Which was beside the point. And exactly the point.

But for the immediate future, I'd landed in her corner of the world. And the only way I could make that corner a little better, include me somewhere in it, was to understand it—understand her.

"Your turn." I pegged her with an unyielding stare. "Why so different?"

She'd taken a big bite of pizza. And didn't bother hurrying through her slow chewing to answer. After she swallowed, she took a couple of pulls of soda through her straw, watching me the entire time. Then she wiped her mouth with her napkin.

Hard eyes stared me down, then narrowed. "It's hard to explain…" Eventually, the beginnings of a mischievous smile pulled at the corner of her lips. "*You'll see.*"

My words—from days ago, when I'd expertly dodged her question—tossed back at me.

I ran my tongue over my teeth, then shook my head. She was good: quick-witted and full of play. Which I fucking loved. "Fair enough."

We finished eating our food in relative quiet. I observed the dwindling late-afternoon crowd in the joint, an even mix of tourists and locals, three of which sat at the bar within earshot debating the cost of various cell phone companies.

On occasion, Leilani would dart a glance at them or at a newcomer walking in the door. When anyone strolled down the sidewalk, she'd stealthily scan the entire street outside, briefly landing a gaze on the pedestrian as she pretended not to check them out.

With every passing minute, she grew more and more agitated.

And I got it. I'd crashed her party. Hadn't really given her a choice in the matter.

Not wanting to see her suffer further on my account, I stood the moment I signed the credit card slip. "Ready to head out?"

"Yeah." She blew out a relieved breath, wasting no time to bolt toward the door.

We headed back out onto a street that could've been dropped from a California beach town with its clear surfing vibe. However, a deeper energy hummed under the surface of the pastel storefronts with contrasting trim. And an eclectic mix of people filled the laidback sidewalks, from clean-cut golfers to hippies in bell-bottoms, surfers with boards strapped to all kinds of vehicles to artists walking by with canvas and easel.

Leilani gave a gentle tug to my elbow. By the time I glanced forward, she'd begun to walk quickly back across Hana Highway through a break in traffic.

I jogged after her, staring at her beat-up red Tacoma as she pulled open her door. "I need some wheels. Know anyone who's wanting to sell an old truck?"

She glanced at me as I got in. Then she shut her door and started the engine. "No. But I'll ask around. How old?"

"Doesn't matter, as long as it's been cared for. And has character."

Absently nodding, she stared over her shoulder, then began backing into the roadway. "There are car shows on different Saturdays. Think the one in Kihei is tomorrow."

"Good." On our left, we passed a Minit Stop with white painted sides and green trim, and I took note of the two gas pumps under a pull-through island for future use. "We're going."

"*Nooo…*"

"As my assistant." Yeah, I planned to milk that dollar-cow for all it was worth. "Without wheels, I need a ride."

A long pause followed. Then she let out a measured breath. "Fine."

"Need a place to stay tonight, too."

She flashed me a priceless put-out look. "You just rented a house."

"I rented a roof with walls. No bed. No appliances. Didn't run the tap, but I'm guessing the water's off. In fact" —I glanced at my phone— "there's forty-five minutes left of the workday. Let's grab my gear at Makani's. You talk to Evelyn and make calls to the water and electric companies, then we'll head back to your place."

Shaking her head, she began to drum an impatient thumb on the steering wheel. But her argument had nothing to do with the list of near-impossible tasks before the end of the day. "You're not staying at my place."

"I am."

"Not *my* place. Makani's place. And we don't have another...bed."

Her hesitation with that last word wasn't lost on me. The last time we'd argued about who slept where, it had been an intimate time for us, alcohol or not.

In the silent seconds, the thumb-drumming had stopped; she strangled the steering wheel with a white-knuckle grip. Once-easy breaths had shallowed. Slender shoulders had ratcheted up, inching toward her ears.

Saving the day, so she didn't have a complete meltdown, I diverted our convo toward safer places, "Couch. Floor. Chair out on the front porch...hammock?"

"Lanai."

"What?"

"We don't call it a covered porch or patio here. It's a lanai."

I tipped my head back against the headrest, half-closing my eyes. "Works for me."

When she didn't argue, when only the gentle rumble and occasional sway of the truck filled the silence, I arched a brow. "Tick tock" I pointed to the back of my wrist, at an imaginary watch. "Time's a wastin."

Yeah, I pushed my luck. But only because all the glorious friction between us got her out of her head. Better to have attitude from her than worry.

The truck skidded to a stop in a cloud of red dust. She didn't even wait for me to open my door before she stormed off. But by the time I walked around the building and entered through the front door, she'd already gotten on the phone with Evelyn and stood halfway down the front worktable.

"...I know it's Friday. Can't we call down? Okay." She heaved out a sigh. "Yeah, we can print it here. Yeah, *makani@ kealohaboards.com*. Yeah, yeah. Sounds good. *Mahalo.*"

When she pocketed her cell phone, she stared at a dust-covered space on the surface of the table. Resigned expression on her face, she lifted her gaze to mine. "Evelyn said she'll make some calls, but it'd be a miracle to have services hooked up by Monday. She's sending the lease paperwork over to Makani's email now."

Guilt fired through my gut. That I'd made her have that defeated expression, caused her distress. "Look, I don't have to stay at your place. I can grab a hotel room or someone's surf shack."

"Bullshit." Makani strolled in from the back room, clutching a handful of papers that he then handed over to me with a pen. "You're staying with us. End of."

Not wanting to get in the middle of it—since I'd already cornered her into a tricky spot—I double-checked the lease, even though I'd harassed her earlier about reviewing it for me. Then I scrawled my John Hancock on the dotted line and initialed and signed the Lease Policy Addendum, Mold Addendum, and Crime Free Addendum.

Leilani gripped the top of the pages as I lifted them up. "I'll fax those over."

"You sure?"

"I'm your assistant, yeah?" She dropped me a defiant glance, arching one brow. A beat later she turned and went to the back desk, stuffed the lease into the automatic feeder on top of the machine, then pressed a button making the machine chirp before it sucked the pages up one at a time with a low hum, the only sound in the space for those tense seconds.

I grinned. *Yeah.* Pissed off or not, in spite of the fact she wanted me but wouldn't admit it to herself, let alone me, she wanted to take ownership of the job she'd agreed to.

"You take the truck." Makani turned and disappeared into the back again, voice growing louder so we could hear. "I gotta finish shaping this order. Henry can drop me off later."

She stared at the empty doorway where Makani had walked through. Her back was to me, but I could almost hear the silent argument echoing in her mind.

Then without a word, she squared her shoulders, went to my bags stacked in the corner, grabbed the two duffels with a grunt from their weight, then stalked out the front of his shop again. I grabbed the wheeled board bags and followed her out.

The first few minutes of the drive to Makani's passed in silence.

No biggie. I'd suffered her silent treatment in the car with the real estate agent; I could handle it alone. Nothing to say, anyway. I'd bowed out, but Makani had insisted. And although I could've given her one more escape hatch, no point in getting between siblings—more importantly, I didn't want to.

My monochrome preordained life had suddenly brightened with vivid color. Why make things more palatable for her? "Easy is overrated."

"What?"

Oh. I muttered that aloud? "Nothing. Just doing some internal philosophizing."

"Enlighten me."

"Easy is overrated," I repeated, noticing familiar structures passing by as we drove.

The muscle in her jaw tightened. "I wouldn't know."

Hmmm. She referring to me? Gut instinct told me her struggle ran deeper than today's events, than me turning her life upside down. "So, then you agree. Hard is better?"

A tiny crinkle appeared at the corner of her eye, before it narrowed as she focused more diligently on the next turn.

We entered a narrow street we'd been down before. With Evelyn.

"Don't bother answering. I can see it in your eyes. You want my kind of hard."

Finally, a well-earned, indignant glance flashed my way. "Do *not*."

"Yeah, ya do. Keep denying it. You'll only want the hard more."

"Will not."

"Atta girl. Denial. Best kind of temptation."

After turning into a short cement driveway, she jammed the truck into park, got out, and stormed across the small lawn toward the front door of a small plantation house that had a green metal roof and well-maintained yellow paint with white trim.

"Uh, Leilani," I called after her before she disappeared inside.

"Yeah?" She whirled around, irritation seething from her posture as she planted her hands on her hips.

"This street. Isn't it…"

A satisfied smile broke out on her face. "Yeah, yeah, *it is*. For sure."

Gears turning, pieces falling into place, I took a few steps *mauka*, to clear my view from a wide mango tree. And there it was: the first house Evelyn had showed us, in Haiku. Where I'd gotten under Leilani's skin. "The neighbors are close," I muttered, repeating my earlier complaint. "Too close." She hadn't mentioned one word about *her* being one of the neighbors.

"Well played, Leilani. Well played."

Turned out, she didn't like easy either.

The greater question? How hard were we both willing to go?

14
FORBIDDEN

Leilani…

"This is a mistake."

"No, it's not." Makani opened his takeout container and jammed a fork into the mountain of steamed vegetables and rice. Then he stuffed his mouth with food.

I stared through the open windows across the room, at the back of Mase's blond head. After stowing his bags in the front corner behind the door and his gear at the back end of our carport, he'd chosen to hang out on the front lanai alone in the growing darkness.

Didn't matter how much distance he put between us, though. The power of Mase's presence pressed in on me. "You don't know."

"You're right." Makani swallowed his food, tipped his

beer bottle to his lips, then chugged down a few gulps. "I don't. Neither do you."

He didn't understand. "I'm freakin'."

"You're fine."

"He's too much like me."

Makani huffed out a dry laugh. "He's the right amount like you."

Risk-taker, he meant. And a dreamer, a wanderer at heart.

Except Mase and I came from two worlds, oceans apart. "But different in all the wrong ways."

He gave me a reflective look. "This is the kind of change we've wanted, yeah? What we've always bitched about. Things won't be different till someone sticks their neck out."

I leaned on the counter we stood behind, pulled a mango out from a large bowl of fruit. "Why does the 'someone' have to be me?"

"You tell me. You brought him here." He shoved another loaded forkful of food into his mouth.

"*Nooo...*" I shook my head, then began slicing up the mango with a paring knife. "You sent me to get him."

"Not to bring him back like a found puppy. All I wanted was to sponsor him."

"Coming here was the only way he'd agree." But what had I wanted? Had something I'd done provoked Mase to push the issue? I replayed the conversation from days ago, one I'd felt out of control of—even as the lack of control had exhilarated me...like riding an unknown wave.

"And you working for him?"

"A nonnegotiable condition." What Mase had said.

Makani tossed his empty food carton into the recycle container. "You didn't have to agree to that."

"He wouldn't have come." I'd believed it at the time. Or maybe I'd wanted to. Because I wanted the challenge of taking the job he'd offered. *Not* because I'd been tempted to keep the most interesting man I'd just met in my life a little longer.

"So?" Makani folded his arms over his chest, staring hard at me.

He understood things about me that Mase only guessed at. My brother knew me better than I knew myself. Which meant he knew the main reason I hadn't blown Mase off, even though I could have, had *really* wanted to: I would've disappointed Makani, the only family on my side. Maybe a year ago I might've been reckless enough to do that, wouldn't have cared.

Not now. Not after he'd protected me. "It's fine."

"Not a mistake," he repeated.

Biggest mistake evah. I didn't say anything further. My fears had no place between us. Makani would boldly swim out and rescue me from shark-infested waters. I had to take care of him too.

Makani kissed my forehead, then went off to bed.

Mase didn't come back in. Fine by me; I needed the space.

I turned out the kitchen lights and fled to my own room. The door closed with a soft snick before I tumbled onto my bed in the dark, hiding away from the outside world and the problems in it that I couldn't fix. Eyes drifting shut on an exhale, I thought about the soothing colors surrounding me that I couldn't see in the shadowy darkness: pale green on the walls in a shade called celadon, wainscoting halfway up painted a soft buttercream, cerulean blue on the pillow I hugged to my chest.

My favorite among them? The repurposed oak desk and chair in whitewashed gray.

If only the world embraced itself in shades of gray. "Why can't everyone see what I see?" I whispered. Beauty in them all, how they blended together, shone brightly apart. Each vital, electric.

The longer I laid there, the more my mind came alive— wishing all people valued every last person. One race, a human nation. Earth and its inhabitants. Wars would cease. The destruction of the planet would halt. We'd all work toward the common goal of helping mankind more than just survive…we'd seek to flourish as our best selves.

Frustrated at the impossible fantasy, I huffed out a breath, tossed the satin pillow aside and flipped over. Makani's words echoed in my head: *Things won't be different till someone sticks their neck out.*

Me. Somehow Makani believed *I* could make a difference. I didn't see how.

My brother of all people knew the uphill battle I'd face to even introduce Mase to the rest of my family. If I still lived at home? I'd be immediately grounded.

But what was the worst they could do to me?

What's the worst they could do to Mase?

I cringed at the thought. Not just my family, but others like them. Intolerance ran deep toward foreigners on our islands. With good reason. An overpowering reason, in their minds.

Unable to work out a solution in my head, I sighed.

For over an hour, I tried to quiet my mind. Did my best to sleep. But my thoughts kept drifting to Mase: my personal shade of gray. Because every next time I thought about him, the color of his skin became less and less of a problem, grew to be the last thing I focused on.

Instead, an image of him naked—only a split second of time that had forever seared into my brain—kept taunting me. The lean muscles of his body. The carefree way he moved, comfortable in his own skin.

Soon, other memories flooded in. The way he'd laughed when I'd teased him. Held me close when I'd jumped into his arms, protecting me against sharks…or my fear of them. The heat in his voice when he'd teased me about other things—sexual things—but held back, protecting me from his own predatory moves.

Even deeper moments shimmered to the surface. How he'd held me when I'd gotten so drunk I'd been sick, even though I didn't remember it. What he'd finally said when I'd asked him "why" again: *Because you're worth it.*

Why had I been afraid to hear his answer? Because there had been more to giving in to Mase than an obligation to my brother. And hearing Mase say the words aloud, voice it from his side, made the unnamable, indescribable, impossible-to-have-happen thing *already happening* between us all too real.

The loop replayed in my mind, more memories merging in at the end. His hand flowing through the water, almost touching my bare bottom. His lips hovering less than an inch from mine.

When had my room gotten so hot?

The air had grown stifling. My skin felt feverish. Once-slow breaths had shortened.

On a restless huff, I slapped my hand down on the bed and sat up. *Need to get busy.* Work. Mase had given me a list of construction materials to order; I needed him out from under the same roof. Something to occupy my mind and get him off it.

I stared at my beloved desk, realizing one thing was missing. Something my new paycheck could afford.

Padding barefoot on the hardwood floor back out into the living room, I fired up Makani's laptop that sat on his desk along the wall.

A muffled sound came from the vicinity of where Mase hung in the darkness, in a hammock behind a screened-in corner of the lanai. Forcing my mind off all things *not* normally under our roof, I began clicking away, surfing the Web.

"*What the fuck?*" Not muffled at all. A hard thump echoed behind me. Then the door opened, slammed shut. "What the hell is that piercing sound?"

I'd gotten so used to the high-pitched noise, I'd drowned it out. Or gone deaf. "Coqui frogs."

"Damn things won't shut up."

"Be thankful you weren't here a year ago when they were

worse. They're invasive, but U of H just got over a million dollars to try and wipe them out."

When he didn't reply, I turned.

My breath caught, mouth falling open.

The sexual mental image from earlier stood there in the flesh, only a few feet away, eyes half-lidded, scraggly hair rumpled. My gaze drifted over his bare chest, down sleek abs, between a defined V of muscles that angled from lean hips, arrowing into a faint line of hair that trailed low, *lower…*

Board shorts hung on his gorgeous body now—but my sinful mind filled in one *very big* blank. Skin flushing hot again, I forced my gaze to meet his. One side of his mouth quirked up, then he yawned and rubbed a hand through his hair.

Seeing him without a shirt for the first time since…*that first time*…I noticed something different, even in the dim light. "You get new ink?"

He glanced down at a black tribal band that circled his raised biceps. "Yeah. In Tahiti, day after you left."

I nodded, gaze stuck on the intricate design that caressed his skin. Then I crossed my arms, aware my nipples had hardened, rasped against the thin fabric of my dress.

"Can't sleep?" His intense gaze held steady with mine.

"No." *Not with sexy* haole you *under the same roof.*

My whole world had turned upside down in under a week: new job handed to me on a platter, new guy totally into me, who I couldn't stop thinking about, travel I'd wanted so badly—all revolving around surfing, which I loved almost as much as breathing.

All because of Mase.

In slow motion, greater understanding sank in. I forced out a shaky breath, admitting to myself why my sex drive had blown off the charts. Not only because of who he was versus who I was. And not as simple as his chemistry meshing with mine. It was because he was here—and wasn't supposed to be. He wanted me and shouldn't. Yeah, I wanted him too… but couldn't.

Mase is taboo.

Biting my lip so hard I nearly drew blood, I tore my gaze from him and forced myself to stare at the glowing laptop screen. A single word broke free, from my childhood, from all the things drilled into my head from the moment I could talk.

Forbidden.

Yet coming clean about that? Knowing the dangers drew me in—had become a part of it? Only made me want him more.

15
WISDOM AND FOOLS

Mase…

Do or die.

The silent seconds as Leilani sat at the makeshift desk became pivotal.

Tension between us grew thick with sexual need, with promise.

Her breathing shallowed.

My pulse raced.

But the instant she forced herself to look away, the only right move flashed brighter than a Las Vegas Strip sign: give her breathing room.

So I sucked it up, spun on my heel, and plopped down onto their white slipcovered couch. *Lighthearted*: where I needed to steer things… "Whatcha doin'?"

Her brow wrinkled in concentration as she stared at a

136

blank Google search screen that awaited her command. She began typing, expression relaxing as if she'd finally remembered. "Ordering lumber and a computer."

And in under five seconds, we were cool again.

Relieved, I stretched my arms across the back of the cushions and dropped her a deadpan look. "Uhhh…aren't you *on* a computer?"

"Not my computer. Makani's. I'm getting a MacBook with your money."

"*Your* money," I corrected.

"Yeah. *My* money." Defiance rippled through her tone. "Then I'm ordering all the supplies on your list that I can. Saw horses. Lumber, tiles" —she suddenly yawned wide— "drywall sheets."

"Construction materials putting you to sleep?"

"Even better than counting sheep." Her gentle smile gave her an innocence that made her look far younger than nineteen.

Which made me want to give her all the space and time she needed. Unable to stop the contagious yawning—tired as fuck—I stretched my mouth wide open again with a deep yowl, then stood.

A glint flashed in her eyes as she watched me, then she held out a hand toward me, palm up. "We'll need your credit card."

"We?"

"Lowe's, Home Depot…and *I*."

"Go easy on me." I went to my duffle in the corner, then retrieved a Visa from my wallet. "Those your only shoes, flip-flops?" I nodded toward the entryway, where half a dozen pair in her size were gathered, some flat and basic, others wedged or fancier.

"Yeah. And we call them *slippahs* here."

"Uh-huh." Not the point. "They're a work hazard. Buy yourself a nice pretty pair on me."

Her eyes narrowed. "What?"

I winked at her. "A nice pretty pair...of work boots: steel toed. Can you have 'em overnighted to be here on Tuesday?"

Her suspicious expression softened, gaze dropping to the floor while she thought. "Depends. Amazon's been sketchy with Prime and certain manufacturers. I'll see what I can find. What's on Tuesday?"

"We begin demolition."

Her mouth fell open, a fierce argument written all over her face.

I held up my hands. "*The boots*. Focus on the boots." *One step at a time.*

A split second later, determination washed over her features. Then she turned back toward the screen and began typing, pulling up separate tabs for Amazon, eBay, and a couple of sporting goods stores.

Before I turned to leave her to it, I lightly rapped the desk beside her hand. "Hey, thanks again for letting me crash here a few days."

She slowly glanced up at me, eyes widening, expression a bit stunned.

Hasn't anyone ever shown you respect?

Apparently unsure of what to say in reply, she simply nodded.

And I silently vowed to show her more of what she'd been missing out on.

I startled more alert when a muffled sound came from inside their house. The activity marked the first sign of life since everything had gone lights-out well over six hours ago.

Leilani?

Shaking my head, I tamped down the school-kid excitement. Slow and steady would win the race with her. And the noise could've easily been the other occupant in the house, the one who'd insisted I stay with them.

Grateful for their hospitality, and not wanting to intrude into their routine, I settled back into the hammock and stared through the screened porch. No...not porch...*lanai*, Leilani had said. *Lanai*, I mentally repeated, rewriting my hardwired thoughts into island-speak.

Morning wound to life in lazy minutes. I'd been wide awake all night. No surprise there: Every first night in a new place went sleepless. The endless high-pitched *woo-weeps* of the coqui frogs? Fucking maddening, no doubt. But they'd kept me company like a nosier band of crickets. The frogs started to quiet down when bird calls began to dominate the morning sounds while the sky incrementally transformed from pitch-black softening into shades of purple, then gray brightening toward blue. A steady northeasterly wind kept the humidity tolerable.

The front door swung open. Makani popped a head out,

his long black hair falling over his shoulder. "You wanna drop me off at work? Leilani sleeps in. We can grab coffee and *grindz*. Then you can catch some waves. Surf's up, six-to-eight from a distant storm."

"Yeah." I grabbed the edge of the rope hammock and rolled out. "Sounds great."

Fifteen minutes later, after a short drive with other vehicles heading west on Hana Highway, our headlights reflected on the front window of Honolulu Coffee in Pa'ia.

We placed our orders, grabbed our steaming mugs of coffee, then took seats at one of the bistro tables by the front window. A couple of girls walked in, faces lighting up when they saw my companion.

"Hey, Makani," they chimed in near-stereo.

"Hey, *howzit*." He gave them a chin-up, then glanced at me. "So, *brah*. First time surfing here?"

"Yeah. Any tips on where to go?" He'd told me to bring my surfboard only. I'd already scoped out spots in *Maui Revealed*, a guidebook I'd brought. But nothing beat firsthand knowledge.

"My crew...we text each other morning surf reports; I'll loop you in. But today? Ho'okipa." He pegged me with a serious expression as he sipped his coffee, eyes dark as his sister's, near-black. His long hair had been cleanly tied back at his nape. "You'll be safe alone there as long as you don't bring your sailboard into the water before 11:00 a.m. and obey the sign about the ten-man rule. No matter what, surfers have the waves in the morning."

"Safe?" I sensed hesitation in his casual tone...and an undercurrent of warning.

His expression hardened. "From locals. Enough other surfers from all over the world go to Hoʻokipa, even in summer and early morning."

"Locals a problem?" Breakfast arrived, and I took a big bite of my egg-and-bacon-filled breakfast wrap.

"Some can be." He started in on his egg sandwich, then pointed his fork to the granola-covered açaí bowl he'd talked me into.

I hooked a spoon under a banana slice, dove through the granola layer, and scooped up some soft-frozen açaí hiding underneath. The tart-sweet flavors were a great match with the savory wrap and perfect to carbo-load for surfing.

"Just keep your head on your shoulders." He continued after he swallowed another bite of his sandwich. "Anyone gives you trouble? Stay out of their way."

"Got it." Sort of. I'd never had problems with locals. Couldn't imagine any issues now. Respect and gratitude went a long way.

Grateful for the pointers, I thought to ask about another. "Where are best places to stock up on things for my new house?"

"Like?"

"Everything. A bed. Sheets for it. Coffeemaker. Toaster. Plates and silverware. Couple of chairs, to start with." Basics to get by on until the house was fully renovated.

"Costco…Target. I think Leilani got some of our stuff at Pier 1…you'd have to check with her."

At the mention of his sister, the convo stalled while I finished my food.

He drank his coffee, assessing me with a critical eye.

After a few minutes, he put his empty mug down. "She won't go easy on you."

"Wouldn't be interested if she did." Didn't bother denying I wanted her.

"She's worth it." A brother's approval. A green light from him to me.

I know. "Don't doubt it for a second."

His eyes narrowed. "Make sure *you* are." Threat laced his deeper tone.

I gave him a solid nod. "I will." Not *I am*. Because worth got earned, every day, with each action. Only fools thought otherwise.

The critical stare from him continued, though. Like he refused to be convinced so easily.

Looks like you *won't go easy on me either.* And I was cool with having to prove myself. Would've questioned things if it were otherwise.

When I arrived at Ho'okipa, a couple dozen other cars and trucks were already parked in the lower lot. I backed into a space along a grassy lawn, then waxed up my board in silence while another guy did the same at the other end. After pausing a few minutes to take in the vibe of the place, I headed past a line of picnic tables under a covered area and approached cement steps that led down to the beach.

However, a trio of local *groms* holding their boards

on their heads—all boys no older than fourteen—walked beyond the steps, cutting between a freestanding shower on the left and a low facilities building on the right. I followed, figuring they knew the lay of the surf break better than I.

We picked our way along rough lava toward a sea-beaten point. They paused halfway, glancing down toward the corner of the bay. Tracking their gazes, I spotted ten adult sea turtles resting on a roped-off section of sandy beach. When the *groms* continued on, so did I, following their lead from a respectful distance.

Beautiful sets flowed in from the near horizon, not huge, maybe seven-footers when cresting, but nicely shaped and coming endlessly.

At the end of the weathered lava point, one by one, the *groms* tossed their boards off the edge then disappeared out of my line of sight. When I reached the jumping-point, I timed the waves, launched my board like a missile out toward a calmer spot, then dove in after it. Being respectful to the building lineup, I paddled farther out and around, taking a deeper spot.

Before long, once the lineup had taken theirs, my wave came. Already positioned well, with no one else charging forward, I paddled hard as it rose, pushed the nose of my board over the lip, then dropped in. The smooth drag of my board sliced through a sweet eight-foot wall.

The wonder of a new land from a first wave always struck me. But this time? My breath caught, heart thumping heavy in my chest. At that moment, beyond the unforgiving black lava coast, above the golden crescent of beach, past green fields and surrounded by lush forest…slept an extraordinary girl.

My curving line on the wave felt natural—right. In those seconds, I reclaimed my piece of heaven on earth, where everything flowed in balance. Even the impossible seemed real…even a girl from a world different than mine. Because deep in our hearts, we rode similar waves.

As my first ride in Maui began to close, water rushed over the seafloor, revealing glimpses of dangerous dark rocks below me. But I stayed true to myself—true to my line. I glanced *mauka*, toward Haiku—toward Leilani. Then I shot my gaze higher until it rested upland over my new home, a first place in the world of my own—one that fit me.

On a determined exhale, I resolved to keep my focus out there.

Not on the rocks below.

16
THE WEIGHT OF ARMOR

Leilani...

Exhaustion pulled hard at me.

I'd tossed and turned, falling in and out of fitful sleep—the first time since...ever.

It isn't *because of the blond surfer sleeping just outside of that wall.* What I'd tried to convince myself of all night.

With a frustrated sigh, I rolled to my side and imagined him lying in the hammock, like I'd done countless times for hours. The sleek muscles of his arms and shoulders gleaming in the moonlight, tousled hair brushed over his brow, arm bent back with a hand over closed eyelids, hiding those expressive ice-blue eyes that seemed to see right through me—understand me.

However, bright light now streamed in through the window. Had been for hours. Nothing I'd done quieted my mind long enough to find sleep, no matter how wiped out I felt.

But when I finally pushed out of bed, excitement tingled under my skin.

Not because of him. The lie stuck only for the instant I forced my mind onto other things. The surf. My friends. My new job, that I'd gotten from…*him.*

"*Ugghhh…*" I shoved my hands into my hair, gripped the roots hard, then pulled strong enough to pinch my scalp. "Men." The species that had always caused me grief.

When my bare feet padded over our hardwood floor into a silent hall, I didn't think twice about claiming the sole bathroom for myself. I locked the door and took a luxurious shower.

And the entire time, I *did not* think about him. Exactly like I hadn't all night.

By the time I wandered into the kitchen for coffee, all remained quiet. No different than any other day when Makani left at the crack of dawn. But what about Mase? Had he passed out, exhausted after his long day of travel and house-hunting?

Pouring the steaming brew Makani had programmed for me into a mug, I tried not to imagine how sweet Mase had looked in the South Pacific as he'd slumbered against the bathroom wall of his *bure*…after he'd apparently nursed me when I'd gotten sick. A twinge of guilt pinged deep in my gut as I sipped my dark roast coffee. What had I done to help him since he'd arrived? *Not a damn thing.*

But back then had been different. We'd been strangers, on

a remote island, for one night—a free pass from reality. That fleeting hazy gift in time had come and gone. And reality glared brightly when I pulled my head out of the clouds and stared honestly at home.

After five minutes of zero movement out on the lanai, I took slow steps forward, working to convince myself that my concern was only out of duty as a host; that I didn't care whether he'd gotten good sleep, how he felt about being on Maui, or what he had planned for the day.

Through the open front window, I tried to make out details through the bug screen in front of me then across and through the second screened wall which enclosed the corner of the lanai. But I sighed in frustration when all I could distinguish was the shadowy outline of a motionless hammock. The whistled up-and-down song of a cardinal sounded seconds before a gray-winged male with his flashy red crest flew by.

But from the screened-in lanai?

Silence.

I sipped more coffee.

More silence.

My pulse began to thump harder as a war within me raged.

Go out there?

No, ignore him.

Do I really like him?

Doesn't matter. Stamp it out now. Can't have him anyway.

On a scowl, I ignored all common sense and opened the front door. One of my reckless stunts had gotten me into the bring-Mase-into-my-world mess—why stop now?

I paused, hand on the screened lanai door, staring harder at the hammock. It appeared empty. Then I barged into the ten-by-fifteen space, to make sure.

"Seriously?" I grumbled, walking back out. "All that agonizing, and he's not even here?"

At that moment, our Tacoma rumbled up the driveway, blond surfer behind the wheel with a big grin on his face.

"Speak of the devil." My own demon. Temptation in the flesh.

"Good morning, sleepyhead!" he called out as he came to a stop.

I tipped the coffee to my lips and guzzled back a couple more fortifying swallows. Then I lowered the mug, walked down the steps, and drew closer to the truck...to Mase.

Something looked different about him. Same messy hair. Same smug smile. But...exhilaration vibrated off of him. Pleasure sparkled in his eyes. He practically glowed with happiness.

"You are...*stoked*." I finally smiled. "You went surfing."

"Yep. Ho'okipa." He gripped the steering wheel, bouncing like a little kid. "Grab a board. We're hunting down foo... *grindz*, shopping, then surfing."

I pressed my lips together to stifle my smile. "In that order?"

"Man's gotta eat. And I already have some stuff to drop off at the house."

Going with the instant thrill that sizzled through my veins, ignoring every last thought in my head, I ran into the house, changed into a swimsuit and sundress, and toed into a sporty pair of *slippahs*. Then I grabbed my favorite longboard and squeezed it alongside his into the back of the truck. "What kind of stuff?" The rest of the bed had been jam-packed with boxes and bags.

"House stuff," he said as I got into the truck. "I hit Target, then Costco."

"All before...*wow*." I gripped the edge of the dashboard as he tore backward down the driveway."

"Before 11:00 a.m.," he finished for me. "I'm glad your Tacoma-theory rang true: no one messed with my shit."

"Lucky." I shook my head at the *haole* who had much to learn. "Stealing a Tacoma's one thing. New stuff left in the back? Begging to be lifted."

By the time we arrived up in Kula thirty minutes later, my stomach growled.

"Where's a good place to eat?" He drummed impatient thumbs on the steering wheel, head craning back and forth to take in both sides of every street.

"And not get our stuff stolen?" I glanced at the overflowing truck bed as we passed by the turnoff for his house, heading instead toward the heart of Kula. "Kula Bistro. Park on the street, and we'll be able to see the truck from their front tables."

His knee bounced the entire time we ate our early lunch. I chewed slow bites of a roasted turkey and avocado panini while he devoured kālua pork egg rolls, crab cakes, and a grilled mahi mahi with pesto on homemade focaccia. Then he ordered a second double espresso.

149

I arched a brow, sipping my iced tea. "Sure you need the caffeine?"

He stilled, his entire demeanor changing on a slow exhale. "Are *we* going too fast?"

Yes. "Do you ever *not* think about sex?"

"No. Should I?"

I shot him an exasperated look. "Yes."

My head still reeled from the dichotomy of the last hour: him in my every thought when he wasn't in front of me to him invading my senses in person—while I tried to suck in steadying breaths of air.

Balancing on the razor-edge of control, I stood the moment Mase paid the check.

"Time to shop, surfer boy." My armor solidly slid back into place.

After we swung by his place and emptied the truck bed, including the surfboards for the time being, we hit Kula Hardware, entering through the lower nursery area. He walked the few lower aisles on both sides of the register, scanning the items for sale from weed killer to potted orchids, then we went upstairs.

He grabbed two five-gallon buckets, then handed me one.

I watched him begin to load various items into his. "Why do you need two tool belts?"

He walked farther down the aisle. "Don't."

Confused, I followed.

Two wood-handled hammers went into his. Two sets of leather gloves got tossed into mine: one extra large, the other extra small.

Shaking my head, I pulled out the smaller gloves. "I don't do manual labor."

"You do assist, *assistant*. And *I* decide what you assist *with*."

A heavy snort escaped before I could stop it. Would've stomped my foot and crossed my arms if I thought it'd help. But appearing to go along with his plan now and giving him shit later had to be easier than going head-to-head with his stubborn ass. "Fine."

"Good."

As our buckets continued to fill with matching tools, I got an uncomfortable his-and-her vibe in my own local hardware store. I tried not to read into the implications of that.

When we passed the locks, he dropped a few different kinds into his bucket. He then counted out ten that closed with a small thumbscrew. "For the windows," he explained when I gave him a questioning look.

Back downstairs, he veered us toward the pesticides. "Not that stuff." I tugged his arm, leading us toward the other side. "We need different things."

"Okay. Lead the way, oh valuable assistant."

I scowled. "Stop calling me that."

"What do you want me to call you?"

"My name works; it's Leilani."

Silence followed.

Ha. Happy I'd shut him up for the moment, I chose what he needed and dropped it into the bucket resting at my feet.

"A machete?" His gaze traveled a few feet to the right, landing on a red Radio Flyer wagon. "Seriously? My inner Indiana Jones is diggin' the retail organization they've got goin' on here."

When I brushed up against him, he stilled.

"Hmmmph." The low contemplative sound ruffled my hair as he pressed in closer. "I prefer Lani."

A hard ache punched into my gut, flared up through my chest. Even though I vaguely remembered him calling me Lani once when we'd first met, it hadn't impacted me then— when we'd been strangers, when it hadn't been so real. In Maui, however, everything became painfully real as bruised emotions I'd stuffed down long ago boiled to the surface. Through a shaky exhale, I struggled to find my voice, make it strong. "I don't."

"I think you do."

I whirled around, raw emotion sparking into anger. "You don't get to—" My words got stuck in my throat.

The overwhelming compassion in his expression stunned me. Tenderness shone in the depths of his eyes. My heavy breaths grew short and choppy as I suddenly felt lost— and found.

He stared hard, eyes narrowing, like he tried to decipher the secrets I held tight inside, buried down deep. His head tilted, then he exhaled on a slow nod.

Somehow I felt exposed, like he *knew* without me

uttering a word. Which was stupid. But felt real all the same.

"You don't…" My voice cracked.

Do not lose it in front of him. Not in the middle of Kula Hardware.

"I don't get to." He agreed, tone so soft I had to strain to hear him. "It's true. Nothing gives me the right to take anything you don't want to give. But if you let me—if you take a chance and trust what we had on a beach thousands of miles and a handful of days ago—you don't have to be afraid."

Arms crossing, I took a step back with a frown. "I'm not afraid." Then I took a deep breath. *I'm not.*

"Okay, then. Stop flirting with me, and let's get the rest of what we need."

My mouth fell open as my arms dropped to my sides, fists clenching. "*Mase.* I'm not flir—" His name echoed in my head, and he watched my expression as a sudden revelation hit me. *He'd* insisted on being called by a nickname. I railed at the idea with mine. Yet something undeniable told me both were for the same reason—family.

He leaned forward, the scruff of his jaw brushing my cheek.

I shivered from the touch, closed my eyes when his warm breath danced over my ear.

"It's okay, *Lani.*" He spoke my name on a hushed tone, as if weighting it with significance. "I won't tell if you don't."

On a slow inhalation, he drew back, brows slightly raised. As if he hoped I'd take a chance. And promised to keep my secrets safe.

My chest twanged again. Only not for things lost long ago. For what I stood to lose in the here and now. So I didn't argue with him; I gave him the tiny thing he wanted that felt so enormous.

Because some long-dead part of me wanted to be able to trust again.

17
CLEAR MINORITY

Mase...

Leilani's eyes sparkled with tears.

The slightest tremble shuddered through her.

Her lower lip quivered until she bit one corner.

But finally, on a deep breath, her lips tugged into an almost smile, and she shook her head. "You're impossible."

Good. We'd delved into all the seriousness she could handle. And in the middle of it, even if she hadn't actually verbalized it, she'd granted me permission to call her *Lani*—a nickname clearly personal to her; I wouldn't squander the privilege. But I did feel obligated to keep things upbeat. "Wrong. I'm not only possible, I'm probable. I think you meant incorrigible."

"Incorrigible?" Her brow wrinkled, then she smirked as she lifted her lighter bucket onto the counter beside the register. "Ohhh…you mean hopeless."

I pegged her with a deadpan expression. "Relentless."

The male cashier wisely ignored our nonsensical debate and began to ring up our items as I added my overflowing bucket to the counter.

Lowering my head, I murmured above her ear. "Annnd…maybe you meant irresistible."

She shivered, then stepped back a good three feet before her gaze locked with mine. "Unbelievable." The right corner of her lips twitched up before she pressed them together, forcing the smile away. "And ridiculous."

"Tenacious."

"This conversation," she clarified.

"Me." I insisted, taking a step closer, showing her I wouldn't give up.

The cashier cleared his throat. "That'll be one-eighty-five fifty-three."

Neither of us reacted…to him.

My attention strayed to the tempting rise and fall of her chest, the hard swallow at the base of her throat, the way she licked her lips as she stared at me with those endless almost-black eyes.

You want me.

Too bad we were in the middle of a hardware store.

I arched a brow at her. "Didn't realize tools would be so stimulating, did you?"

She coughed out a laugh. "Hammer."

"Nailed it."

"So very screwed."

"Yeah, ya are." My voice lowered. "Because I drill…with serious power."

Deafening silence followed.

The credit card slip printed.

Then the cashier let out a heavy sigh. "Just sign here and you're all set."

Dude probably wanted our lame-ass word-association porn-comedy out of his store.

Saving the day, I winked at Leilani and grabbed the buckets off the counter. Then we headed back toward the truck. Weaving our way between rows of one-gallon plants, she tugged her bucket from my grasp. "I've got mine."

Up the asphalt parking area, toward the front of the hardware store, two older male teens stepped out of a pickup as they waited in line for gas. The driver glared at us. "Go home, *haole*!"

Leilani froze in her tracks, body rigid. She sucked in a sharp breath, closed her eyes, and shook her head. "This isn't gonna work." Dread sank into her tone.

All the headway we'd made, the lightheartedness…the intimacy? Gone.

I frowned, unhappy with her instant about-face. "What isn't?"

"You" —she pointed a finger at me then aimed it at the silken skin between her breasts— "me."

"Sure, it is."

Her expression hardened further. "No, it's not."

"Why not?"

"Because you're white."

"So?"

"I'm not." She gestured her arms wide, palms tilting upward. "*We're* not."

"So? What's that got to do with anything?"

"*Every*thing." She thumped her bucket onto the ground below the tailgate of her Tacoma, then plopped her hands on her hips. "Look, this was a colossal mistake. Keep your money. Get out while you can."

"No." I hoisted my bucket over the tailgate before looping a strap through the handle. Then I crossed my arms, staring her down. "I'm in. That's *your* money. Work is work. And paychecks have only one color: green."

Furrows etched into her forehead as her brows pinched together. "You aren't safe here."

"Where is anyone safe? Wayward sharks, texting drivers, stray bullets." My voice broke on the last syllable. What the hell had made me say that? I sucked in a steadying breath, then pressed on, refusing to back down. "Safe is overrated, anyway. I played it safe for a while. Nice and expected, protected. Pre-med, remember? No thanks."

"It's just…"

"So what if I'm white?" I stepped closer, then dragged a finger up her bare arm, lingering on the smooth skin over her shoulder. "You're the most gorgeous shade of honey-dipped bronze I've ever seen."

"But—"

"So, I'm a minority."

She glanced up toward the gas pumps, even though the verbal bullies had already pulled forward, out of sight. "It goes way deeper than skin color."

"Enlighten me."

"You're not just white. You're *haole*…outsider."

She paused, as if the simple explanation made a difference. When my impassive expression told her it didn't, she continued with her case, "Couple hundred years ago, outsiders stole our islands. Enslaved Hawaiians. Later, the egotistical sons-of-bitches *gave us* sliced-up pieces of our land back. White means outsider; but it runs deeper than that. Corporations steal our land, pollute the water.

"But you? You're more than *haole*. You're a surfer. Surfing's a beloved thousand-year-old piece of culture the Hawaiians reclaimed. Then some punk Australians showed up and, in the blink of an eye, turned the sport pro, shared it with the world."

She crossed her arms, angling a glare at me. "Every year, more *haole* surfers come into our turf, wanting to make a name for themselves."

"Hey" —I held up my hands in surrender— "you invited me. *Makani* offered *me* the sponsorship."

"I know." She heaved out a sigh, then broke apart her arms and ran her hands through her hair. "His heart's in the right place. My brother thinks he can fix everything. One person can't fix all this. Even a handful can't. It's too big."

I stepped into the shade and leaned a shoulder against the wall. It made her face me, turn her back toward where the hecklers had been. "Maybe that's the problem. If someone believes they don't make a difference, they're right. But one person does matter. Look at Ghandi. Look at Mother Theresa. They believed in what was true to their heart, against hatred

159

and indifference—against all odds."

"They *beat* Ghandi."

I snorted. My plight didn't scratch the surface of his. "I think I can handle it."

"Can you?" She did that arm-cross thing again, jutting her hip out a couple of inches—her attitude stance. *Fucking adorable.*

"Yeah." I didn't kid myself. I'd seen the ratio here. I'd entered a region where my skin color made me the clear minority. "Doesn't matter. I've traveled the world growing up. And a big part of my inner bearing believes being a part of the land means being a part of the community too. Means I respect the locals, support them. I intend to continue that philosophy wherever I go."

And no place on earth—nor any people on it—would deter me from the freedom I sought.

Her eyes narrowed a fraction, her head tilting slightly to the right. "Fine."

After a decisive nod, she bent to pick up her bucket of supplies. She swung it up into the truck with a grunt and dropped it down into the back corner with a clunk. As I secured it with the strap, she walked to the passenger side of her truck. Hand gripping the door handle, she paused, glancing over her shoulder. "You coming?"

"*Fuck* yeah."

Wherever she agreed to go *with me*? I followed. Even if tension sparked the air between us; I got the strong feeling I needed to get used to it.

We headed back to the house, unloaded the hardware

supplies, then spent twenty minutes focused on changing out the door locks. When I dusted my hands off and looked around, she headed toward the truck.

"Ready to hit the surf?" she asked.

"That question *better* be rhetorical."

She leaned against the side of the truck bed, then dropped a heavy stare at me. "Let's see what you can handle." Challenge sizzled through every staccatoed word.

Not one cell in my body had been programmed to back down. Not to her. Not to a wave. Most definitely not to any idiotic prejudices, no matter the dumbass reason—*especially* not because of race.

We loaded our boards, then she got behind the wheel. The early-afternoon ride lasted well over an hour. We blew past Hoʻokipa, heading farther east. And the entire time, she played the quintessential tour guide: pointing out where she'd gone to elementary school, food joints she and her friends preferred, sweet spots to go surfing if the waves were setting up right.

But the last thirty minutes fell mostly silent as she concentrated on Hana Highway's hairpin turns. I gaped at impressive waterfalls that tumbled from lush green cliffs before the rushing water disappeared below bridges we drove over. "This is what Disneyland tries to emulate."

She glanced at me during a rare straightaway. "I wouldn't know."

"Never been?" Surely Hawaiians visited mainland California from time to time.

A short headshake. "No."

I made a mental note to sneak a detour into one of our travel itineraries to hit The Happiest Place on Earth.

A few minutes down a nondescript turnoff *makai* of the highway, she pulled over and parked on a grassy shoulder behind a handful of other cars. We grabbed our boards, then negotiated our way down a slippery path covered in vines that seemed eager to trip us. The humidity had doubled with zero air current, signaling mosquitos to hover over every exposed inch of skin like miniature fairies with gnashing teeth. I forged on, lured by the boom of crashing waves and the scent of fresh salty air.

Before long, the jungle opened up to reveal a narrow swath of beach.

A group of six surfers waited in a lineup right as one of them dropped in on a sweet seven-footer. Four Hawaiians stood at the water's edge, turning to fully face us when we moved into their peripheral sight.

"Hey, *howzit*." Leilani gave the shoreline group a chin-up, then splashed into foamy water that flowed over her feet.

"Go home, *haole*!" one of the group shouted.

Original. The racist broken record seemed to be a theme.

Following Leilani's lead, I greeted the welcoming committee with my own friendly nod, then ignored them, heading straight toward the waves after her.

In the span of time it took to stride forward three steps, a big Hawaiian blocked my way. *Big.* I tilted my head back, gaze rising from his massive pecs up a thick neck until we finally stared at one another eye to eye. "Where you goin', *haole*?" His dead-calm tone was unnerving.

"Fuckin' *haole*," another heckler spat out from somewhere behind me.

I nodded toward the ocean, where Leilani had stopped and turned in shin-deep water. "I'm about to surf."

"No." Big Guy lowered his head an inch, glowering at me from under dark brows. "Not heah, yo' not."

"Go home, *haole*!" the heckler repeated, closer, as if he'd crowded into my right-hand blind spot. "Go swim wit' da *groms*."

With quick splashes, Leilani jogged back. Then she planted the tail of her board into the sand beside me and dropped a hand to her hip, narrowing her eyes. "Leave him alone, Koa."

Feeling a sudden need to protect her, I took a step forward, angling her behind me. "I got this, Lani."

"*Lani*?" Koa shot a death glare over my shoulder. "Whooziz fuckin' *haole* callin' you 'Lani'?"

The situation had raced zero-to-sixty dangerous. Unnecessarily. "Look, *brah*—"

Blind Spot stepped around me, revealing himself: another seriously muscled Hawaiian. "He ain't yo' fuckin' *brah*," he snarled. "And you ain't hangin' wit' *Lani*. Got it? She's *our* girl."

Suddenly she stepped between Blind Spot and me, and she slapped a palm on his chest. "I'm *no one's* girl, Ke'eaumoku."

After leveling a glare filled with challenge at Ke'eaumoku, then at Koa, then toward the rest of their gang who'd gathered around us, she waited for a reply. When nothing but heavy breathing followed, she grabbed my hand. "C'mon." She stared at them while speaking to me. "We've got plenty better surf spots."

"Keep 'im off our beach, Leilani," Koa growled. "Don' wan' pretty city boy ta get all fucked up."

Everything in me railed at the idea of backing down, but I reminded myself their fight wasn't mine, had nothing to do with me.

Then a message flashed into my brain: *What would Ghandi do?*

The moment I turned, a bright light flashed into my peripheral.

Pain exploded into my temple. The world spun, and I stumbled. Black dots fuzzed the edges of my vision.

Leilani stepped in front of me, shouting, fear and anger washing over her expression.

But I couldn't fully see her.

Didn't actually hear her.

My lungs seized from shock. Memories from another horrific time blurred with the present. Pinching my eyes shut, I tried to block out the onslaught of emotion. Then I gasped in a burning breath.

It isn't the same. I still stood.

Guilt flared through me that it wasn't…and that I did.

18
POWDER KEG

Leilani...

Mase stumbled forward, struggling for breath.

I grabbed his forearms and pushed hard up against him, leveraging him upright.

Don't pass out. Do not *pass out.*

Frightening images flashed into my head of him hitting the ground, then those idiots surrounding and beating the shit out of him while he was down. But when Mase almost tipped over onto me like a tree, the stupid *kanaks* faded back toward the water, uninterested.

When Mase finally found his legs, he gripped my shoulders and pushed me away from him.

I assessed him closely. "Can you carry your board?"

He gave a nod, then teetered right, planting a foot out for balance. On a sharp wince, he pressed a hand to his temple.

"Maybe you could hand it to me?"

During the seconds it took to retrieve both boards, Mase had leaned against a rocky outcropping in the sand a few feet away. Somehow, we managed to get our boards on our heads and pick our way back up the narrow trail, him in the lead.

Every few seconds, I glanced forward, making sure he didn't sway off trail. "You better not fall."

"Not planning on it." Anger darkened his tone.

Eventually, we made it to the truck. He tossed his board in, then got into the cab. I climbed up into the bed, opened the built-in metal toolbox that Makani kept stocked with first aid supplies, and found an icepack. Bending it back and forth, I broke the rigid tube in the center, then massaged the granules inside, waiting for its chemical reaction to make it cold enough.

When I handed it to Mase, he stared at its white cover for a beat. Then he jammed an elbow onto the doorframe at the base of his open window and rested his head into his hand against the icepack.

I walked around back, then got into the driver's side. My fingers pinched the key. But I couldn't start the engine. Every breath I took burned with regret. Deep shame churned in my gut.

He got hurt because of me.

But he'd needed to understand, see the hatred in person. And better with me there than not.

"Didn't mean for them to hurt you," I murmured. No better explanation came.

He cut a harsh glare toward me. "You *knew* that would happen?"

"Well, I didn't know your face would take a hit from a loaded beer can."

"Really? What did you expect?" He shouted. "A fist? A knife? A *gun*?"

His last growled-out word echoed so loudly, I jumped in my seat, startled at his fury. "No. L-l-look" —I stammered as my throat locked up— "I didn't think they w-wo—"

"That's your problem." His tone lowered, bitterness turning it sour. "You didn't think. Try it next time. I'm a person. I have a life. Random shit happens all on its own. You don't need to be throwing someone you care about into a powder keg when they have no clue *they're* the lit match."

"Look, Mase, I'm sorr—"

"Maybe you don't care," he muttered as he shifted his gaze away from me to stare out the windshield. Then he closed his eyes and rested his temple against the icepack again.

"No. I do. I care." The hushed words came out before I gave any thought about them.

I do. I care. Maybe a little more than I'd been willing to admit to myself. A whole lot more than made any kind of sense, given who he was…who I was.

"Then show it. Think."

Got it. Not the first time I'd heard it.

I started the engine and began the drive back to my place, wishing I could find some reset button to start over with him. "Okay. Okay, I get it. I fucked up."

What else was new? Yet another half-baked Leilani idea with consequences I'd failed to consider—that could've been much worse.

And he was really bent about it. His hands shook. Breaths had shortened. Brows remained drawn low. Beneath the dark-blond stubble on his face, his jaw kept clenching.

I'd hurt him—more than physically. And hadn't meant to.

Chest still burning with regret, I heaved out a sigh. "I'm sorry."

"It's okay." Gruffness edged his tone.

Clearly, it wasn't. But nothing I could do about it now; I'd disappointed him.

The hour-long drive passed silently. For the first half of it, I'd taken the turns as easy as I could while his head had stayed propped on his icepack-pillowed hand. With every glance his way, I'd verified he hadn't fallen asleep, but his eyes had stayed shut, even when he'd finally pulled his hand down and tipped backward against the headrest.

Seconds after the engine cut, he got out, went up the steps, and disappeared into his screened-in portion of the lanai, tumbling into the hammock. I pulled our boards out and put them with the others in the back of the carport.

The house fell dead-silent. Which I noticed for all of two seconds before I buried myself into work; he hadn't taken his offer back, so the job was still on. Over the next two hours, I researched out windsurfing competitions and outlined a potential schedule, including days in between for training.

When my hips began to cramp from sitting too long and time had run out before we needed to leave, I got up, grabbed our small icepack from the freezer, then brought it outside. His long legs didn't move when the front door thudded shut.

After hesitating for only a moment, I knocked on the screen-door frame.

"Yeah?"

"Mind if I come in?"

"Nope."

"Single syllables are a good start." When he made no move to get up, kept his back toward me, I stretched my arm in front of his face, offering him the icepack.

He took it with a swipe, then pressed it to his head. "Thanks. Still pissed as fuck at you," he grumbled.

"Got it." I'd earned the punishment, would grin and bear it like always. "Still goin' to Peggy Sue's?"

"What?"

"Peggy Sue's. The car show."

"Oh, shit. I forgot about that." He sat up and swung around fast, then planted his feet when he wobbled. "Got any ibuprofen?"

"Yeah."

"Then we're goin' to Peggy Sue's. If you're drivin'."

After the pills, we drove the thirty minutes to Kihei in silence. Well, almost. He'd asked about the closing sugarcane mill, and I'd filled him in on what little details I knew.

But I hardly noticed the lack of chitchat. I grew distracted by how public we were about to be. And since I didn't exactly frequent car shows, I had no idea what to expect.

Will Maui's car collectors treat him differently? Will their crowds?

After we parked the Tacoma and walked toward the colorful cars, a group of familiar faces who'd gathered at the nearest end caught my attention.

RULE BREAKER

Dread curdled in my gut.

Because I got the feeling Mase's lesson in our cultural diversity hadn't ended yet.

19
ONE ACT AT A TIME

Mase…

Anger seethed just under my skin.

Not toward Leilani anymore. With everyone: generations who'd come before us, world leaders, local influencers, *parents*—mine included, mine especially.

The world gets saved one kind act at a time.

What I kept telling myself. The change I wanted began with me.

During the ride over, my attitude toward Leilani had softened. She'd only known what she'd grown up around. And she *had* asked me a question under the influence of alcohol: *"Ever feel like you're living someone else's life? Like what everyone wants for you, expects for you…isn't for you?"* Only I hadn't bothered to learn more.

Until the evidence had knocked me upside the head—welcome to reality.

With every step we took farther away from her truck, Leilani grew more agitated. She kept casting nervous glances toward a group of tuners our age, all Hawaiian, who'd gathered near an entrance up ahead.

When I put a gentle hand on her shoulder to slow us up a second, she flinched.

"You're jumpy."

"Yeah." Her glance shot over toward the group of guys again. "Sorry."

"Hey." I touched a fingertip under her chin and gently lifted until she looked up at me. "Stop worrying. This isn't your fault." She needed to hear that. To know I felt it. "Earlier…it just caught me by surprise. I *did* tell you I could handle it."

She gave me a weak smile, remorse in her eyes.

I shook my head. "Don't apologize again. I'm good."

After she sucked in a shaky breath, she gave me a nod. "N'kay."

Then I hooked my arm into hers and purposefully got between her and them. "Think we'll make a scene?"

Amusement sparked in her eyes. "No."

"Not enough?" I glanced their way, then back toward her. "I could dip you" —I wrapped an arm around her back, swung her sideways and down low, then bent my head until our lips were a few millimeters apart— "and kiss you."

Her shallow breaths fogged over my lips, dark gaze locking with mine. She swallowed hard.

Before she could answer, I spun her back upright. "Think I'll save the kiss for later."

"Why?" She blinked, clearly stunned.

"Because the dip was enough."

"For what?"

"Getting your mind off everyone else." I nodded toward the group as we passed by them. "Didn't stop 'em from mad-doggin' me, though."

"Mad-doggin'?" She glanced back. "Oh, you mean stink-eye."

"Stink what?"

"We call it stink-eye here: dirty look. They think they're hot shit. C'mon, let's keep walking. No flying cans yet."

"Atta girl."

As we strolled down the aisle of bright paint and curving fenders, a polished chrome bumper stood out at the end of the angled spaces on our row. A beautiful shiny grill fronted what at first looked like a rust-bucket of a truck. But a deeper story unfolded if you took the time to look. Islands of weathered green paint had surrendered to large patches of intentionally preserved surface-patina rust. A soft shine along the curve of the nearest fender told me a clear satin sealer now protected what years of nature had created.

Fixated on the truck, I drew closer, skirting around her front until I stood beside the driver's door. I stared in at an impeccable, refurbished cab interior.

"*Niiice.*" A red-and-white FOR SALE sign sat on the camel-colored leather bench seat.

Not thinking twice, I pulled my phone out and began

snapping pictures from every angle. "You got your Notes app handy?" Couldn't get a decent pic of the sign.

"Yep." She plucked her phone out of her dress pocket.

I read the vehicle info to her, "1954 Chevy restomod. New drive train, 350 V8, auto-trans." Then I rattled off the price and phone number.

"You said you wanted 'character'" —she tilted her head a little, squinting her eyes at it— "this *definitely* has character."

"Sure does. What d'ya think? You like her?"

"Yeah." She stepped back, crossing her arms as she titled her head a fraction to the other side. "Maybe. A Maui cruiser, for sure."

"I heard 'yes.'" I dropped her a knowing look.

"Maybes and noes are yeses, now?" She arched a brow. "Fine. I'll be seen in it. But no capital *Y* and no exclamation points."

No sex, she meant. "Uh-huh. We'll see."

An older Hawaiian gentleman with a white T-shirt and mirrored sunglasses approached us. "You like 'er?"

"Yeah, I do." I stared longingly at her. "She's a beaut."

"'Nuff ta buy 'er?"

"Maybe…" I winked at Leilani. "Let's talk price."

He broke into a wide smile, extending a hand toward me. "I'm Kaleo." He nodded toward the truck. "This is Halia, means 'in remembrance of a loved one.'"

Damn. I froze for a second as I thought of Deke. Then I recovered and shook his hand. "I'm honored to meet her, Kaleo. I'm Mase. This is Leilani." She gave him a brief nod.

Then Kaleo and I negotiated while I looked under Halia's

hood, examined her undercarriage, asked how long he'd had her and the modifications he'd made since ownership. In the end, after learning all the painstaking details Kaleo had lovingly put into his truck, I paid his full asking price—well worth it, and then some.

With banks closed for the weekend, we agreed to meet at the Bank of Hawaii in Pukalani late Monday afternoon, a ten-minute drive from my rental house. Leilani offered to drop me off.

Afterward, Leilani and I wandered through the rest of the cars. Then we got burgers and milkshakes at Peggy Sue's. When we finally left, things had almost gone back to normal between us. I'd cooled off from my earlier pissed-off and she'd relaxed about the whole thing. To a point.

As we headed toward her Tacoma, passing by the same tuners whose group had since doubled in size, I stealthily slipped my hand into hers—my compromise on a dip-and-kiss encore.

But she unclasped before we ever reached full contact, then crooked her arm into mine.

When I arched a brow at her, she dropped me a deadpan look. "*Friends.* Remember the rule? No dating my boss."

Uh-huh. Fat chance, sexy island girl.

Because when I'd thrown her off-balance, dipping and almost kissing her? When her breaths had shortened, lips parting on a gasp?

She wanted *way more* than friends.

With a definite capital *Y.*

And page full of exclamation points.

20
SPINNING IN NEUTRAL

Leilani…

"How am I supposed to work like this?"

"Like what?" Mase's warm breath skated over my bare shoulder.

I swallowed hard, then pulled in a steadying breath. "With you so…*close.*"

The gleaming drywall nail balanced between my pinched fingers; I had the blunt end of my brand new hammer aimed at its circular head.

But I couldn't concentrate.

His body heat seemed to warm my skin no matter where he stood. The earthy ocean scent of him nearly overwhelmed me, made me struggle not to exhale on a sensual sigh. And the thin black V-neck T-shirt that clung to his biceps? Deadly.

He stepped back, giving me breathing room. "Consider my house neutral territory."

"What?" I glanced at him, dropping the nail I'd been obsessing over.

His ice-blue eyes were more vibrant above the black of his shirt. A healthy tan colored his face, light pink dusting his cheekbones. Tousled hair, once dark-blond, had lightened after only a week of daily surfing.

His stubble-covered jaw clenched a beat. "Like Switzerland." Full lips quirked up a little as he stared at me.

Easier said than done. In the five days since the car show, we'd danced around each other. We'd gotten his few belongings moved into the house, had spent two days demolishing what he'd wanted to get started on—in my steel-toed work boots—and had begun organizing materials, all while almost brushing up against one another.

The sexual tension? Thicker than ever.

But I wasn't about to admit it. Or give in. Switzerland? Challenge accepted. "Fine by me. No flirting. No advances. No teasing or sexual innuendo."

He rolled his eyes. "No fun."

I punched his shoulder.

"Ow. What?" He rubbed where I'd made contact. "That's all I heard."

Ignoring him, I grabbed my nail again, positioning the point where he'd shown me. "Seriously. I've never done this before."

"Swung a hammer?"

"Yeah."

"Okay. So you see this here end?" He ran a finger down the wooden handle. "You hold it. And this tiny metal end here? That's where you make impact."

"Ha. Ha. You want me hurt, smartass?"

"I'm just teasin'. Look" —he pulled his hammer from his belt, then fished out a nail from a pocket and pressed the point onto his next penciled *X* along the edge of the drywall sheet— "it's not in the swing; it's all in the aim. You're holding your nail too low. That's how people miss and smash their fingers."

He pinched his nail under the head, then gave a few short taps. "Hit the head of the hammer squarely on the head of the nail."

After the nail sank down a third of the way, he removed his fingers, then finished with heavier pounding. "Use your whole arm and elbow. Keep your wrist straight; let the weight of the hammer do your work."

Nodding, I placed my nail, then imitated his swings with a few easy taps.

"You're choking up too high on the handle. Rookie mistake." He stepped in behind me, slid his palm over my forearm, then covered my hand, my fingers.

I gasped from the intimate contact, then kept inhaling to cover my instant reaction.

When I relaxed my hand, he guided it into proper position. "Grip lower down. Gives you more leverage."

On a hard swallow, I gave a short nod. Only when he stepped back, breaking contact, did my brain cells fire again, did my lungs remember to breathe.

Focusing all my pent-up energy on my task, I tightened my hold, then followed his instructions, hammering in smooth easy strokes.

"That's it. You don't have to do it fast. And you don't have to hit hard. Accurate is what we're after."

After forty-five minutes of cutting to fit and hammering into place, three drywall sheets filled the first wall of his bedroom. With that warm-up, it took another hour and a half for us to hang the remainder of the bedroom walls. A breeze filtered in from the open window but didn't do much to ease the stifling air inside.

I slid my hammer into my five-gallon bucket. "When's break time?" Deciding *now*, I unfastened my tool belt.

"You hungry?" He reached his arms over his head, stretching.

"Tired. Hot. And yeah, I could eat."

"Then, now." He pulled off his tool belt, draped it over one end of a saw horse, then went into the hall.

I followed him to a kitchen that had wooden frames for cabinetry, square openings where drawers would slide in or doors would cover, and loose plywood sheets where countertop would eventually lay. A brand-new stainless steel refrigerator hummed in one corner.

He opened the fridge door. Bright colored food wrappers sat on shelves. Bottles of cold beer stood in cardboard six-pack cases.

"*Niiice.*" I nudged him out of the way, stealing all the cold air. Then I grabbed the nearest sandwich and a beer. "You got *grindz* and didn't say anything?" I pressed the wrapped sandwich to my nose. Tangy mouthwatering spices made my stomach growl. "What is this? Beef?"

"Korean beef with kimchi slaw…like a sloppy joe—with attitude," he replied as he followed me outside. Then he sat beside me on the other fraying beach chair we'd confiscated from Makani's storage room.

A steady cool trade wind flowed through his yard, clearing my head, relaxing my rioting body. *Almost.*

Because our forearms touched as we ate and admired the killer double-coastline view. And although Mase was right-handed, he ate with his left, maintaining our skin-to-skin contact. And even though I wanted to keep my distance, I didn't pull away.

Without a word, we both edged into a distinctly gray area—very *non*neutral territory.

The following day, preparing for another round of pretending that neutral existed in our construction-Switzerland, I took a fortifying deep breath then stepped through Mase's front door. But I didn't find him in any of the areas we'd been working on.

"Mase?"

No answer.

With nowhere else to search inside, I pulled open the back sliding glass door and stepped onto the covered lanai. The tattered beach chairs were empty. Walking onto the grass, I finally spotted him, hunched over a weathered wooden picnic table near the garden. An old jacaranda tree swayed in the wind, dancing shadows over him as it sprinkled down purple flower petals.

"What are you doing?"

"Researching," he murmured. He didn't glance up. Just continued to scan a page in a thick book, sliding his finger from left to right. After a nod, he wrote down a quick note on a yellow lined legal pad.

My gaze landed on seedling trays, then lifted to a couple of rows of foot-tall plants covering the roughhewn table. "Sure you're not starting a reforestation project?"

"Certain."

I glanced down at a pile of seed packets, began to rifle through them. "Oregano, basil, cilantro...marigolds." With a snap of my fingers, I spun toward him. "You're starting a farm."

"In a way..."

"Such as, Mr. Vague?"

"The chickens."

Blinking in confusion, I turned toward the decrepit hen house...correction, *refurbished* hen house; he'd obviously been busy between yesterday and today. Thinking I missed something walking over from the lanai, I spun in a slow three-sixty, scanning the property, then cocked my head at him. "*What* chickens?"

"The dozen day-olds being shipped to me."

"Of course. Day-old chicks." My tone flattened with disbelief.

"Yep."

"N'kay." Not certain what to think about the sudden development, I focused on the books. "What about the chickens…*chicks*," I corrected. "Don't you have to put them in a…?"

"Brooder. Got one of them comin' too. And there's a healthier way to keep them fed, happy, and laying without chemicals." He flipped a page, then scrawled another note. "Applies to people too."

"Where'd you get this book?" When he abandoned the larger book, reaching far to the side to grab a slim hardcover, I lifted the heavy reference book with two hands. "*Healing with Whole Foods*. Looks very…*doctorly*."

He let out a soft snort, finally looking up at me. "Back in Philly. While I studied pre-med, I researched alternative medicine on the side."

"Chickens," I repeated, floored. Couldn't wrap my mind around someone spending so much time on…fowl.

"Yep. Check this out…" He flipped halfway through the slim book, then nodded. "Centipedes. Chickens love centipedes. Need to order me a few guinea hens."

"Because…"

"They love ticks. And spiders. So do the chickens."

"We don't have ticks here. I don't think."

"Hmmm…" He went silent again, reading.

I stared at the nearly finished coop. Roofing shingles were stacked on a new plywood roof. Rolls of chicken wire stood beside it.

"Any snakes on the island?" he asked.

I scowled, shaking my head. "No. Better not ever be."

"Why?"

"We don't need another non-natural predator."

"Damn," he breathed out.

"Now what?" Thrown by his sudden intellectual side, and wanting a closer look, I sat beside him on the bench. What I didn't mean to do was brush my leg against his. Too late, the heat of his skin and the soft hairs on his calf had an electrifying effect on me. And yet, I couldn't bear to pull my leg away. Swallowing hard, I leaned into his side, making an attempt to take control. Deliberate seemed to calm me more than accidental.

"Not a damn thing likes millipedes," he grumbled.

"Smart chickens and hens. *I* hate millipedes." My whole body shuddered.

"Me too. Found one little fucker curled under my arm in bed the other morning."

The detailed image revolted me seconds before it excited me. Because the heat-seeking insect vanished from my mind. Instead, I fantasized about the warm, protective space beneath his arm…with me curled under it.

No! Switzerland, I reminded myself as I struggled to find a balancing neutral.

Think about the bug, Leilani. Visualize a nasty skittering bug under his smelly armpit. "Yuck," I vocalized for emphasis—for him and me.

But then I inhaled. And Mase smelled incredible, earthy. *Distract yourself!*

I searched for something—anything—to take my mind off how much I enjoyed being so close to him. *How about why you came, genius.* "I booked a flight for you."

"For *us*."

"Us?" I blinked again in confusion, then stared at a knot on the surface of the table, rethinking our conversation from a few afternoons ago when we'd strategized a plan of action: him storm-chasing both surfing and windsurfing for the rest of the season unless we could nab a wildcard entry. "We're talking about the same thing, right? *You* flying to the Mentawai Islands next week?"

"Yep. You're my assistant. You're my liaison. My PR girl. You are *most definitely* coming."

"Oh," I whispered.

All I could manage, still adjusting to facets of him I hadn't anticipated. He'd gone from adventuring surfer boy to academic and…*farm* boy. Which neutralized my ability to hold up a worthy debate.

Because part of me wanted to argue against traveling with him. But the other part, the adventurer in me, began to vibrate with excitement.

21
ABOUT THE JOURNEY

Mase...

Our feet hit solid ground—on a different part of the planet.

Literal neutral ground.

No baggage...metaphorically.

After twenty-four hours, four planes, then a bone-jarring speedboat ride across the Mentawai Strait, Leilani and I stood shoulder to shoulder, wordless. A trickle of sweat rolled down my back under my T-shirt. Three black canvas board bags towered over us as they leaned against a wall.

"Why am I here again?" She crossed her arms, raising one slender dark brow at me.

"On a speck of land in Sumatra?"

"Yeah."

"To surf." I grabbed the lightest board bag from the wall, then laid it at her feet.

She toed the bag, as if she suspected it might sprout legs. "I don't need to surf. You do."

"You're my assistant."

She shot me an exhausted look. "Assisting can be done remotely."

"Can it? Did you get us a car?"

"*You* a car. And there are no car rentals here. Gotta barter with the locals."

"Exactly."

Brows drawing together, she propped her hands on her hips. "You expect me to barter?"

"Why not?" Trying not to crack a smile, I grabbed the handles of the other two bags, one of which held the masts and rigging, as I waited for her to agree.

"What's in this bag?" She again toed the first bag I'd pulled down.

"Our surfboards. You grabbin' 'em?"

"*Our* surfboards?"

"*You* catch on quick. Remember that job description we didn't nail down?"

"Stupid endless job description," she grumbled as she grabbed the handle and swiveled the long bag on its wheels.

"I'm sorry, what was that?"

"Yes."

"Well, you're coming with me—everywhere. I go? You go. You wanted to travel? Here's the world, right at our feet. Life is right in front of us. All we have to do is step out and grab it."

After I got to the curb, she didn't appear beside me.

When I heard no sound, I glanced back.

She stood a few feet behind, staring at me. The bag she'd wheeled over soundlessly fell from her grip. Her expression changed, eyes widening. The corners of her mouth twitched, then relaxed. Amazed? Impressed? Shocked? I couldn't tell. Maybe a mixture of all.

"You made me come...*for me*?"

"Watch it, Girl Friday. That smacks of sexual innuendo."

She glared at me, then huffed a breath out as she squared her shoulders. "That was platonic."

Uh-huh. *Says the blush pinking your cheeks.* "Not a damn platonic thing about that."

I dropped my two bags, stepped closer, and got up in her space, calling her bluff. Our clothes touched: my shirt and shorts pressed against her flimsy dress.

Brave girl didn't move an inch.

Hands at our sides, chests rising and falling together, a little faster with every inhalation, we stared at each other. She swallowed, took a deeper breath.

The wind suddenly swirled around us, blowing her hair across her face. Unthinking, I reached up and tucked the silken black strands behind her ear.

I kept my fingers there, cupping her jaw. "When I make you come, it will be for you...*and* for me."

Her eyes glittered. The pulse at the base of her throat thumped.

She wanted me. No doubt about it.

But we weren't there yet. The rules separating us were

too fresh. The reasons too important. However, the checks and balances we honored would only remain a short time longer. Enough to let both of us know it was okay to break them—that we'd be safe to cross over.

Because we didn't need to have the conversation to know we'd blown way past the possibility of being just physical, and it had begun to happen almost from the beginning. Which scared the fuck out of her. And me, if I was being totally honest.

Want something for myself? Begin to value it? It becomes something to lose.

We remained standing there for a long while. My sensual promise hung in the air between us. She didn't dispute it, didn't argue, simply continued to stare at me with a look of wonder and bewilderment.

Good. Her being both impressed and confused gave me the advantage in the game we played. And kept her on her toes.

With every passing breath, the gravity of the moment settled down into us.

And slowly, the outside world crept in.

The growl of another boat engine grew louder as it approached the dock. Untamed jungle crowded in from both sides of a narrow dirt road. The humidity vanished as cool winds from the ocean swept in from the strait.

I stepped back, giving us both space to breathe. "Car?"

She didn't respond at first. Then she blinked and scanned our immediate surroundings.

Five vehicles were parked in view: three rust-bucket

sedans, all with their windows rolled down, a dilapidated truck with two crisscrossed bungee cords where a tailgate used to be, a newer dark-blue Jeep with beads of water from a fresh rain sparkling over its perfect paint.

Abandoning me and our bags, she passed the Jeep without even a glance at it, then began to examine the truck. From an area across the road in the shade of a tree, where half a dozen young men sat on battered lawn chairs drinking out of bottles and playing some kind of board game, a gangly teenager popped up and lightly jogged toward her.

I lagged behind to give her plenty of room. But not far: within earshot. And close enough to protect her if needed.

Not that the place felt threatening. I'd gotten a friendly vibe from the beach locales I'd traveled to on my own so far. Everywhere I went, the local people were welcoming. Smiles were common. Generosity, even more so. Like their fortunate lives were a tapestry woven with experiences and newcomers were a brightly colored thread they'd been gifted.

But I understood the people whose paths I crossed in remote locations didn't have it easy. Theirs might be simpler lives, free of cutting-edge electronics and expensive brand names, but they still had to provide for themselves, for their families.

As I watched Leilani speak to the Indonesian boy, I grew more impressed with how she communicated—and the details she asked. He spoke broken English. She explained what she wanted to know in her regular easy cadence, no slower. When his brows had drawn in confusion to something she'd asked, she'd repeat it, adding hand gestures when she pointed to the tires or gave a lifting motion in front of the hood.

When she finally glanced back at me, I walked over.

"He said the truck's sound. Good tires. Engine is rusty, but runs well. Spare gas tank in the back is full."

"How long can we have it?"

"All weekend. Two hundred dollars." She pulled her backpack from her shoulder.

Not a bad deal. And not like we had a lot of choices. "No, I got it." Safe-feeling or not, no need to have her exposing herself as a target as she pulled out her wallet. I reached into my pocket, peeled off ten twenties, and handed them over. The kid took the money, then pointed at the keys dangling in the ignition.

We climbed in, drove back to the board bags, and while she sat inside, I loaded them in back. Then we were off. To parts unknown. Were there more popular surf resorts on other islands along the Mentawai Strait? Sure. But I wanted roads and more remote places to explore.

Her legs began bouncing before we'd clocked in a mile. "Where we goin'?"

"To the beach."

"Point it in any direction till we hit sand?"

"Not exactly." I'd done some online reconnaissance. Called a few New Jersey surf buddies who'd been down before. Got the lay of the land.

"A plan, then?"

"Kinda."

Really, it didn't matter where we went first. Most islands

had a few good rippers if you looked long enough. But knowing where to search before hitting the road saved time. And although I hadn't consciously thought about the benefit when I'd called them, I realized it now.

Being on autopilot more, meant I got to appreciate the company along the way. But appreciation became a benefit with a cost; it turned into a challenging heightened awareness. Of her…so close to me. She hadn't settled into the seat near the door. No, she'd sidled right up next to me, her thigh pressed against mine.

No matter how hard I stared at the road, my attention stayed riveted elsewhere: the gentle swells of her breasts as the low neckline of her thin dress clung to them; the smooth bare skin of her toned thigh and how when a pothole rocked her, separating us by even an inch, she'd readjust, pressing her side back against mine; the intoxicating floral scent of her hair and how it tickled when a crossbreeze blew strands over my face then swirled them away again.

Seconds dragged into the best torturous minutes as we drove down a winding one-lane road. Thick jungle pressed in on either side, giving way every now and then to bright stretches of sand and endless blue ocean.

A tug at my shorts had me look down. She'd wound one of the white canvas ties of the cargo pocket above my knee around her finger. I glanced up and met her gaze; it sparkled with humor. "What's your 'kinda' plan?" A teasing tone edged her voice.

Excellent question. On a hairpin turn, I glanced back at the road. "No idea." The quiet reply slipped out before

I could stop it—and had nothing to do with our road trip destination.

"Wherever we end up?" Her words softened, as if maybe the hidden meaning hit her too.

"Yeah."

Without thought. No fear. A new adventure possible at every turn. Even though there were no guarantees we wouldn't hit a dead-end, or worse.

Even with all the unpredictable risks, I couldn't imagine living our journey any other way.

22
TERRITORY UNCHARTED

Leilani...

At a *T* in the road, when a clear path went right, toward the ocean, Mase hooked a hard left.

The symbolism wasn't lost on me.

How he wanted me, but waited. Out of some sense of correctness.

Heading *mauka* on a bumpier dirt road, we passed by a group of local women and kids. Many carried baskets on their heads. All wore cotton dresses in bright colors. When a few glanced our way as we passed, they flashed us wide smiles.

"Still 'kinda'?" I asked. He spoke in riddles. Like so many of the aunties and uncles on Maui who loved to talk story.

"Yep."

"*Riiight…*" I got the sense he knew exactly where he was going. With the truck—and me.

At least one of us has a clue.

My worries about us began to fade away as the road ended where a grouping of huts began and more villagers greeted us, surrounding the truck. Mase jumped out, rummaged through one of his bags in the back, then brought out a bottle that glistened in the sunlight.

The friendly group guided us to their chieftain in the center of their community. A smaller man with wrinkled dark skin and a shock of white hair smiled up at us.

Mase extended his bottle. "A gift for you."

The chieftain nodded and took the bottle of clear liquid, appearing to be vodka. Whether the man spoke English or not never became clear. But when a couple of teenaged boys shouted in excitement, pointing at our surfboards, communication had been struck. They ran off. A few minutes later, they returned, each with a board balanced over their head. After gleefully shouting words I didn't understand, they jogged down a narrow path.

"What do you think they were saying?"

He gave me a one-shoulder shrug, then grinned. "Surf's up?"

I laughed. "Works for me."

Mase didn't worry about our gear, so neither did I.

And ten minutes later, every thought faded away behind turquoise walls of glass, misty sea spray, and heavenly barrels that lasted until our legs gave out.

Later that night, we sat around a dying beach campfire

with our two new friends. They'd settled down on the other side while Mase and I enjoyed the slight chill of the ocean breeze.

The air was crisp and clean. And each next inhalation tasted like rebirth…felt like freedom. I'd come with Mase, on my first adventure to fulfill my lifelong wish of traveling the world, without expectation of what the experience might bring. Yet the reality blew me away.

An unnamable magic, distinct and beautiful, swirled in the air around us. Among strangers, instant friendship bonds had formed with our common love of wind and sea; trust and joy abounded, plentiful and free.

"This," I whispered to Mase. "This" —I nodded at our friends, toward the village behind us, then swept my gaze across the ocean before landing an intense stare on the one man beside me who'd made it all possible— "is the reason I wanted to travel."

A content sigh escaped him as he gave a slow nod. "The fabric of the world. All of us unique threads within it."

"Makes for a richer life for all involved." Most Hawaiians honored connectivity to all. The soul of nature, and our oneness with those who heard it, sang loudly in our blood.

His chin dipped in another nod, his gaze going unfocused off into the horizon toward the west. After long beats of silence, his voice turned reverent. "Deeper…and stronger."

A sense of importance pierced my heart, spreading warmth through my body until it settled heavy in my bones. Mase had wanted my realization to happen, wanted me to see. And the satisfaction I felt—from him, from me, from our connection to one another and everything and everyone around us—hung palpable in the air between us, intimate and delicate, yet vibrant and growing stronger.

And as I relaxed into it, the difference between our remote location and my home—his home now, too—became clear. I didn't know how to get beyond that disparity. When we'd been at the beach on a faraway Pacific isle, the night we'd first met, I'd discovered the beginnings of the same thing—an escape from reality.

Every little problem in the real world had vanished.

Almost like…the way it felt to ride a wave.

Comfortable with the philosophical path my mind had wandered down, and trusting that I could be safe there with Mase, I asked the first question that came to mind.

"How do we go back to reality from here? From a world of total acceptance to…"

Challenges…

No need to clarify. He knew.

He folded an arm under his head. "On a beach in France, when I was a kid, I met a cool guy named Freddie once. He was a follower of Zoroastrianism."

"Zoroastrianism? How did you even remember that word?"

He smiled. "Back then, I didn't. Remembered the 'Zoro' part. Looked it up when I started college."

"Where was Freddie from?"

"Iran, I think. I might've been twelve at the time, he had to be pushing thirty. But my broth…" He paused and took a deep breath. When I glanced at him, he cleared his throat, then continued, "I surfed with Freddie for a good five hours one day. And while we waited for our turn at the wave, he said a lot of things that went right over my head. But one of his phrases stuck with me. Humata, Hukhta, Huvarshta: Good thoughts. Good words. Good deeds."

"Elegant."

"And simple."

"What does it mean to you?"

He gazed up at the stars. "I think the world is more complex than we could ever imagine. And we can't even begin to fix everything happening around us, let alone political issues happening globally. But we can be the best selves we were meant to be. We can be pure and good. Forgiving and relentless. And when an obstacle lies in our path?"

He paused, then glanced at me. "Be like water."

"Be like water," I repeated, loving the modest phrase.

If only the world were so simple.

23
WATCHED OVER BY STARS

Mase…

"They've gotten so big." Leilani cupped a chirping silver chick in her hand.

"Right?" Only had them a week and they'd nearly doubled in size.

She surveyed the rest of the burgeoning flock that scurried over fresh pine shavings in a large plastic bin. "Who's been watching them?"

"Neighbor. We struck a deal: They take care of the place while I'm gone, I keep 'em in fresh eggs."

After she deposited the fluffball into the container, I handed her a beer and we sat in my borrowed beach chairs, staring up at the night sky.

Head still tilted back, she glanced at me. "Remember when we first laid on the beach?"

"You drunk off your ass?"

She elbowed my side. "I'm serious."

"Yeah, I remember." *Every moment, in vivid detail.* "Kinda miss that girl."

"What girl? She's sitting right beside you."

"No. The girl who'd let herself go. The one who'd let in a surfer boy she'd just met."

Picking at the corner of her beer label, she shrugged. "That was the tequila talkin'."

"What would it take for it to be just the girl, not the tequila?"

She turned and stared at me, eyes dark, jawline hard, chest rising and falling more rapidly at my question, at the unhidden challenge there. Finally, her eyes softened. "What I meant was do you remember the stars?"

"Yeah, I remember. They were amazing." I glanced upward. "These aren't bad either."

"Wanna see better?"

"Of course, I do." I'd seen some amazing skies in my life, but hadn't appreciated them with someone in a long time. And I suddenly wanted to. With her.

With her... I'd do anything.

Suddenly, she popped up from her chair and disappeared. Seconds later, I heard keys jangling behind me. "You comin', or what?"

Thirty minutes later, dressed in several layers of the second-warmest shirts I owned, sitting next to a petite girl practically drowning in the extra-large of my warmest, I did my best not to break out into a grin as we ascended Haleakala.

"Slow down," she ordered in a gruff tone, for the third time.

"Already going five under."

"Slower."

I lifted my foot off the gas as commanded. "This okay?"

"Yeah, sorry." She leaned forward, gripping the edge of the dashboard as she peered over the hood. "It's the nēnē. They're endangered. And careless drivers hit them on this road."

I frowned, slowing down to a near-crawl. "Lemme turn the high beams off."

As soon as light flooded onto the road's surface instead of farther ahead, her shoulders relaxed. Before a full minute ticked by, there stood a pair of the large birds, in the middle of the road.

"They look like Canadian geese." When they waddled off the road, I continued on at a crawl.

"They've evolved from them. Almost no webbing between their toes. Don't fly anymore. Mostly hang out in the higher elevations."

"You into birds?"

She shrugged. "Learned about endangered species on the islands in school. I'm into helping them when I can. Volunteer out at the Nakula Natural Area Reserve sometimes."

"What kind of help do they need?"

"Healthy forest planted, for one. The British and Australians planted tropical trees and bushes they liked, which crowded out all of the indigenous trees that our birds need for survival. Planting new native trees helps where deforestation and grazing wiped them out. Fences have to be built to keep out the boars and deer." She pointed off to the left. "Park over there."

Sounded cool. "If you don't mind me tagging along, invite me to go with you next time."

Surprise washed over her expression, then she smiled and nodded. "N'kay."

"*Brrr...*" I shivered as a brisk wind hit my face the instant I opened the door. At nearly ten-thousand feet in elevation, it felt like we'd traveled another planet away from the balmy tropics just over an hour downslope.

In under a minute, we settled on my new couch cushions that we'd earlier tossed into the bed of the truck. Then we quickly pulled the only two blankets I owned over us, up to our chins, and did our best to fend off the forty-degree wind chill in our makeshift observation deck.

For about five minutes, we laid like that, side by side, bodies huddled. Nothing overtly sexual about it, yet my body pinged with energy. But more than that, my chest felt heavy from the peaceful intimacy between us.

Her leg began to bounce. "You freezin' yo' *da kines* off yet?"

I frowned. "What kinds?"

"Da *kines.*"

"My balls?"

She laughed hard, curling her knees up into her chest. "Remember? We say '*da kine*' to mean anything. You said it's like 'whatchamacallit' in English."

"For the record, I don't say 'whatchamacallit' when

talkin' 'bout my balls. They're *my balls*."

"*I'm* not calling them anything."

"*You* brought it up."

Crossing her arms with an exaggerated drop, she stared intently at the night sky. "Well, I'm *not* talking about them."

"Still are…"

She let out a soft snort, shoulders shaking again. But she said nothing further—giving in or winning, I wasn't sure.

The silence stretched into minutes, but it was nice. Reminded me of our first night on the beach. Just her and me. None of my problems. None of hers.

"Fuck, yeah," I finally admitted. "I'm freezing my balls off."

But I didn't care. Being there—with her—topped every experience I'd ever had.

Our breaths puffed out in frosted clouds, mingling together for an instant before vanishing with the next gust of wind. Countless stars glittered above in an infinite pitch-black sky; we were small specks below, grains of sand at the bottom of an endless ocean.

A deep quiet settled between us. Not the awkward kind where you struggle for something to say. No. What happened relaxed into our bones, turning every next frosty breath into something that warmed my chest, made each heartbeat heavier. And as the comforting silence wrapped itself around us, she reached her arm out, then brushed the back of her knuckles over mine.

The realness resembled what had happened that first night. Only no tequila flowed through our veins. We were ice-cold sober.

"You like our stars?" She'd said it as if they belonged to her. To Maui.

But they were more than that. Personal and private. "Yeah. I like 'em. *Our* stars."

At the emphasis, she glanced at me. A hint of amusement crinkled at the corner of her eyes. Then she stared upward again.

Backs of our hands still touching, her fingers straightened against mine, relaxed with a slight curve, then stretched backward again, interlacing our fingers together.

That tiny act felt huge.

Nervous on a level I couldn't remember feeling before, I let out a slow breath. The moment hit me hard, and I gently gripped her hand, holding on while trying not to shake. Or act like some lovesick teenager. Because I wasn't.

What tempted me, what unfolded between us in gradual turns, was a journey bigger than emotional discovery, greater than hormones pinging out of control. Two people from different worlds had begun to reach across a gap an ocean wide, hoping to find safety on the other side.

For the first time in what felt like a lifetime, I'd truly connected to another soul again.

Never expected it to happen. *Not this deep.*

Cramp forming in the base of my throat at how hard her trust hit me, I sucked in a deep breath, then closed my eyes and exhaled, trying to calm my breaths and pounding heart. After a few seconds ticked by, my breathing began to calm, matching the rise and fall of her chest in gentle rhythm. Rise…fall.

Rise...

Fall...

The simple connection resonated deeply, strong yet fragile. I rubbed my thumb over the soft skin of her hand, suddenly more curious about her, what she deemed important. "What's your favorite memory?"

"This one." Her response, a bare whisper over the wind, held a potent fierceness.

"Mine too." Without doubt.

Another matched breath passed without words, until I needed to know more. "After this one..."

Her fingers relaxed. Then she tucked her other arm under her head as she searched the starry sky for her answer. "My first time on a perfect barrel."

I grinned, knowing the feeling. "Where at?"

"La Pérouse Bay. I was twelve. I'd hung back in the local lineup for years. Caught plenty of closeouts, because it was all the guys would let me have. Then one day, Makani had a feeling."

"A feeling?"

"He gets gut instincts with waves, winds, coming storms...pain in his hand."

"What happened to his hand?"

"He broke it. The outside blade of it; it aches when the air pressure drops. Anyway, La Pérouse tends to rock when other spots die down. Only this one weekend, a tropical storm in October had shifted course, sending perfect barrels streaming in to every sweet north and east shore."

"Isn't La Pérouse south?"

"Yep. Where no one was headed. Makani's always been the cool one. Gave his sister *grom* a chance to catch a decent wave. And damn was it *sick*."

She pulled in a deep breath, tightening her grip on my hand while still gazing skyward. "Perfect right-hander, arched up a sheet of blue-green glass" —her lips tugged into a slow smile— "trailed my fingers through the most beautiful wall made just for me."

I nodded. Knew exactly what she meant: totally stoked for that first time—in awe of the power of it all.

"What about you?" She nudged my arm with hers. "What's your favorite memory?"

Easy answer. I tightened my grip with hers, gave her a meaningful glance. "Being connected like this, but with someone else." Difficult as fuck to talk about, though. "My brother." Voice catching, I continued to suck in a breath, then swallowed hard. "Deacon. I called him Deke."

She waited as I paused and huffed out a harsh breath. Grateful for her patience, I thought about the best time I'd had with him—focused on it.

"He and I used to stare up at the night sky, first person I ever did it with." I glanced at her again. "Only person I watched the stars on the beach with besides you." Hadn't really thought about it back on our tiny island that first night, but the truth hit me right then: how much I'd trusted her from the beginning, clicked with her from the start.

"As kids on our parents' stuffy vacations, we'd have to find our own entertainment. Surfed all day long. After sunset, we'd grab a quick bite, then race back to the beach.

Planted our scrawny asses on the sand, then stared up at the sky for hours."

"You ever fall asleep out there?"

"Yeah. Pissed my father off. Because my mother got worried sick. Only time she did, though. Like her motherly instinct couldn't see through all the greed and glamour she and my father had packed into their schedule. But the moment nothing else distracted her, and empty twin beds stared back at her, her brain finally kicked in. Then she'd have a screaming meltdown."

Leilani's hand tightened then loosened again. Like she silently supported me.

"But we always ended up okay," I added. "Because Deke always smoothed things over."

More silent minutes ticked by. The cold wind whipped into the truck bed, then spun back out. But down on the couch cushions, under our blankets, we kept warm enough.

And in the protection of the two of us sharing secrets, my mind wandered into a replay of the best memories of Deke and me: As two kids bored out of our minds in the middle of the night amid the shiny retail shops in one of Chile's beachfront towns, we'd broken into an ice cream shop at the end of the street, then sampled every colorful flavor in the case.

When we'd been teens in a beachside town in Andalucía, Spain, and he'd liked a pretty older girl for the first time, he'd conned a street florist to "loan" us a bouquet of roses for a few minutes. When Deke had presented them, taking her hand while trying to lure the smiling girl to surf with him, her boyfriend had arrived in a sideways-sliding green Torino, lunged out of the door that swung upon, then shredded the roses by beating the flowers over our heads while shouting foreign expletives.

"What's your worst?" Her voice softened.

Thoughts dangling on Deke with red petals sticking out of his messy blond hair, I fought a smile. *Not that one.* Or a million other great adventures I'd had with him.

No. The worst was *much* worse…

"Losing him." I struggled to suck air into my lungs. Then I blurted out the memory as quickly as I could…before I couldn't. "Random gunfire. We were standing on the street outside his new dorm. All of a sudden, a deafening crack fired out. Blood exploded onto his shirt. He grabbed on to me. Stared into my eyes as the life faded from his. He couldn't speak. Only looked at me with shock…fear…and love. I clutched his shoulders, holding him up as his legs gave out. Screamed for him to hold on. *Hold on!*"

"I'm so sorry, Mase." She offered words I'd heard before. But they'd never felt as soothing. Gave me the courage to tell her more. Confess all of it.

"Later, the police asked me if I saw anything. Any small thing, they'd said. A license plate. A car make and model. An unusual sound from the engine. Words said or shouted out. *Anything.*" My voice cracked.

Familiar pain flared in my chest. "I struggled with huge guilt that I hadn't done anything. Hadn't even glanced up for a second." I forced a hard breath past the choking cramp in my throat. "Couldn't tell the police a damn thing."

"You did exactly what you were supposed to. You were

there for a brother you loved." Her hand tightened around mine.

A slight tug made me glance toward her. She'd shifted to prop onto her elbow, facing me. In the darkness, her barely discernable features were blurred by the tears in my eyes. I blinked them away. "Damn wind," I muttered.

"It's okay, Mase." She slowly shook her head. "Not everything has a reason. We don't get to solve it all. And maybe we don't have to. Maybe we just live for them."

I stared at her. With all the psychiatrists I'd churned through on my own—because the *Prices* never had problems—none had explained it quite so simply.

And I'd begun my journey chasing waves, which had led me to her, because I'd finally realized I was happiest on the wave. Waves I'd discovered with Deke. "How'd you get to be so wise?"

Her chin dipped on a headshake, hiding her face behind the dark silk of her hair. Then she settled down, pressing her shoulder against mine. She tucked her bent arm under her head again and stared skyward. "I'm not. I've just…I've been there too."

Her voice quieted with every word. Then she sucked in a stuttered breath.

I braced myself. Then I tightened my hand around hers. She'd supported my heartfelt confession. I would be a rock for her.

"My worst moment?" She paused, then let out a shaky breath. "Watching my mom die."

208

24
A FRAGILE STEP

Leilani…

'd never said that aloud…until Mase.

Everyone else knew. How much my *makuahine* meant to me, how closed we'd been.

The devastation I'd suffered when she'd gone.

Attached to her long skirts, I'd harvested every gourd with her. Together, we'd shopped at every farmer's market, played in the ocean. I'd learned to trust in others from her.

"Oh, wow. Lani…"

He breathed out my name with sadness, but I reached over and silenced him further with a gentle fingertip touched to his lips. I couldn't handle hearing him say he was sorry, even though I'd expressed it to him over his brother only moments ago.

I would not break down.

Not again.

His gentle whisper of my name, thick with emotion,

reminded me of something. An important something. My eyes drifted shut on memories that flooded in. "*Makuahine*, my mom, she's the only one who has ever called me Lani. Before you."

He needed to know why I'd been so sensitive about it. Everyone had known. But not him.

A brush of fingertips trailed over one corner of my lips, then his hand cupped my cheek. "Leilani is a beautiful name. What does it mean?"

Finding strength in who I was, in the love for the woman who'd named me, I opened my eyes to meet his gaze. "Heavenly flower. My mom loved rare orchids."

Mind drifting, I recalled the lyrical sound of her voice: "*You're my rarest flower of all.*"

"Thank you," Mase whispered, "for sharing your name with me. I'm honored, Lani."

My breath caught at the reverence in his tone, at the unexpected tie I'd formed with the man only inches away. Yet vulnerable as I felt in the intimate moment, I wanted him to know more about her. "She taught me the meaning of aloha spirit, the importance of sharing our love with others."

"What happened?"

I paused, then drew in a shaky breath at the memory of those last days.

He turned onto his side, propped up on an elbow. "It's okay if you don't want to tell me."

"No." I partially sat up. Distanced myself, but only because I needed the space to breathe; talking about *Makuahine* brought her right there with us. "I want to." I hadn't talked about it with anyone since it'd happened and a part of me wanted to share it.

And something about Mase made me feel safe enough to do it.

"She died of cancer, non-Hodgkin lymphoma. It happened fast, and she didn't want treatment." My thoughts drifted to the day she'd broken the news to me. "I was eight. In my first weeks of third grade when she told me before school. She was deep in the rows of orchids that she raised."

"She raised orchids?"

"Yeah. Orchids. Water lilies. She loved flowers. Supplied them to local restaurants for bouquets. She had a deep love for our land—'āina—like so many Hawaiians do. '*Aloha 'āina*,' she'd say: Love and respect the land."

"Maui's an amazing land. Clean water. Pure air. Can't imagine how you get cancer here."

"Easy. A lot of people I know blame the GMO seed companies. And the pesticides they make and spray here to test them. Back then, trucks would spray our roadsides with Roundup. Near schools, churches, and homes too."

"They sprayed Roundup everywhere." Disgust weighted his tone.

"Used to. Turns out, the ones applying weren't following the labeling instructions. Supposed to keep people and pets away after spraying until it's dry."

"It's never dry here."

"Yeah…" My lungs burned and I let out a heavy breath. "Her getting sick is another big part of why my brothers are so angry at outsiders. It's not just surfers coming in and taking the waves. Big corporations snatch up our lands then think they can do whatever they want with them—like they did over a hundred years ago."

In my mind, I focused on *Makuahine's* face, trying to remember the small dimples bracketing her mouth with her smile, her plump cheeks, skin the color of creamed coffee, eyes dark like the richest curls in heartwood koa. "She taught me to live, to discover what makes me happy and ignore the rest."

"The rest?"

"The anger. It's what my father has. My brothers. They're filled with such hate for all the wrongs done to them, they seem to have forgotten how to do right."

"Wait…did you say *brothers*?" He put his hand on my forearm.

"Uh…yeah. Koa on the beach? My oldest brother."

"How many brothers do you have?" He pushed himself more upright, enabling me to see his puzzled expression more easily. His brows furrowed as he cocked his head. "Ka…moku?"

The possessive idiotic *kanak* he'd met. "Ke'eaumoku. And *no*, he's not my brother."

Mase's eyes narrowed. "Ex-boyfriend?"

I huffed out a laugh. "*No*. He wishes. And I have three brothers, which is plenty. You haven't met Holokai."

"Big as Koa?"

"Bigger. And more protective." When his eyes widened, I grabbed a fistful of the front of his shirt and tugged him back down with me, grateful he hadn't focused on my brother being a part of the group who'd lobbed a beer can up against his head. "No more talk of others. Let's just enjoy the sky."

As we settled back down, a silence fell between us again, deep and comfortable. I rested my head into the crook of his shoulder as we gazed at the stars. Different constellations than those we saw halfway around the world sparkled overhead, yet they seemed to be woven of the same fabric, connected—blanketing us tiny humans down here on this lone planet with their splendor.

I sighed, emotionally spent. Yet with Mase, I felt safe, protected...happy.

After about five minutes, he cleared his throat. "You know we're gonna date, right?"

"Date?" I fought a smile at his left-field statement.

"Yeah."

Amused at his formality, I nudged into his side. "Not a 'beach-bunny fuck'?"

He snorted. "Not even close."

Pondering the idea, I glanced at him through the darkness. "What's dating like?"

"You've never been on a date?"

"Nope."

"Uhhh..." He turned, clicked on his phone, then pointed the screen at me. A bluish glow illuminated his face while he stared hard at me, narrowing his eyes. "You *have* had sex, right?"

"*Yes.*" I shoved his phone against his chest, hoping he couldn't see my embarrassment. "But not anything that counted."

He cocked his head, confusion wrinkling his brow. "What kind of sex doesn't count?"

I shrugged, trying to be casual about it. "The kind that doesn't matter."

"Oh." He continued to stare intently at me, like he tried to read my thoughts.

I did my best to show only a blank page. But then, I began to wonder what *he* might be thinking *I* was thinking. "I'm not a slut."

"Never thought that."

"Good." I frowned, unhappy with the tension between us. "It's just…guys I know here…"

"Guys you've been with?"

"Only a *couple* of guys."

"Okay." His tone softened.

"Three," I clarified. "*Only* three."

"Leilani, it's okay. I don't need a headcount. Or the details."

"No." I let out a heavy breath. "I want you to know."

"Okay…whatever you want me to know."

I struggled to find the words to describe my lame encounters. Had no idea why they'd been so disappointing. "They…" *Did what?* It'd been more what they hadn't done. "I didn't…"

Heat fired my face. Talking to Mase had seemed so easy about everything else.

"How 'bout I guess?"

I huffed out laughter. "You wanna guess the deets about my awful sex life?"

"No." He gave a gentle headshake. "I really don't want specifics." He took my hand in his, gave it a gentle squeeze. "I'm guessing none of them gave you an orgasm?"

Oh, God. We were *actually* going there. "No."

"No, they did? Or no, they didn't..."

"No." I pulled my hand from his, dropped my heating face into it, then mumbled, "I have not had an orgasm."

"What?" He leaned his head down close. "I can't hear you."

I repeated it, but the wind whistled around me, protecting my confession.

"Leilani." His stern tone made me glance up. He grasped my shoulders, then pulled me up into a seated position in front of him. We were face-to-face, his inches above mine but close enough that his breath fanned over my lips as he stared into my eyes. "This is important. And I can't hear the words you're saying."

The moment felt right and incredibly raw. Standing on a precipice, toes gripping the sharp rocky edge, I sensed the wind pushing at my back, urging me to jump, trust that I'd land in safe water.

Mase was the water...

"I didn't have an orgasm."

"With them?"

"With them." *Be brave. He's got you.* "Or ever."

The intensity of his stare stole my breath. I closed my eyes, afraid I'd said too much. The lightest touch brushed over my eyelid. *A kiss.* Another feathered across the bridge of my nose, danced over my brow. When I inhaled deeply,

215

his scent, salty and of the earth, poured inside me.

With the softest touch, his lips pressed to mine. I gasped at the pleasant shock, then he gently sealed his mouth over mine, deepening the kiss.

When we broke contact, it was for a split second. Only long enough for him to whisper a promise between our lips. "*Ours* will count. We matter. *You* matter."

My body relaxed at the conviction in his tone and I fell forward into his strong embrace. When tears sprang to my eyes, I buried my face into the crook of his shoulder and took a deep breath, holding tight to the man I hadn't seen coming.

No one had ever said anything like that to me.

"And we *will* be dating." He kissed the top of my head.

I smiled through my tears at his perseverance. And I finally gave in to the idea.

Yeah, I guess we will.

A tiny part of my hardened heart melted. The rest clung to the hope that he wouldn't crash it over the jagged rocks.

25
THE THRILL OF THE RIDE

The following week…

Mase…

Taking on a wave is a tricky thing.

No two are the same.

Skills and experience come into play—to a point.

Because the forces of nature heavily influence the outcome.

That's why even the best surfers get hurt…some get killed. But every last one paddled into the situation unable to help themselves, living life on the edge of adrenaline, passion in their hearts for the thrill of the ride.

Incredible risk. Euphoric reward.

When I glanced at Leilani, my heart filled with pride, because the brave surfer girl who sat beside me in my truck, had decided to paddle with me toward an enormous swell building in our future.

We didn't know how things would turn out. No one ever did. Yet when I tore my gaze from her beautiful face and stared at the roadway, I threw out a wish that we'd make it in spite of our personal storms edging in on both sides of the horizon.

Then I remembered our teasing banter in my kitchen less than an hour ago.

> *"Whatcha packin' there for our date?" Her curious gaze remained fixed on the frozen water bottles I'd worked into the cooler bag.*
>
> *I zipped the bag shut. "Packed. And not tellin'."*
>
> *"Where we goin'?"*
>
> *"Not tellin'." I gave her a pointed stare.*
>
> *When we stepped outside and she rounded the side of my truck, I opened the passenger door for her but she paused at the back corner. She turned my way, gaze tearing reluctantly away from the gear in the back.*
>
> *She tipped her head toward the boards while watching me. "The date is us surfin'?"*
>
> *"Nope." I nodded toward the cab.*
>
> *"But…"*
>
> *"In." I arched my brows, amused that she questioned so much, challenged me on almost everything. "Not. Tellin'."*

Mischief flashed in her eyes. "Not even if I tempt it out of you?"

Damn. Maybe...

"I dunno. You well-versed in interrogation techniques?" Couldn't help pushing her buttons. Unexpected things happened. Like her letting her true self out to play.

"You wish, surfer boy."

Hell yeah, I do. *But no rush. We had plenty of time. And I didn't want to scare her from the path she'd agreed to. One small step at a time had gotten us to this point. And waiting for her? Worth every second of patience.*

"Watcha smilin' at?" Her voice tugged me back into the present.

"You." *Always you.*

I tried to wipe the grin from my face as we slowed for traffic. The wind from our open-window driving calmed and the tropical scent of plumeria filled my lungs. I closed my eyes and blew out a controlled breath.

Think about non*sexual things, Mase.* Like her brother. *Brothers*, plural...who would beat the shit out of me if they knew where my thoughts kept going about their baby sister.

"Hey, you never told me what Makani has on you." The reason she'd had to fly down to recruit me in the first place, why we'd even met.

A sudden scowl crinkled her face. *Adorable.* Then she gave a one-shoulder shrug and slouched down, resting the ball of her bare foot on the dash.

Silence filled the cab as she stared out the windshield.

"Not talkin'?"

"Don't see the need to."

"Because it's a family thing? 'Ohana?" Maybe she needed to protect someone.

"In a way…"

Couldn't fault her for wanting to be vague. Had my own demons with 'ohana that I hadn't opened up about. "You'll share when you're ready." We both would.

"Yeah." Her tone held doubt.

"You can tell me anything, you know. No judgment." She had to know that by now.

"N'kay."

Serious topic change needed. "What's with the zipped lips on the tour-guiding?"

She straightened in her seat and spun toward me. "Sorry. Am I on the clock or we on a date?"

Aha. There *you* are. Just needed to rile her a bit. "Date."

"Then, I am *not* your tour guide."

"What if I asked you to be? I'd love to know your favorite places." *Teach me about you.* "Off the clock."

I held her gaze until I had to tear it away again to drive. But not before I saw her eyes soften, the hint of a smile. Like she understood I wanted today to be different and she wanted that too.

She finally settled back on a nod. Only the distance between us had lessened, her bare leg only a couple of inches from mine. "Well, you don't want to go in the water out there."

I glanced right, stared at nothing but gorgeous blue. "Sharks?"

"Well, yeah. That too."

"Worse than sharks?"

"Sewage runoff."

"Uck." The bane of a surfer's existence. Some locales had corporations who viewed unspoiled tropical paradise as expendable. Others had local wastewater treatment practices that failed to protect the water due to carelessness, ignorance, or cost. No coastal area fell immune. Everything eventually washed out to sea.

"Where's it safe?" Acting as nonchalant as possible, I lowered my right hand from the steering wheel, then casually settled it in the empty space between us on the seat.

"Anything south of Cove Park is safe. She nodded ahead, down the coastline. Big resorts are coming up: Four Seasons, Fairmont, Grand Wailea. Golf courses. Some of the priciest homes on the island sit on beachfront there."

"There's Peggy Sue's." She pointed toward the shopping area where I'd found Halia, my truck, then ran her fingers along the edge of the dash panel. "You talk with Kaleo after you bought her?"

"Only once." I stroked my knuckles a couple of inches up her thigh, then down—not much contact, but enough to gauge her reaction. "He called to tell me where to get gas for it."

Her only reaction? Amusement. "A *gas* station…"

"*The* gas station."

"Really? There's only one Kaleo approves of?"

"Yep. Pure gas, without ethanol. Joe's place. I think Kaleo said it's called Joe's Kula Auto—"

"—at Historic Calasa Garage," she finished. "In Upcountry." She gave a short nod. "I've seen it. Really cool old green building."

I only half-listened to her words. Because her whole *non*reaction thing stopped working for me the instant she'd brushed off the intimacy: I wanted to have an effect on her.

Testing boundaries, I twisted my wrist, then spread my fingers higher over the soft skin right below her short hemline.

"Been there since nineteen thirty-t—" A small gasp cut her last word short.

"Thirty-two," I completed for her, doing my damnedest not to smirk. "How ya doin' there?"

"Good."

"Don't want me touching you?"

She blew out a measured breath through pursed lips. "Can't *handle* you touching. Not now. Not…yet."

"Why?" I wanted to hear about the danger. "What will happen if I keep touching?"

"You *know* what would happen."

"Do I?" I didn't actually know. Would she shut me down? Or…would she spur me on?

When we came to a stop at a red light, I glanced at her. Her breaths had quickened. Pink colored her cheeks. Lust glittered in her eyes, but she didn't seem embarrassed by it.

"Keep driving." She slid her hand over mine, weaving

our fingers together. Then she lifted my hand and planted it onto *my* thigh. With forceful pressure, she left hers there, as if guarding against any future attempts.

I chuckled. "Guess I don't get to find out what happens when you get incredibly turned on in a moving vehicle." *Not yet, anyway.*

She glared at me with as much irritation as she could muster while both amused and at least *a little* turned on. Then she crossed her arms, which gave me a scandalous view of her breasts above her low clinging neckline.

Topic change...

"*Sooo...*" The mystery had to end sometime. "Where exactly is La Pérouse?"

Her lips parted on a slight gasp as her expression lit up. "No *way.*"

"*Way.*" Yep. I'd been hoping she'd like where we were headed.

"Oh my God." She clapped her hands together. Then she leaned forward to the edge of her seat and stared farther ahead, legs bouncing. "You'll go past the curve, then it's before mile marker seven on the right."

Manicured greenery quickly surrendered to a drier landscape. To our upper left, Haleakala's southern slope rose above us in undulating hills of brown and black with only occasional spots of green. Maui's leeward side revealed her starkest landscape. And within minutes, the extremes became even more pronounced.

"Wow." Brownish-black lava stretched ahead on both sides of the road, then flowed down toward an impossibly blue ocean. "Looks like the moon…on beachfront property."

"Wait till you travel from Hana on this side…it's even more desolate."

"Not *to* Hana?"

She scowled with a hard headshake. "Too many miles of bumpy one-lane road. Some parts? Dense jungle so close you can touch vines on one side and see sheer cliff drop on the other. I've never driven it, but Makani refuses to drive it counterclockwise, says it feels like his tires are hanging halfway off the cliff edge."

No thanks. But she acted like she'd been there firsthand. "You were the passenger with someone else?"

She sucked in a deep breath. "Yeah." Silence followed, tense and awkward. Like she'd fallen into deep thought. About something that bothered her.

"Did something bad happen?"

"No." Another pause stretched out. "Not to me. Right before I went with a guy, some friends had driven from this direction. They'd been drinking. Didn't end well."

No elaboration followed.

And I didn't press the issue. Lots of secrets rattled around in her head, but I sure as hell wasn't going force her to untangle them.

"There's a small area ahead where we can park, but be careful where you drive her." She gave a nod toward the jagged blackish-brown field that stretched along the coastline to our left. "It's *aʻa* lava: sharp enough to puncture your tires."

Ahhh… Why Makani had insisted I pack us good shoes— when he'd helped me plan the date behind Leilani's back.

When we got out of the truck, I balanced the cooler bag against the back window, then handed her her thicker *slippahs*. "Volcano's dormant, right?"

She gave me a knowing smile as she took them, then exchanged out her shoes. "Yeah. Last erupted, right in this area, over two hundred years ago. They don't expect it to again." She stared up at Haleakala, but then her gaze drifted toward the surfboards in the truck bed. "Seriously, you brought boards but we're not surfing?"

"Not planning to."

"Why'd you bring 'em?"

"Seems wrong to go to the beach without something to ride..." The last word trailed off as the innuendo hit me. "Unless we're a sure thing on a first date."

She replied with a gentle punch to my shoulder. "*No.*" All of a sudden, she cocked her head in thought, then faced northwest for a beat. When she turned back around, she tugged her lower lip in with her teeth, before releasing it. "You cool leaving the boards here?"

My gaze got stuck on her plump lower lip, how it glistened.

On a hard swallow, I focused on her question. "Are you?" They weren't my most expensive, but I didn't want them stolen either. I squinted and stared back along the empty roadway. We hadn't seen one other car coming or going. The small parking lot stood empty, and we'd parked behind some greenery...but still.

"How long's the date?"

Smooth. "Nice try."

Her mouth fell open, innocent expression washing over

her features. "What?"

"Not giving any hints. You planning on it being over before it starts?"

Instead of a smartass barb back, she crossed the few feet between us and placed her hand on my arm. The small action spread warmth through my chest.

"It's my first real date. I hope it never ends. Can't wait for it to begin."

I gently grabbed the loose fabric of her dress, then tugged her against me. "If you can't tell it's started" —I gradually dipped my head down for a kiss— "I need to up my game." By the last word, we made contact, barely touching. In no hurry, I brushed my lips along the seam. She sucked in a slow gasp. Then I pressed in a fraction more, gently molding our mouths together.

A low moan rumbled from her throat when the kiss deepened, her tongue sliding over mine.

Lazy seconds later, when I pulled away, I let out a slow exhale, trying to calm my heart.

Her lower lip had plumped further. Her breaths came in shallow bursts as she stared up at me, dazed.

Damn. I liked putting that amazed satisfaction on her face. "And it lasts as long as it takes."

"As long as it takes for what?" Her voice had turned breathless.

"You'll see…"

The corners of her lips twitched into a smile.

Perfect.

The board decision suddenly clicked into my head.

"We'll take 'em with us."

"N'kay." She looped the canvas strap of the soft-sided cooler onto her shoulder while I tugged the boards from the back of the truck, inverted one, then sandwiched them and, with a solid hoist up and lunge under, balanced both on my head.

"Where to?" A dusty cinder path forked into a couple of different directions, both heading down toward the ocean.

She stepped into my view. "I can carry mine."

"Nah, I'm good."

After a pause, she nodded, then stared west again, squinting. "Up for a little lawbreaking?"

Not at all what I expected.

"Sure." Why the hell not? I wanted to make a memorable first date? She apparently did too.

Without explanation, she turned away from both worn paths, heading instead through dense brush a couple of feet beyond the grill of the truck. She pulled back thicker branches for me until I followed and lowered the boards to work my way through. A house appeared seventy feet *mauka* from us, with a couple of beat-up Tacomas parked in the far corner, closer to the road. With quick steps, we continued on until lava hills and thicker foliage blocked us from view.

Once I caught up, she nodded toward the structure. "We have to be careful."

"Says the hardened criminal."

She glared my way, then smirked as a brisk wind danced the dark strands of her hair across her face. "Even though we have a legal right to the shoreline, they own the land."

"Not friendly about trespassers?"

"Is a hello-by-shotgun friendly?"

"*Sooo*…that would be a no."

Expertly balancing in her *slippahs* on an angled outcropping, she gave a quick headshake. The she turned and picked her way across a short lava bridge that spanned over the foaming surf.

"Where's their aloha spirit?"

"*Nowhere* near their privacy."

We wound our way *mauka* again, traversing through the sharp lava outcroppings. A brighter patch of shoreline up ahead caught my attention. The farther we hiked, the more the anomaly revealed itself until a wide swath of pristine golden sand stretched for a good thirty yards.

My feet sank into perfect spongy sand. "This doesn't look natural."

"Right?"

Four white chaise lounges lined up in a row, empty, but seeming to wait for specific occupants. "Or legal."

"Scared?"

"No." Not a chance.

Thrilled? *Hell, yeah.*

And intrigued. Because the woman seemed totally comfortable with breaking the law. After she'd made a clear rule about *not* dating me—and had now broken that too.

On a wide parcel of land, bordered on its far side by a field of unnavigable lava rock, a manicured lawn stretched up to a palatial Tahitian-style home. Where the grass ended a hundred feet upslope, an infinity pool spilled water over its exposed edge and spanned from one corner of a large lanai to the other. Another dozen white chaises peeked out from under its covered shade. Exotic blooming plants lined a stepping-stone path that led up to an informal garden where a verdigris metal sculpture stood beside a stone bench that angled toward the ocean.

Off right, a giant lava rock waterfall bubbled water down between ferns and small plants that were nestled into its crags and holes. The water spilled into an in-ground spa large enough to hold ten people, swirling currents across a bluish-black surface.

"Wow." I set the boards down where grass met sand, then glanced at Leilani. "You been here before?"

"No. Saw it the one day I'd been surfing. Always wanted to check it out."

"You've never been back after that first time?" Makani hadn't mentioned it when I'd grilled him for ideas.

Her expression softened as she stared at me. "No."

Perfect.

"Bag?" She tucked a thumb under the canvas strap at her shoulder, arching her brows.

"Yep." I lifted it from her. "Now we can open the bag."

Scanning the ground for fire ants but finding none, I nodded toward a partially shaded spot under two swaying palms near the beach. She sat on the lawn's edge, legs bent in front of her, feet in the sand, then leaned back on outstretched arms and closed her eyes, angling her face toward the sun.

I stood frozen for a moment, struck by her pure beauty: smooth bronze skin, silken dark hair, gentle tempting curves. But the most captivating of all? The delicate smile on her lips.

Everything around us, land, sea, sky...all of it...was home to her.

And with every passing second, it transformed into home for me—*with* her. Somehow the distinction began to blur, like *she'd* become home. The sudden realization took me by surprise.

She squinted an eye open. "You opening that bag, or what? Better be some food in there."

I planted my ass on the lawn beside her, then unzipped while she watched. Feeling her intense scrutiny, I handed her one of the paper takeout containers. "Fish and poi," I blurted, afraid she'd be disappointed if she thought it was something else.

Her eyes widened a little, then the beginnings of another smile tugged at her lips. "I love fish and poi."

"Yeah?"

I acted casual about it, but I'd known. Makani had said it was her favorite. What I hadn't been sure about was whether takeout on a first date would be a good idea. But every time I'd considered the two of us dressed up in a restaurant? Anxiety had frozen my lungs until I'd remembered to breathe.

Instead, I'd opted for what came natural to me, to her. Where we felt most ourselves.

In each of our containers, crispy poi-battered fish tenders were stacked on a bed of greens on one side, a round cup filled with creamy purple poi sat in the other. I reached back into the bag and pulled out a third cup, thumbing off the top. "They insisted on more poi."

"Can never have too much."

I frowned at the purple paste. "Really." When I shook the container, it jiggled. I lifted it to my nose and took a good sniff. Not much of a scent, earthy maybe.

When I glanced at her, she pressed her lips together to hide her amusement. "Try it." She dipped one of her fish tenders into her paste, then dropped it onto her tongue.

A low groan vibrated from her throat as she closed her mouth and her eyes drifted shut.

My body instantly reacted to her sound, blood rushing southward, fast. I had to force out a steadying breath. *Patience.* "Well, damn. That sounds pretty good."

"It's the *best.*"

Good. My shoulders lowered in relief. The best fish and poi to her? Worked for me.

Remembering all the crazy food Deke and I bravely tried as kids, I grabbed a piece of battered fish, swiped it through the poi, then took a bite. Complex flavors burst over my tongue, the perfect balance of savory and rich, salty with a hint of mellow sweet. "*Mmm…*"

"Seeee?" Satisfaction sparkled in her eyes as she grabbed her second piece, dipped it deep into her poi, then popped the covered bite into her mouth.

We ate in companionable silence, relaxed on the lawn with our toes buried in soft sand. A low hum of comfortable energy surrounded our idyllic to-go picnic. Nothing needed to be said. No minutes of time that passed felt unfilled. We simply became two people well-suited to one another hangin' alone on a beach.

She licked her fingers clean, making tiny lip-smacking noises at the tip of each finger. "What else you got in there?"

I got distracted, mind stuck as I watched her thumb disappear deep into her mouth. Her cheeks hollowed slightly as she licked and sucked, while slowing pulling it back out.

"Mase...?" She snapped her fingers in front of my face.

I blinked. *Right. Earth to Mase.*

"Where'd you go?"

On a heavy exhalation, I gave a slow headshake. "Nowhere..." *that I'm elaborating on.* "Just thinking how much I love fish and poi too."

Then she killed me all over again as she peeked out the tip of her tongue and licked her lips, but her expression held pure innocent joy.

My mind? Not a damn thing innocent going on there.

"Anything else in there?" She nodded toward the bag.

"I *dunnooo*..." Tuning down my charged-up libido, I made a big production of rooting around in the nearly empty bag. Then I flashed up a hand and waved it, crinkling the clear plastic wrapping. "Maui's best banana bread?"

"Really." Skepticism riddled her tone while she eyed the thick slice in my hand with suspicion.

"So they say..."

She narrowed her eyes. "Who's this 'they'?"

"The royal council of banana bread tasters."

"Uh-huh...aka: not telling."

"Yep. You have your secrets, I have mine." I peeled the wrapper back from the moist cake, then broke off a bite-sized corner. "Eat. You decide." Because really, her opinion? Only one that mattered.

She plucked the bite from my fingers, dropped it into her mouth, then chewed slowly. Her expression relaxed. Then a smile began to form.

"And?"

"World's *best* banana bread." She swiped the rest of the slice from my hand. Then she broke off half and offered it to me.

"Because you've tasted all the banana bread ever baked in the entire world?" Because, really, who were we to pass on poking fun at a legitimate and verifiable claim.

"Well, yeah." She gave a decisive nod.

Not caring about manners, I bit off half my piece. Buttery sweetness melted over my tongue. A groan escaped my throat. "Yep. World's best." Made even better since it was *our* world.

As we scarfed down our banana bread dessert, a sudden odd sound crackled in the distance, unnatural over the rustling palm fronds overhead and crashing surf along the coastline. The noise grew louder and sharper.

Crunching rock.

Under tires.

Lots of tires.

I darted a glance behind us and spotted three white-and-blue police cruisers come to a stop at the end of the gravel drive beside the house. One door flung open and an officer jumped out. "Hey, you, down there!"

"Time to go!" Leilani lunged up from the lawn, then reached for the bag.

"Leave it." It only held our trash anyway. "Grab your board and head straight for the water."

Because our golden beach sat at the protected end of a small bay, only gentle waves lapped the sand. But without watercraft, and nowhere to run but over dangerous lava, it was our only escape.

I pulled up the rear, jogging after her as she waded into the water. Then she popped onto her board on her belly and began paddling. When I glanced back, two of the three officers had made it halfway down the lawn.

"Stop!" The nearest shouted. "You're under arrest!"

Yeah. Not.

I splashed into the water, jumped up in the air holding the board to my chest, then landed on the surface, already paddling. Swift and steady, I stroked with all my power until my arms burned, then kept going. Those officers had been in shorts. And I didn't have any clue whether they'd chase into the water after us. Or whether they had partners in watercraft anywhere nearby.

But their shouts silenced once I'd almost caught up to Leilani, our position even with my parked truck but an easy hundred yards out from shore.

When I pulled alongside her, she started laughing, then wiped her hand across her wet face. "*Oh. My. God.* That was awesome."

"Which part? It was the banana bread, wasn't it?"

She huffed out more raw laughter and cocked her head slightly, trying to suppress a smile. Then she slowly stroked one hand, turning her board until it pointed at mine. She paddled a few times to coast alongside me. Staring intently at me, she lifted her hand, then slid it into mine. Her top teeth tugged at the corner of her lower lip before she released it, expression softening. "All of it."

"*Yeah*, it was." On a sucked-in breath, I gripped her hand, gave a light pull, then adjusted for impact as our lips gently collided. Hers softened, sucking and nipping at my lower lip. Closing her eyes, she sighed into the kiss, then molded her mouth with mine.

Rolling waves flowed under our boards. Heat from the midday sun warmed our backs. Nearby waves crashed with powerful bass tones onto the hardened lava shore. The power of the place, our moment in time, hit me; it belonged to us and us alone—private and protected.

Minutes stretched by as we explored each other's mouths. Her hand gently tightened, then released. After a time, we broke apart, and she stared at me for a long moment, as if wanting to make sure I was real.

I smiled at her. "I'm here."

"I know." Her voice had gone breathless with wonder, as if she had read my thoughts: that we'd found each other in spite of our differences—maybe because of them. "Can't believe it." On a heavy sigh, she rested her cheek on my arm.

That makes two of us. Never would've imagined someone could make me feel that way. Restless and settled all at once, craving more, yet satisfied with what I'd been granted.

235

My body hummed with energy, taut and aroused—by her, by the day, by the undeniable perfection of it all.

"C'mon!" She suddenly burst with excitement. "I'll show you the wave."

"It's going off? Now?"

I'd checked the surf reports. Only two-to-three footers had been forecast for the bay today. But no other place would've worked. And I'd brought the boards only in case another spot on the way started firing.

"No. But I want to show you."

She wanted to share it with me. And I wanted to see it.

"Over there." She pointed toward mounded lava that jutted out, forming a sweet point break. "Lotta great swells roll in during the summer from tropical storms."

"Except today."

With a nod, she tore her gaze from the spot. "Except today."

Didn't matter. Not to me. And judging from her happy expression, she didn't care either. Sometimes a great day doesn't only have killer waves. Every now and then, it's what's between the waves that counts.

A line traveling along the surface caught my eye. "What about over there?" I tipped my head toward a long turquoise ribbon as it glided toward shore.

"Sweet. I think it bends around the break."

I stared at the white foamy crest as it steadily curled over, then kept going. "It's got a nice steady twist to it."

"Let's give it a shot." She began paddling without waiting for my reply.

Atta girl.

Took us about ten minutes to reach the waves. "Not big." She judged the most recent one. "Maybe three-footers."

"Wait for it."

She nodded, turning with me as we stared at the horizon. Sets of waves followed patterns. Another ten minutes, or so, could yield a group of nice ones. *I hoped.* The waves flowed toward us from the south, generated by winds and storms thousands of miles away.

"There." A larger set headed our way, distinct from the rest.

"*Nice.* Pass on the first, take the second." It had the most defined line, and I wanted her to have it. When the first wave came, she turned and began to paddle, timing her speed to catch the second. Faster and faster she went until the wave lifted her up as it began to crest under her board.

Yes.

She popped up and began to carve, finding a natural fall line. Her body twisted, arms gracefully spread as they angled with her turns. Then she undulated, bending low to sweep up under the lip then slide back down the wall again.

Nice. Her silhouette appeared beautiful as she danced through the green glassy wave.

Keeping her in my sights, I swiftly paddled to catch the next one. As the wave rose, I stroked hard enough to feel a decent burn. Right at the peak, I popped up, then dropped in. Skating across the face, I raked my fingers through the water, connecting to the wave. When the spray increased around me, I carved upward, then angled down, shooting farther out from the curl. As the wave began to close, I scanned ahead for Leilani.

She'd paddled up shore and had traveled a good hundred yards away. I planked my board, then followed with swift even strokes.

Cool water, warm sun, steady breeze, and a girl worth chasing. Life didn't get any better.

The waves rolled under me, lifting and falling, as I watched her disappear behind a steep lava formation that jutted into the ocean. After I rounded the corner, I spotted her as she angled into a narrow cove.

When I finally caught up, she dunked down into the thigh-high water, then walked onshore. She towed her board behind her until she safely beached it a few feet in.

Eager to reconnect with her, I splashed down into the water, then followed her up onto the shallow beach made of disintegrated black lava peppered with white specks of crushed coral. The high walls of an ancient lava flow surrounded the intimate space, casting it in partial shadow.

"Sweet ride." Nothing technical, but a gift from nature all the same.

White dress plastered to her body over her swimsuit, she plopped onto the sand, turned over, then propped up on her elbows as she stared out to sea. A serious faraway expression washed over her face, but the slight crinkle in her eye and a hint of a smile warmed it into a look of satisfaction as she let out a heavy sigh. "Yeah."

I moved, casting her in shadow as I blocked the sun. "Room for me down there?"

Not taking…asking.

"Yeah." She glanced up at me, then patted the rough sand

beside her.

But I didn't move.

Our gazes remained locked together. Her breath caught. When she finally exhaled, she licked her lips. Then she tugged the lower one inside her mouth, breaths quickening, as if the saltwater that coated them tasted good, but she wanted something more.

I wanted to be the one to provide it.

My pulse kicked up as blood began to flood south. I sucked in a shaky breath, then stretched out beside her. "This too close?"

"No." The soft-spoken word rippled with the undercurrent of an order.

"Want me closer?"

"Yes," she whispered on a slow nod.

"How close?"

"All the way close."

"Like this?" My mouth hovered over hers.

Air fogged between our lips, warm and tempting. But we didn't touch.

After a hard swallow, I turned my head a fraction to the right, over the corner of her luscious mouth. Careful not to make contact, I floated left, tracing the contours of her decadent lips. I took my time, learning her, breathing her in, savoring her wild scent. All the while, an intense ache pulsed through my body, heavy in my chest, an insistent throb in my groin.

I paused when I reached the center of her mouth. My eyes drifted shut as I lingered there.

The slightest gasp escaped her parted lips.

Then she touched her forehead to mine. "*Honi,*" she breathed.

"Was that a request in Hawaiian?" I murmured as the tips of our noses touched.

"It means to kiss. But like this" —she clasped my hand, wove her fingers together with mine, still connected forehead to forehead, nose to nose— "when we inhale as one." Our chests expanded together, her essence filling my nostrils as mine filled hers. "It's *hā*: the breath of life."

The sacredness of the act was evident in her tone.

My chest burned with emotion, and I tightened my hand around hers. "I'm honored."

On the next breath, she shifted, tilting her head, then brushed her lips over mine. Soft, sweet, and yet, the power of it all hit me with the unexpected force of a rogue wave.

She pulled back, staring into my eyes as hers glittered with unshed tears. "And *mana*: the spiritual connection between us."

We both let out a slow breath as the weight of the moment—of what we shared—sank in. Then we gave in to the pull, lips gently colliding.

But we clasped our hands tighter together. Because we both knew not all great rides came easy.

26
FLEETING MOMENT

Leilani...

Sensations flooded everywhere, from the top of my head to my curling toes.

Soft lips caressed mine, begging me to lean closer.

Mase's hard muscles tensed, then relaxed, as if his body wanted to do more.

I wanted to do more. *So much more...*

But before things got overheated, before they really even got started, our movements slowed. The urgency faded as hard kisses melted into tender nips and slow sucks.

His essence felt animalistic: tamed yet wild just below the surface.

Like me.

"Thank you," I breathed when we parted. I dropped my forehead to his once more.

"For what?" His nose touched mine, a gentle rub.

I couldn't believe he was here. With me. The boy I'd been waiting all my life for. Only he wasn't a boy. And I was no longer a little girl with fairy-tale dreams. We laid on a remote lava beach as man and woman, a part of my ʻāina, one with the world of my Hawaiian ancestry.

But only *one* of us was Hawaiian.

I pinched my eyes shut, refusing to mar the *pono* day with my lifelong struggles.

"For giving me time, for waiting."

If only patience was the solution to everything.

No. I refused think about what we couldn't be.

Makuahine's words shimmered into my mind: *All that ever exists is now, the fleeting seconds we pull breath into our lungs. Seize the precious moment, for happiness is found there.*

My awareness drifted back to the man in front of me.

Mase *is my now.*

Before I overanalyzed for one more wasted second, I lunged forward, capturing his lips with mine—*to be in the* now *we'd stolen for ourselves*. His strong hands smoothed up my back, holding me close. Eyes closed, senses flaring to life, I skimmed my fingers along the lean muscles of his forearms, over his biceps, across his broad shoulders, then up into the blond curls at his nape.

Our kisses grew unhurried, like we owned the day with nowhere to go. Stubble on his jaw scratched my face a little, but I enjoyed the roughness, his raw maleness. A reaching wave bubbled up over our toes, then retreated.

"Leilani," he murmured with reverence against my lips

as we paused to catch our breaths.

"Say my name again."

"*Leilani…*" he breathed before brushing his mouth over mine.

I savored the way it floated from his lips, as if he took great care with a fragile gift he deemed sacred.

The sun dipped behind forming clouds as I settled against him, resting my head below his shoulder with one hand draped across his chest and my other on his arm. Silent as we embraced one another, I stared out across the vast ocean.

Somewhere out there, over thousands of miles of endless water, then thousands more miles of continent, were Mase's people, the world he came from.

On a hard exhale, I tightened my grip on his arm. "You're in my world now."

The afternoon had wound to an end with the sun splashing brilliant corals and pinks across the sky as it touched the unseen horizon. We'd lain for hours in the shade on the tiny beach we'd claimed for ourselves, kissing, laughing, and talking, sharing inconsequential things—grateful to even be together. Then we'd paddled back and had even caught a decent three-footer as it spiraled in, not far from his truck.

In the darkening quiet of his cab, reasonably dry in fresh clothes we'd changed into, I scooted closer to him as we drove up the highway. I threaded my fingers into his, resting my head on his shoulder. "*I'm* planning our next date."

He squeezed my hand, then glanced at me, amusement dancing in his eyes. "We're not done with this one."

"Good." I gave him a soft kiss, then pointed toward the road where a YIELD TO ONCOMING TRAFFIC sign indicated a one-lane section.

A cozy buffer wrapped itself around us, as if only the two of us existed. Yet as he made each turn, through eucalyptus forest, across grazing lands, climbing into the misty clouds of Upcountry, a sense of urgency began to press in.

Because once we got out of the private space of his truck, the rest of the world waited—one that didn't accept outsiders, one that only saw the color of his skin without bothering to hear the beat of his heart.

I want them to care. I wanted him to be accepted.

After several more curves, he pulled into his driveway, then parked beside my Tacoma. He left our boards in the back, grabbed the bag of wet clothes, then clasped his hand in mine as we walked toward his front door. "So, how'd I do?"

"Not bad."

"Not bad?" He dropped the bag on the second step. Then his hands began to roam over my hips, up my ribs, as soft kisses trailed up my neck. "I'll have to do better."

Every cell in my body zinged to life as his breath and lips teased my skin. Then heat tingled downward, turning into the most delicious ache. He folded his body around me, warm and solid. His scent filled my lungs, of the earth and ocean and something unique to him, incredibly male.

When he tugged on my earlobe with his teeth, I shivered

on a sharp gasp. "*Pono*," I breathed, as the righteousness of the moment took hold. I wrapped my arms around him, holding him tight. "Most amazing date ever." My heart filled with gratitude; that he'd been the one to take me on my first.

Headlights suddenly flashed over us, seconds before a vehicle pulled up behind Mase's truck. Temporarily blinded, it took a few seconds for my eyes to readjust to the darkness as a car door opened. Then my heart sank when I saw who got out: a police officer—who I knew.

"That your truck there?" He nodded toward Halia.

Mase stepped forward, partially blocking me. "Yeah, so?"

"A truck matching your description was parked near the scene of a crime."

Narrowing his eyes, Mase tilted his head a little. "What crime is that, exactly?"

"Trespassing. Onto imported sand owned by a private party."

I sidled in front of Mase. "Onto a beach? C'mon, Kanaloa. You know that's public land."

"Onto the lawn." Kanaloa swung his gaze toward me.

Mase crossed his arms. "How do you know it was onto the lawn?"

"Motion sensors were tripped."

"What evidence do you have?"

"We saw you."

"How could you have seen us? We weren't there."

"Two people matching your description? Blond hair, tall, dark board shorts? Hawaiian girl, white dress? With your truck parked nearby? How stupid do you think I am?"

"I have no basis with which to evaluate your intelligence, so I'll leave that to you. But lots of people on Maui match that description. And my truck was parked there because we were surfing at La Pérouse."

"There weren't waves at La Pérouse today."

"Says you."

"There was a bag there."

"Didn't have my name on it."

"How do you know?"

"Because I wasn't there."

"There were fingerprints on a banana bread wrapper."

"Fingerprints. And you ran those fingerprints and they matched one of us?"

"Partial fingerprints. And we can send them to a lab for analysis."

"So…you're going to waste valuable police resources to run a fingerprint analysis on a banana bread wrapper? To… catch a perpetrator who walked on the grass?"

Kanaloa ignored Mase's common sense. His hard eyes stared at me. "Watch it, Leilani. You misstep once, and it's over."

My jaw clenched, shoulders squaring back. "Are you threatening me?"

"Only making sure you clearly understand what's at stake here." Kanaloa held my gaze for three long seconds, before glaring at Mase. Then he turned and walked away.

Mase and I stared silently at the car as it backed down his driveway until headlights flashed in an arc across his ʻōhiʻa bushes then disappeared.

He turned toward me. "What's that all about? What's at stake here?"

"Nothing." Total lie. But I didn't want to ruin things further.

On a deep breath, his eyes slightly narrowed as he did that whole see-through-me thing, as if trying to ferret out my secrets.

"I should go." Before I get buried under my past any deeper.

"Wait." He closed the remaining space between us and gathered me into his arms.

On a slow exhale, I relaxed in his solid hold, settling into the safety there. Closing my eyes, I imagined that Mase had the power to erase everything that had come before.

That I could start fresh.

Soaking in his protective warmth, my thoughts drifted back to our laughter earlier on the waves, the freedom of floating on the water, the blissful feeling of his lips on mine.

"I had a good time today," I whispered.

"The *best* time." He rested his chin on my head.

"Yeah." I wrapped my arms around his waist, then clung tightly to him. "It was."

Mase didn't mention our next date again. Not when I said good-bye minutes after our last heartfelt embrace. Not the next day when I'd spent time on the computer in his living-room-office researching rules for competitions and booking flights. Not as we continued fixing up his house during the daylight hours when he wasn't surfing or windsurfing.

And not in our phone call each night when we talked about every little thing—work related and not—but nothing *big* was said.

I felt it, though—all the questions he wanted to ask but didn't when his intent gaze lingered on my face a few seconds too long as he tried to figure me out. And with every passing hour spent with him—learning and trusting that he'd do me no harm, that he'd actually protect me—the pressure to share my secrets began to outweigh the reasons to keep them.

And we hadn't kissed again. We'd gotten close: inadvertently stepping into each other's space in the hallway while trying to avoid contact; him hovering just behind me while I booked the tickets, his body so close I could feel the heat of his skin, his breath rustling my hair tucked behind my ear.

In some powerful unspoken agreement, we'd both decided to give us some time. Whether or not it was because I couldn't open up, I didn't know. I sensed it had something to do with it.

But I *thought* about our kissing.

And the way his chest expanded sharply whenever we touched, I knew he thought about it too.

At the moment, not one thing about him gave any hint that he was thinking about us. Seconds ago, he'd opened up another one of those big architectural schematics, smoothed out the curling ends, then stuck polished lava rock paperweights on the corners. His hands were firmly planted on each side of the paper. His head hung over the center as he scanned the page, brows furrowed in concentration.

I tore my gaze back toward my laptop screen, back to searching potential competitions while comparing their dates to his schedule. Attuned to every little thing about him, however, I sensed when he shifted. Each breath. Every sigh.

He tapped a thumb onto the paper twice. "Got any time this week to work on the roof?"

"Thursday." Three days away.

Cocking his head while he slid a ruler up the page then made a mark with a pencil, he hummed low. "What's on for Wednesday?"

"We are."

His breath caught, but he didn't move. Stayed hunched over his drawing. After a beat more, he glanced up. "We are?"

"Yep. Second date."

"I was wondering when you'd get to that."

"Oh, really? Could've fooled me."

He stood to his full height, crossing his arms over his chest. "Same goes."

Blessedly, he wore a black T-shirt. A really thin black tee that molded to every groove and ridge, that hugged his biceps right at their widest point. Not that I'd noticed.

I gave a half-shrug, then glanced back at my laptop. "Didn't want you to think you were all that."

Didn't want to risk my heart. Not when too many wanted to lock it up.

"Hmmm," he hummed again louder. "But it must've gone well."

"Maybe…" *So totally.*

A low grunt came in reply. He didn't move. Stood the same five-foot distance away. On the other side of the worktable.

Without looking up, I sensed him staring at me. The heavy tension between us prickled heat over my skin, began to warm lower, more private places.

On a hard swallow, I clenched my knees together trying to get a grip on my rioting body. Concentrating on the same sentence about wildcard rules that I'd read four times without comprehending a word of it, I drew in a slow, deep breath. "You cool with testing out new boards?"

"When?"

"Wednesday."

"So, it's not a date."

"Oh, it's a date."

Silence followed. He stilled to the point I had to look up.

His intent gaze pegged me. Hot. Molten hot. Then it transformed into a smug look.

I pressed my palms onto the table, trying to remain calm. "Boards. Testing. Yes or no?"

"Yeah. That's cool."

"Good." I stood, tumbling the metal stool underneath me onto the ground with a clatter. I didn't care. Didn't bother to pick it up. I grabbed my phone instead, suddenly needing to get out of the room, needing to breathe. "I'll call Makani. Let him know."

In three quick steps, I almost made it out the door. Fresh air breezed across my face seconds before he stood in front of me.

He stared down into my eyes. "Don't be afraid of this… of us. Just handle it like I am."

"Oh?" *Does that mean you're afraid too?* "How is that?"

He lowered his head and brushed his lips over mine, sending a shudder through my body and my pulse soaring. I gasped when he slid his hand over my lower back and pulled me close.

"One moment at a time," he murmured. Then his lips covered mine in a teasing, sensual kiss—better than *any* I'd fantasized about.

27
BREATHLESS LEAP

Mase…

"**W**hoa." I got out of my truck and blinked. "No way."
Coolest shit ever.

"Way." She crossed her arms, smug smile dimpling her cheeks.

A sleek black helicopter sat on the tarmac, rotors spinning. Attached to the skids? Two longboards.

"Sure that'll fly?"

Unconcerned expression on her face, she gave a half-shrug. "Dave said a setup like this flew in a commercial for Pepsi years ago. He grew obsessed about it and built one of his own."

"Untried?" I cocked my head and stepped closer. The boards were strapped to specially made racks.

"Chicken?"

"No." If the pilot felt good about it, I did. And if Leilani had planned the day out with that kind of adventure? "I'm game."

"*Good.*" She grabbed the front of my rash guard, fisted her hands, then pulled me forward. My lips collided with hers into a fierce kiss.

When we came up for air, my pulse humming, I let out a hard breath. My thoughts scattered as blood drained from my brain. "Yeah, beyond good."

On the craft, the cockpit door opened, then a red-headed stocky pilot stepped out and waved us over. We grabbed our two gear bags from my truck before leaving it parked in front of the hangar as the pilot had directed us when Leilani had called earlier.

He held a hand out for brief introductions, then gestured us inside. After Leilani took the third leather seat of four, I tossed our bags onto the floor between our feet and climbed in beside her. The pilot closed our door, took his seat and closed his door, then flipped several switches. The engine revved higher with a vibration we felt through the seats while we fastened our belts and put on our headsets.

The stale air inside had faint traces of metal and jet fuel. Before long, cold air conditioning began to flow over our faces. In the headsets, Dave's voice echoed in a tinny tone as he glanced over his shoulder. "Ready?"

Arching my brows, I glanced at Leilani. She wore a wide grin, then gave a solid nod. "Ready."

I nudged my knee into hers. "Ever flown in a helicopter before?"

"Yeah. Not often."

"Where have you flown to?"

"The place we're headed."

A knife of disappointment stabbed through my gut. I wanted to be the first she experienced things with. But I shook off the childish feeling on a slow exhale. The islands were her backyard. And like the date I'd planned for her only days ago, she would've been most everywhere in it.

I slid my hand in hers.

She glanced up at me and smiled.

Ahhh...but she's never experienced any of it with me.

And I intended to have *that* make all the difference.

The nose of the chopper pointed east, but when we reached the northeastern section of the island, Dave didn't turn us south.

"Seriously." I glanced at her. "Where are you taking us?"

"Somewhere private." Her voice lowered, and I swear I heard her murmur, "A special place."

The high cliffs of the Big Island came into view. Towering monoliths covered in emerald green stretched toward a crystal blue sky. Sparkling waterfalls ribboned down several crags. A rush of white egrets took flight, then calmed, spiraling upward on invisible wind currents.

"Wow. Breathtaking." All I could manage to say. Not that the meager words did the experience any justice. I'd traveled to many places in my life. None matched the naked majesty before me. Pristine. Untouched.

When we cleared the far northern tip of the island then angled southeast, excitement began to thrum in my veins.

Whitecaps were visible on glorious waves, shimmering under the sun. The wind soared toward shore at the perfect pitch, but although small clouds dotted the sky here and there, the sunny day held promise.

Line after line angled toward untouched shoreline: a surfer's call.

I glanced toward the vastness of the open ocean to the northeast, where the currents of the trade winds journeyed from before they coaxed the cobalt sea toward shore.

Turning back toward the island, I pressed closer to Lani, felt her warmth against my side as I watched the rugged landscape of Hawai'i reveal herself.

"Beautiful, isn't it?" Her lips curved into a warm smile.

"Yes." I stared at her, getting lost in dark-chocolate eyes filled with emotion.

Her breath caught and a blush pinked her cheeks. "I meant the island, surfer boy."

I shrugged, then glanced at the landmass. "Eh, it's okay. I've seen better."

A shocked gasp accompanied her outraged expression. She elbowed me hard in the ribs. "Take it back."

"Yeah, it's incredible." Jagged lava cliffs covered in thick green jungle met charcoal sand beaches. Deep blue waters brightened to stunning turquoise where sea met shore.

On a slow, wide arc, Dave angled us into a massive gulch. "Gonna take you back to my favorite waterfall."

Lush green cliffs towered on either side of us. We followed a stream of blue water that occasionally appeared through the foliage below. He pulled back on the cyclic stick and we began to ascend. As we flew *mauka*, he began to s-curve in our flight path, meandering back and forth with a slight adjustments. It enabled us to take in both sides of the wide impressive gulch carved by hundreds of thousands of years of water erosion.

"Up ahead," alerted the disembodied voice in our headsets.

A foamy white ribbon rippled down from the apex of the gulch, splashing over treetops as it plunged several hundred feet down through the jungle. "*Niiice.*" Then I wondered if she'd been back here. "Have you flown back here too?" I nodded out the window.

"No." She shook her head. "Other parts, not this."

My stomach dropped when he rotated around, then I began to feel a little queasy. "Ugh."

When I glanced at her, suspecting my skin had turned a shade of green, she gripped my hand. "Me too. Look out at the horizon; it helps."

As I stared at the thin hazy edge of what I could see, an unusual sense of rightness flowed through my veins—at once buzzing with excitement and settling heavy with a peaceful calm. That she wanted to share an adventure with me, take me where she'd been—and where she hadn't.

After flying back out, then skimming over open water, Dave rotated right. I stared at the edge of the ocean as we headed south along the coastline. Within a few minutes, steam rose up out of the water.

"Kamukona," Dave said. "It's where the lava meets the ocean. Dangerous down there. Tourists shouldn't get too close; the super-heated plumes rising up are noxious, filled with hydrochloric gas and microscopic particles of volcanic glass."

Lifting the bird higher, he brought us *mauka* and flew us over black flattened flows of lava. A few gaping holes had reddish-orange magma rushing through them. "*Wow.*"

"This is Puʻu ʻŌʻō, flowing from Kīlauea's south flank. Its path changes daily."

After doing a figure eight above the amazing otherworldly landscape, he brought us back toward the ocean the way we'd come. He gave us a couple of minutes to view new land being formed, forged from the center of the earth then cooled and hardened by her surface waters. Then he turned us back north. Minutes later, he slowed and descended, then hovered about thirty feet above the water.

"This the spot?" he asked.

I looked down. A gorgeous wave arced with a nice crest below us.

Leilani glanced over my shoulder. "That's the one, Dave. We all set?"

"Roger. Bomb's away." An unnerving scraping clunk sounded.

"What was that?"

"Boards launching."

Leilani grabbed our bags one at a time, tossing them into the front seat beside Dave. "Can you drop these straight out onto the beach?"

"Yep. You got it."

I frowned. "And how are *we* getting down?" Dangling rope? Ladder?

"Jumping." She took her headset off, held her hand out awaiting mine with a nod at my head. Then she secured both into a Velcro loop behind the far seat.

"Jumping." I repeated her word, letting it sink in, but it did nothing to take the shock out of my brain.

She gripped the door handle, then shot me a taunting smirk. "Just don't slip."

With a hard yank, she jerked the handle. As the door slid open, she carefully lowered and took a seat on the edge of the floor. Then she gripped a handle fastened to the metal framework where the boards had been. A narrow step jutted out from the framework, above the skid.

After planting the ball of her foot on the step, she glanced back at me with a wide smile. Raw happiness glittered in her eyes. And it hit me at that instant as I stared into the soul of a girl who set herself free once in a while—what life was about for her, what she needed. Even if she'd bound her true nature by rules for some unknown reason.

What stoked her the most?

Being wild.

Unlike our last date, she'd dressed sportier: boy-short bottoms, rash guard top. Her thick black hair had been pulled back and wound into a tight bun, but the rotor wash caught tiny wisps and danced them over her face. The sun gleamed a healthy shine on her skin. Her smile? Infectious.

I grinned back at her. "You're fucking nuts," I shouted.

"You love it."

"Yeah, I do."

Her smile softened. Then she took a deep breath, turned

toward the ocean, tightened into a crouch, and sprang outward.

My breath froze as she sailed out and down through the air, one second tops, before plunging down under.

She broke the surface seconds later, waving with a big smile.

I glanced at the pilot. He stared straight ahead—probably focused on keeping us steady.

When I paused another moment, I heard a shout. I gripped the handhold, leaned forward, then stared down.

Hands cupped around her mouth, she yelled some unintelligible word again.

Not rocket science to fill in the blank: chicken. *Like hell.*

I planted my foot, leaned forward, then took the leap, aiming toward the wild girl who turned a second date into a crazy adventure—one I wanted to live full-throttle.

After I plunged into the cool clear water, I swam toward Leilani.

The graceful lines of our longboards bobbed on the surface a dozen yards toward shore. With quick strokes, we reached them. She wasted no time, hoisting up onto her belly in fluid motion. I rolled onto mine, then turned my board. On a single-minded mission, she pulled ahead, paddling swiftly toward the sweet reef break we spotted from above.

I briefly wondered what ingredients had created the gift from the sea ahead of us. The perfect rise of a coral formation down below? A strong storm in an ideal location to send percussive winds our way? Maybe the reason leaned toward magic…because we were here to surf it.

When we reached the break, hanging back from where each wave rose to shoulder height, she paused.

"Well?"

"*Sick.*" Impressive. All of it: the insane jump, the incredible day, the thrilling buzz—her.

She stared longingly at the wave. "It is. Doesn't happen often. Was hoping it'd be here."

"What made you think it might be?"

"Time of year. Plus, another tropical storm is churning out there in the same position." She nodded toward the southeast.

I stared at her. Couldn't help it. Dark blue fabric molded to her sinful curves.

She tilted her head as mischief sparked in her chocolate-brown eyes. "We talkin' or ridin'?"

Before I had a chance to give the obvious reply, she gave a sharp angled slap to the water, splashing me. Then she tore off, paddling toward the center of the wave.

I immediately followed, watching what direction she turned. The wave drew up into a beautiful peak, offering up both a left and right break. When she popped up, she angled left. I dropped in, then swung right.

Not the biggest wave, nor the widest barrel, but it had a narrow cleft and smooth glassy wall. The water swept us along, powering mellow rides with our longboards.

No cutbacks or tight tricks. No air. But then, we'd caught plenty on the jump down. And the day wasn't about what *I* could do. It had become about the *we*.

Plus the steady glide gave me a greater gift than

an adrenaline boost; it gave me a chance to absorb my surroundings. Sparkling blue flowed onto glittering black sand. Rich green stretched up to a cloudless sky.

Better than all of that, over my shoulder, a girl surfed the same wave, soaked in the same scenery. I pulled out before the wave collapsed completely. It had been an amazing ten-second ride.

And as I paddled through the clear water, circling around to meet back up with her, I couldn't wait to do it all again. Because she'd let herself go in broad daylight once more. No tequila to get drunk on. No endless stars to wonder underneath, feeling limitless and safe.

When she began to head my way, she wore a look of fierce determination and pride.

On a slow breath, I murmured to the wind. "You should come out to play more often, Lani."

28
FEAR OF THE FALL

Leilani...

My heart hammered as I glided over flat ocean, but I felt like I drifted toward the edge of the biggest sheer drop of my life.

Mase was the reason to jump.

Bold and beautiful as he paddled toward me—toward us—memories of diving off Black Rock as a *keiki* floated into my mind. To jump, you couldn't look down, because fear froze the hesitant, then waves pummeled the foolish.

But if I closed my eyes and took the leap, would Mase catch me? If consequences battered into me, rocking my foundation, would I survive the fall?

I didn't know. And the unknown? Frightened me.

"No one can predict the future..." I drew in a sharp breath as *Makuahine's* sage words echoed through my head as if

she'd just spoken them. "*You have to live in the moment. Live every moment.*"

"You would've liked Mase," I whispered into the trade winds, hoping she'd hear me.

A strange ripple pulsed through me in reply. Like the winds listened today, like she'd heard and approved. I let out a gentle sigh as peace settled into my chest. Then I smiled and paddled over to him, not thinking anymore.

"Doing," I murmured.

"What's that?"

"I'm *doing*."

His smile tilted up into a smirk. "Me, I hope."

"Cocky surfer."

"Would you prefer me to be humble?"

I choked on a laugh. "*Hell* no."

"Good. Because I like what 'cocky surfer' does to mysterious island girl."

"Yeah? And what's that?"

"Makes her feisty, sexy…eventually open up, spill all her secrets."

"Not happenin', surfer boy."

"*So* happenin', island girl."

"We'll see." My attitude flared at the secrets part, but my heart warmed at the feisty.

Sexy. The word described *him*. Fully clothed now in a rash guard and board shorts, his boyish looks—joyful smile, wet blond hair with a slight curl, ice-blue eyes shimmering toward silver in the bright sun—hid the shark lurking just below skin-deep. Apex predator. Fully male. Circling his next meal…

The rest of me heated as I remembered when he'd been *less* fully clothed. Warm turned to tingle, which deepened into an ache. I drew in a quick breath, then dove underwater, needing to douse the fire I'd started simply by letting my mind wander.

When I came up for air, Mase glanced over his shoulder, then began paddling. "Let's ride one together. I surf goofy foot. We can both take the left."

My pulse raced at the idea. Until last week, I'd never really surfed with anyone besides Makani. Had been pretty much a loner in the waves. The gift of *kai*, the ocean, and becoming one with waves that washed ashore onto our ʻaina was sacred to me, cherished—private.

Just surfing with him the other day had been a huge step for me.

To surf the same wave?

I would've thought it impossible only weeks ago.

Live every moment brushed through my mind like the breeze. A command...permission. From her. For me. To just let go and live—out loud, not hiding who I was.

My eyes teared up with how hard the heartfelt emotion hit me. I swallowed past a burning lump in my throat, blinked the unwanted moisture from my eyes, then gave him a nod.

I started paddling, facing away from him—so he wouldn't see my struggle. But with him. And toward something.

We slowed, letting a few smaller waves roll under. But I didn't sit up, wouldn't relax back into anything. Not yet. And I didn't have to. Because the beginnings of a nice set lined up.

I angled toward shore, then paddled with quick, strong strokes.

He glided into position right beside me.

Faster...

My arms burned with exertion.

Wait for it...

My heart pounded with excitement.

Now!

With a shove, I popped up, planted my feet, and crouched low, finding my balance as I rocked my hips forward.

Mase glided up just behind me, and when I glanced back, his grin widened as we both reached our left hands out, trailing our fingers through the arching glassy wall.

"Coming aboard," he warned, seconds before he stepped onto my board.

With a gasp, I twisted my body and moved my feet forward, adjusting my balance for the extra weight as he skimmed his hands over my hips, stabilizing me. For the briefest moments, we faced each other, riding the wave together, and I tentatively slid my hands around his waist, up his back. Then on a slow exhale, I let myself go. Closed my eyes and fully trusted him, to guide us, to see the danger, and navigate us through.

And the feeling? Exhilarating.

For hours we surfed, sometimes carving the left-hander, other times dropping in to the right. Eventually, we swam through schools of darting fish and went ashore. After pulling out our towels and drying off, we shouldered the bags Dave had dropped earlier, then headed *mauka*, onto a path hidden by overgrown foliage.

"Where are we going?" he asked, following close behind.

"Somewhere."

"Want me to guess?"

"Sure."

"Chipped stone path through jungle next to a rugged beach? We're heading to an ancient Hawaiian fishing lodge."

"Nope."

"Stone steps. Interesting. Going higher. And on the northeastern edge of all Hawai'i? I'm going with ancient Inuit fishing lodge."

"Inuit?"

"Alaskan."

"Why Alaskan?"

"Because you said 'nope' to Hawaiian."

"Nope to Inuit."

"Viking? Although, gotta say, Vikings would've had to travel really far to build a fishing lodge all the way out here."

"Why a fishing lodge?"

"What I would build. Did you see all those fish around us? This is what people think of when they imagine paradise."

"That's all you'd want is a fishing lodge?"

"What else would I need? Fire pit. Oh, maybe a hot tub." His eyes widened a bit, then he snapped his fingers. "You're taking me to one of the sacred ancient Hawaiian pools."

"Nope."

"An Inuit pool?"

I turned, unable to hide my grin at his ridiculous guesses. "It's not Inuit. Or Viking."

"Australian, then." The steady crunching of rocks beneath his feet stopped.

I paused, turning.

His mouth fell open as he stared over my head.

I touched my fingers under his chin then lifted it shut. "Careful. Mosquitos might breed in there."

"That is *not* a Hawaiian fishing lodge."

I glanced over my shoulder at the structure. Perched on the side of a hidden cliff, it seemed to sprout from the treetops. "Not bad for a vacation shack, yeah?"

"Whose is it?" He gaped at the sweeping Tahitian-style roofline, swept his gaze across the wide lanai.

I pushed overgrown ferns aside, then rounded the front corner of the building, stepping onto the mossy stone pathway. "Someone I know."

When I flipped open the keypad at the front door, he stared at it. "Someone you know…who gives you the alarm code?"

Right. I hadn't planned on too many questions. And breaking glass in such a beautiful structure would've broken my heart. "I've…been here before."

"Ah." He folded his arms over his chest, then eyed me with suspicion as I paced out eleven steps from the door, spun left ninety degrees, then counted another eleven, before crouching down and overturning a flattened rock.

I lifted the weather-dulled key from its hiding space in triumph.

"This *someone* gonna mind we're here?"

"No."

"He won't come to use his fishing lodge anytime soon?"

"What makes you think it's a 'he'?"

"All your secrecy, the hesitancy before you answered. You have a rich boyfriend you haven't told me about?"

"No. No boyfriend."

"Uncle, then."

I stepped out of my *slippahs*, tucking them against the stone foundation as he did the same. Resting a hand on the door handle, I glanced at him, letting out a heavy sigh. "Fine. It's my uncle's." *Not exactly.* But I needed his questions to stop. Could only expose myself in small steps, with things I was ready to share *when* I grew ready to share, in time, with trust.

In truth, I'd only been inside the house once.

And as I stepped through a counterbalanced front door made almost entirely of glass, the beauty of the open-air space struck me. Natural bamboo planks lined thirty-foot vaulted ceilings. Custom mango-wood cabinetry filled a spacious kitchen. I smoothed my palms over velvety gray soapstone countertops while gazing at a stunning raw-edged monkeypod dining table.

"That a NanaWall?" He stared toward the lanai that faced the waves where we'd surfed.

"A *what* wall?" I watched his large bare feet as they crossed a plush oriental rug that depicted a hazy delicate garden at the golden moment of sunrise.

"NanaWall," he repeated, hand curving around a metal handle on the far end. "Yep. Cade's parents have one at their country house."

"No idea."

"May I?" He raised his brows.

"Sure." I gave a shrug, trying to hide my smile at his excitement over window-walls while I tried to place the familiar name. "Cade..." —I nodded slowly, beginning to remember standing outside a house with Mase creeped-out about cane spiders— "the ex-roommate with your dog..."

"Yep, Ava." He twisted the handle and yanked to a loud unsticking sound. A base whoosh followed as fresh air from the trades burst in. He glided the bifolding glass panels along their track, stacking one panel against the other, until the wall disappeared.

My eyes drifted shut on a deep inhale, as I drew in the mineral scent of all things good into my lungs.

"*Fucking* awesome." Walking onto the lanai, he stretched his arms wide, then clasped his hands behind his head.

"You like, yeah?"

"Yeah. I like *a lot*." He rested his hands on the teak railing outside.

A part of me ached to join him. Drawn to both him and nature, I wanted to be out there, stand beside him...*touch him*.

But I resisted. Safe inside for now, I remained where I stood. Chicken? Maybe. Not sure if it mattered. We would be close soon enough. Close enough to touch. To taste. And... *more*.

My pulse started to escalate as tingling parts of my body warmed, then began to throb with insistence that I move over there now. Blowing out a shaky breath, I smoothed my hands over the cool countertop again, curled my toes against the hard bamboo floor, trying to remain calm.

269

All of a sudden, he whirled around. "Cool to check out the rest of the house?"

"We're here, aren't we?" I followed when he disappeared down the hall. "Already did the B and E. No biggie to keep on trespassing."

"Uhhh…'B and E'?" He glanced over his shoulder at me, then popped a head into an open doorway on our left. "You sound like a hardened criminal." He shook his head, muttering with a smile, "*B and E.*" He continued walking toward a closed door on the right, opened the door and scanned inside, then closed it again. "And technically, there was no breaking, only entering."

"Unlawful entry."

He narrowed his eyes at me. "You been in trouble with the law, island girl?"

"No." *Not really.* "Looking for something?"

"Changing the subject?"

"Maybe."

"Totally."

Not bothering to argue the point, I stopped short two feet from him when he rejected the third room with a dissatisfied headshake; I hadn't glanced into any of them. Skin still flushed from my sensual thoughts while I'd stood in the kitchen with an entire room between us, my attention stayed focused on him, and my slow calming breaths, in the close quarters of the hallway.

"The master bedroom," he finally replied, explaining what he was searching for.

A gasp escaped my lips before I could stop it. "Oh." Right down to business.

He leveled a serious look at me. "You're not scared." The last word held a note of disbelief.

I tried to steady my racing heart, asking myself the same question. Why would I be afraid to be with him? Far from virginal, even if I hadn't been properly pleasured as he'd so eloquently pointed out, there should've been nothing to fear.

And yet, I couldn't take another step closer. Couldn't seem to calm my hammering pulse. Chest rising and falling to keep up with my heart, I couldn't catch a good solid breath.

"Hey." He moved closer. Got in my space. *Touched me.* "We don't have to do anything you're not ready for."

Chin lifting in defiance at his words, at my irritating hesitation, I put a hand on his chest, over his also-rapidly-beating heart. "I'm ready."

I was. Wasn't I?

"Then, what?" In the darkened hallway, humidity stifling the still air around us, he brushed the hair from my eyes, cupped my face. "You can tell me."

"I don't—" Words failed me. Logic did too. I couldn't name the feeling. Fear choked my breath, and yet, it wasn't of going forward. It wasn't of holding tight to him, cherishing him, pleasuring him. It was the *letting go* part—having what I wanted most in the world, admitting it to myself and actually taking hold of it, only to have it snatched away.

Wrapping his arms around me, caging me in his solid strength, he tilted his head down. A soft kiss pressed to my forehead.

Surrendering to the rush of feeling, I closed my eyes, inhaled his scent of salt and earth and man. Gentle pressure

271

feathered over one eyelid, then the other: more tender kisses. "You can," he murmured, brushing his mouth over my cheekbone, dragging his stubble over my jaw.

I clung to him, slipping my hands under the damp waistband of his board shorts, pressing his lower back toward me.

"*We* can," he promised on a whisper before his warm lips covered mine.

The tender kiss surpassed all others, soft yet firm, teasing and serious. When my lips parted on a gasp, he nipped my lower lip, then nuzzled my nose with his. "We got this," he murmured.

His confidence washed away all my fears. I wanted to believe him—needed to.

Unable to speak, I nodded, then pressed my lips to his neck, nestling my face into the crook of his shoulder. *Live every moment.* A gift. The moment we stole for ourselves, in someone else's house, in everyone else's world, had become ours, raw and special. And I wanted to hold on to it, remember every tiny second that had grown monumental.

After a quick squeeze, he pulled away, breaking the spell we'd fallen under.

"C'mon." He kissed the top of head. "Gotta find that master bedroom."

My shoulders trembled with laughter. "Your romance astounds me."

"My determination impresses you."

"True."

"And we're not having sex there."

I frowned. "We're not?"

"No."

"Where, then?"

"Not *yet*," he corrected, giving me a pointed look.

"Ahhh…so it's a matter of when."

"Exactly." He nodded, then turned, heading back the way we'd come. "We could also discuss *where*…"

"Oh, could we?"

"Sure." He paused, gripped a wood-trimmed corner of the wall on the far side of the kitchen, then glanced over his shoulder at me. "Where would you like to?"

"Seriously, we're gonna plan this out? Like a sexual itinerary?"

"Sure."

My mind exploded with so many possibilities, I had to blow out a slow breath to steady myself. "You're insane."

"Insanity craves company." He smirked, then turned and disappeared around the corner.

"Such a philosopher," I muttered, following him.

"Well?" He stood in a massive arched entry that had no doors.

We'd finally made it to the master bedroom. A room in the house I'd never been.

Drawn by finishes I'd only seen in my dreams, I followed Mase in with reverent steps. Sumptuous cream fabric covered two divans, each reclined and angled toward a far wall of glass; the matching his-and-hers low sofas had feet and trim carved of rare translucent curly koa wood. A pair of round jewel-toned pillows had been tossed into a corner of each, on the far one, vibrant emerald and crimson ruby. I skimmed my fingers over the silk of the canary yellow and sapphire blue.

Movement made me turn as Mase gathered back a mass of gossamer mosquito netting that suspended from the ceiling and draped over a massive bed. No color adorned the high mattress, only the sheen of soft ivory bedding. Drawing in a deep breath, I curved my hand around a polished koa-wood bedpost at the foot of the bed.

He stood diagonally across from me, beside two layers of fluffed pillows, watching me with seriousness as something sparked in his eyes. "Is *this* a 'where'?"

Careful not to wrinkle one square inch, I pulled the corner of the duvet between my fingers. Cool to the touch, it sobered me back into the moment. "Definitely."

My skin flushed hot at the idea of being naked in there. With him.

What would it be like to mess a *pono* bed up, that someone else had carefully made, obviously cleaned regularly? Unable to help myself, I squealed and jumped, arms and legs flinging wide before I landed facedown in the center of it. Smothered by thousand-thread-count cotton plastered to my nose, I could barely breathe, but I smiled into the fabric, not caring.

"Now?" Amusement rippled in his tone. "You want all the mind-blowing sex now?"

A soft rustle sounded in his vicinity.

I tilted my head, peeking up at him.

He'd grabbed the back of his rash guard in a fist and was pulling it over his head. When he curved his shoulders down, contracting his torso, my gaze lowered to take in the bunched muscles of his abs, the low V angling down from his hips, and the dusting of blond hair that disappeared under his low-slung board shorts.

I blew out a slow breath, wanting to touch...taste...feel. But not yet. We had a whole night. "No. Not now. And..." I blinked, then glanced at him, propping my head up with a bent arm. "Mind-blowing?"

He fought a smile. "Well, something's gonna blow. That's for damn sure."

For damn sure.

"Shower?"

Confused at his redirect, I frowned. "Where is—" *it?*

My mind froze and I blinked more heavily as he shoved down his shorts. At my eye level, hung his impressive manhood, thick with a pale golden hue. And I stared at it. I'd seen it before, only a flash when we'd first met. But inches away, its *many inches* stole my breath away. If that's what he looked like *not* turned on, however would he...fit...when he was?

"I'm guessing over there?" His voice softened to a low murmur.

Breaths coming faster no matter how hard I tried to control them, I glanced up. He reached a hand toward me, then nodded at the far corner of the room, beyond a lava rock wall. "The question was an invitation."

"Oh," I whispered. So not sex *in the bed* yet.

Trusting in him like I'd never trusted another man before, I slowly swung my legs to the side of the bed and took his hand. Staring into my eyes, he pulled me up, then guided me forward before folding me into his arms.

He pressed a kiss to my temple. His lips lingered there a moment, tender yet firm, before dragging lower until they brushed the shell of my ear. I shivered under the intimate warmth of his breath as his hands smoothed up my back, over the thin material I still wore.

"*Relaaax...*" His whispered suggestion dragged out like a buttery caress as his thumbs rubbed over the tight muscles between my shoulder blades. "No sex yet."

"No?"

A low chuckle rumbled from his throat as his lips teased over my jawline before they drifted lower, over the sensitive skin of my neck. "No. Only foreplay."

I blew out a shaky breath, not fully understanding what he meant but very much wanting to find out. "How will I stand long enough to shower?"

"I'll hold you."

I smiled. "Is this your typical foreplay?"

"No."

"Never?"

"Only with you."

The admission stunned me. And pleased me. That I'd be special enough for him to take his time with me. To allow me to savor the slow buildup. That he'd want the same thing too.

With a slow glide of his hands, his fingers wandered under the hem of the rash guard that covered my swimsuit top. His breath floated warmth over my neck, my shoulder. "May I?"

"Yes." The word came out on a croak.

A final kiss brushed over my collarbone before he leaned back and tugged upward.

Cool air rushed over my skin as the clinging fabric peeled away from my stomach, my chest, my shoulders, then up over my head. I shivered when he took a small step backward without removing his hands from my upper arms.

His gaze roved down my body. "Gorgeous."

And though I still wore a tiny bikini top and boy-short bottoms, I felt completely naked. Because he didn't only see me skin-deep. He *knew* me, every part, down to my beating heart. And he liked what he saw.

Even though fear still hovered, it faded toward the edges of my mind; I grew bold with him. That someone might know me for who I was deep inside, who I yearned to be out loud for the whole world to know with every fiber of my being.

Could you grow to love me?

And…will I be able to keep you if I let myself fall?

29
IN PLAIN SIGHT

Mase...

Leilani shivered in my arms. But not from cold air. And I didn't need to ask her why.

Her expression gave her away...

Fear.

Strength.

Doubt.

Courage.

Countless emotions were in the trembling of her lower lip, the hesitation in her eyes. But her hardened jaw as she straightened her shoulders made my chest swell with pride. And hope.

Because the girl who'd hunted me down across the ocean, the one who'd hidden behind a mask of propriety and rules for some undisclosed reason, had grown. She'd ventured out of her shell, shed the restricting mask.

And I stood before her, naked. In body and heart. Whatever she would have of me, for however long we were lucky enough to have it—brave enough to take for ourselves no matter the consequences—was hers.

"Let me." Soft words were steeled with determination as she stepped just out of my reach.

I clenched my hands, aching to pull her back, claim her as mine. But I waited, knew she needed to take the leap on her own.

On a deep inhale, she arched her back, hands disappearing, breasts pulled taut beneath the small triangles of her suit while she undid the tie between her shoulder blades. Her gaze lowered, as if she'd gone shy.

"I see you." I stared hard at her, not moving a muscle.

She blinked heavily, then lifted her gaze until it locked with mine.

"*All* of you." Not only the tempting curves, but what lay hidden beneath. Just for me.

"What do you see?" Innocent curiosity softened her face, but she didn't stop undressing. Her hands lifted to her nape, untied the last knot, then the flimsy covering twirled to the ground.

I stared deep into her dark wide eyes. "Your wild heart. Your bright soul."

"You don't want to tame my wildness?"

"Not even a little. It's what I love about you. You're a beautiful, intelligent woman who knows what she wants and has finally allowed herself to have it."

Her hands curved over her midsection in a self-hug. "What do I want?"

Fear held her back, but she was ready; I sensed it. "You tell me."

"*You*." Force weighted her steady tone. "I want *you*."

"Why?" I needed to hear it. Had to know whether her desire and need had gone deeper than a physical craving—like mine had.

"Because…" Her gaze went unfocused. On a swallow, she pegged me with a hard look. In silence, she smoothed her palms out over her lower stomach. Her fingers wedged into the material hugging the widest part of her hips. "Because you understand me."

"I do." I let out a slow breath.

In her, I saw myself. We were the same: harboring an inner child who'd struggled growing up, wanting desperately to be loved. As new adults, we practically vibrated with a need to find ourselves, to accept who we were first in order to have what we ultimately wanted.

"And…" She shoved her hands down, shedding the last bit of clothing she wore along with any remaining inhibition. "I want you to know me. To *love* me."

Bared before me stood the most incredible sight. Vulnerable and strong. Humble yet proud. A fierce female warrior with a soul brighter than the sun.

And all mine—because she offered me her heart.

"Come here, island girl." When I held out my hand, the corners of her mouth twitched, but she wordlessly obeyed, sliding delicate fingers over my palm. "I know you, and I want to know more. *Everything* there is to know..." I dropped a kiss on her temple, traced my lips along her cheekbone, rubbed my nose to the tip of hers. "You ask me to love you…"

"Please," she whispered on an exhale.

"I already love you." Our breaths mingled, lips hovering. At the slightest touch, hers parted on a gasp. I molded my mouth to hers with a sensual kiss that grew in intensity as her body fell lax in my arms. Breathing hard, I pulled back, touching my forehead to hers as I admitted the truth to myself, to her. "Started falling when you stormed away from me the first time we met."

With a contented sigh, her head tilted to the side until her cheek rested on my chest just below my shoulder. We stood naked in each other's arms. It should have been sexual, and it was. But for the first time we stood bared to each other as our true selves. Fears and all. The effect was both thrilling and frightening. And I wanted to let it sink in, find my foundation in it.

"Got thrown for a tailspin when you opened up that night."

Soft laughter tickled over my skin. "When you got me drunk?"

"*We* got drunk."

"I began to fall then too," she admitted.

"You didn't make it easy on yourself."

"No."

"Stubborn woman."

"Yeah." Her hands flattened over my lower back and she pulled me close.

"So, we getting clean, or what?"

"I feel like we just did. Like I've cleansed my soul." Her hold tightened further. "Will it stay that way?"

Unmarred by the world, she meant. I couldn't promise that. We didn't have control over outside forces. We could learn how to react to them though. "Only if we fight for it."

She gave a nod against my chest. "Only if we do it together."

"Exactly."

"To the shower, yeah?" She stepped back, biting her lip. Then she whirled around and smacked my ass before darting around the corner.

A hot sting smarted over my skin, then fired deeper, heating my blood. "Oh, so we're playing it that way."

When I rounded the corner, moist air flowed over my face. Warm wood floors gave way to cool polished black stones. Weathered lava rock surrounded a fifteen-foot square outdoor space. Ferns and colorful orchids sprouted out from cracks and pockets in the wall. Palms and jacarandas swayed in the strong winds overhead, dancing shadows across filtered light.

And an exotic beauty with silken dark hair flowing down her back stood at the far end, angling up a faucet lever.

At the sound of a low hum, then sputtering an instant later, she glanced around as our surroundings came to life. Tiny waterfalls gurgled out from hidden openings all over the surface of the wall. Green lily pads and purple lotus flowers floating in a shallow pond that skirted the bottom of the wall began to sway with the sudden current. Water droplets began to fall from a wide copper latticework that spanned above the entire space. A heavier shower rained down from solid sheeting near her end.

As I walked farther in, she slinked around the edge of the shower, light on the balls of her feet.

"Looking to escape?"

"Could I?" She feigned slightly left, then right, causing her breasts to sway.

I swallowed hard, then sucked in a slow breath at the incredible sight. "No."

Could either of us? And why would we want to.

Gazed fixed on me, she stepped under the stream, tilting her head back with no modesty. Like we'd been reborn together in the sacred place we'd trespassed into, neither of us willing to hide any longer.

I closed the ten-foot distance between us, then pulled her into my arms as a delighted smile lit up her face.

"I've got you," I murmured before my lips covered hers.

No escape. Because I'm never letting you go.

Soap suds.

I blame the soap suds.

And the naked.

And all the wet.

Very…*very*…wet.

Because after Leilani and I got clean, we got very, very dirty.

Her lips parted on a gasp, eyes drifting shut, as my fingers slid down between her folds. Hands gripping my shoulders, chest heaving for breath, her entire body began to tremble.

Rock hard and straining for her, I sucked in deep breaths, dangling by the barest thread of control. I tucked her close with one arm while I pressed a little harder, rubbed a little faster...

The sexiest low moans quieted into whimpers with each of her quickening breaths. Her bronze skin flushed into a gorgeous shade of pink. Dark, wet eyelashes covered eyes that had pinched closed under her tense brow. After a sudden deep gasp, her body went taut, grip tightening on my arms as she bit her lush lower lip.

I almost felt the painful pleasure with her as she teetered on that edge, about to fall over.

Flattening my hand, I glided my fingers farther down, pressed the knuckle of my thumb over her clit where my fingers had been, then plunged a finger into her slick heat. I stroked over her inner nerves with a curling thrust, circled my thumb, then gripped together with firmer pressure.

She gasped then screamed, body shaking from head to toe, inner muscles clenching my finger in tight spasms as she tumbled into sweet release. Over the next seconds, I continued stroking while slowing the pace, taking every quaking wave her body wanted to give.

Head tucked under my chin, her arms moved around my waist, hands sliding up my back. With a tight hold, she clung to me, letting out a low satisfied groan.

With a heavy exhalation, I wrapped my arms around

her, breaths slowing on pace with hers. The moment hit me hard, her level of trust, the gift of her body, her heart, and it took me a bit to recover along with her.

Water still raining down on us, she began to stir back to life. "*Damn*," she breathed out.

Then she pulled slightly away, testing her legs for strength as she found her balance.

I didn't say a thing. I couldn't. The gorgeous woman who'd just come apart in my arms had taken my breath away and stolen all my words.

She stared up at me with amazement. Then she gave me a shy smile. "You *did* hold me up."

"Told ya I would."

She bit the corner of that plump lower lip again, fire sparking in her eyes. "Your turn."

"Nah, it's okay." I wanted to give her time. Make sure she was ready.

"*Ohhh*, no. No more waiting." She wrapped her hand around my cock.

I hissed in a breath as it kicked against her touch, hardening again for her. "Well, okay. If you insist."

"I do." Her breaths shortened, her excitement growing again as she gripped the base, then stroked upward. "I insist."

I groaned, brain cells frying, every inch of skin she stroked throbbing. When I leaned back, my shoulders pressed against the jagged lava rock wall. Then I blinked and quickly looked around. No chairs in sight. Only hard ground and rough walls.

Covering her hand with mine, I gently removed her hold

from my body for the moment. I slid my hand into hers, then tugged her back toward the bedroom. "We need a location change."

Back through the entry, in an alcove on the left, upper shelves held stacks of thick folded white towels. On the wall across, two plush white robes dangled from hooks. I tossed a bathmat onto the ground, then wrapped her in a soft bath sheet, gently toweling her off.

"We've done this before," she said, gazing down at me.

"We have?"

"You taking care of me, toweling me off."

"Ahhh…shots of tequila, a near-shark encounter, then you about to pass out."

"Yeah, but I remember what a gentleman you were. Me naked. You not taking advantage."

I swept her into my arms, towel and all, then carried her over to the bed. "And now?"

"You *better* take advantage."

"Don't have to tell me twice, woman." I gently dropped her onto the thick bedding, and her body gave the most incredible bounce, curves swaying, then settling.

She stared up at me, happiness in her expression.

"Oh, damn. Hold that thought." I backed up, committing the way she looked to memory, all flushed contentment turning into shocked amusement as I began to retreat. Then I strode out of the room.

"Where are you going?" She shouted, laughing.

"Condom!"

In the fastest retrieval known to man, I raced through

the kitchen leapt over two pieces of furniture, dumped the contents of both our bags, scattered everything until I pinched a foil packet between my fingers, then raced back, slowing my steps to act all casual as I approached the bed.

The moment she saw me, she let loose a wide yawn, eyes half-lidded.

"*Ohhh*, no." I jumped onto the bed, then began tickling her. "No teasin', then sleepin'. I'm taking advantage—you said. There're no take-backs."

After her laughter died down, her hands slid back into position, gripping my shaft with renewed force. My body reacted, beginning to harden for her once again. "No take-backs." Arching up, she kissed my chest, dragged her lips up my neck, then clipped her teeth onto my earlobe. "Only *taking* me."

Once I'd grown hard again, which took only a few seconds under her touch, she plucked the condom from my grasp and began to roll it on. I slowly kissed a trail over her body from ear to navel, charting every curve, dip, and plane, taking note of which spots made her gasp, tremble, or moan. Her legs eased open, knees bending, calves brushing over my hips, then across my ass as she welcomed me into her most private space.

When my lips clamped a nipple, her breaths shallowed. As I sucked the hardened bud through my teeth with steady pressure, then flicked it with my tongue, she squirmed and softly moaned.

I pulled my head up when I finally drew my hips back, though. Gaze locking with hers, I caught my tip at her entrance and stared into her sparkling eyes as I gently thrust forward, connecting with her deeply in every way.

Fingers digging into my arms, she let out a soft whimper as I glided into her slick body.

Not yet fully seated, but concerned, I eased back and searched her eyes. "You okay?"

She gave a quick nod. "Yeah, tight." Then she curved her hips up, pulling me deeper again.

"*Yeah, tight.*" I gasped for air. "So *fucking* tight." I kissed her slowly, driving forward as her inner muscles gradually began to adjust. "Amazing," I growled against her lips.

Her hips undulated right as I thrust one last time, causing me to slide all the way in, balls-deep. She clung to me and gasped. My head fell to her shoulder as I struggled for breath. Sparks of pleasure zapped from deep in my lower back into my groin. On a hard swallow, I eased back, then thrust forward. When I pulled back again, she arched. Then she matched my every movement, my draw then thrust, her arch then curve, as we found our perfect rhythm.

Soon, her moans grew louder. Pressure built in me the closer she got, the harder she gripped. Breathing deeper, I did my best to hold back, wait for her once more. But the feeling was too intense. She flashed hotter all around me. Then I snapped, ache firing hot and fast until my nerve endings detonated. I growled out as I came. Her nails dug into the back of my arms as her muscles went taut, back arching, hips grinding; then she screamed, spasms clamping around me as her entire body shuddered.

In that moment…

Heaven.

After a few beats, my senses began to sharpen in slow motion, awareness of our surroundings settling back in. I collapsed around her, falling to the side as I caught my breath. Then I gathered her in my arms and held her close as our breaths slowed together.

Time seemed to warp as we drifted in and out, light fading into darkness.

At one point, I remember her kissing my arm and hearing her murmur, "I want to keep you."

I tightened my hold. "Try and take me away."

In the far reaches of my mind, I understood what she meant. But I ignored the fear. Because it could only hurt us if we let it.

30
IT ALWAYS CATCHES UP

Mase…

"**L**ike hell. You're coming." Kristen Michaelson, oldest sister to my ex-roommate, Cade, gathered her dark hair together with calm strokes of her fingers then fastened it into a ponytail all while glaring at me with her electric-blue eyes in vivid liquid crystal from my laptop screen.

"Sorry. Not my gig." *Politics?* No fucking thanks.

Thirty minutes after Leilani and I had returned from our amazing twenty-four hour escape, Leilani had run out to Kula Marketplace to grab some sandwiches when Kristen had texted me to call. And I'd only been video-chatting with Kristen for ninety seconds when she dropped the bomb that the Michaelson's party-planning business, Invitation Only, had been hired to run an upcoming fundraising campaign for the *illustrious* Senator Price. Bile had risen into my throat the split second she'd suggested I fly out for it.

"*Ma-son*…" Silence followed the staccatoed syllables.

"*Ye-esss*…"

A growl vibrated out. "What's your middle name?"

"Kinda loses the intimidating punch when you have to ask."

More glaring silence.

Aw, what the hell. I stifled a grin and played along. "Alexander."

"Mason Alexander Price, you get your too-skinny ass out here for this party."

"My ass is not too skinny."

A groan sounded out. "I can't believe we're talking about your ass."

"You brought it up."

"Fine." She rolled her blue eyes. "Your ass is *not* too skinny."

"It's not?"

"No. It has just the right amount of muscle."

"*Okaaay*…this just got weird." Kristen was a *mom*-like bossy sister to me.

"Oh, yeah?" Her brows raised, the beginnings of an evil smile forming. "Ass. Balls. Di—"

"Holy fuck, Kristen. *Stop.* I do *not* want to hear body parts coming from your mouth." *Jesus.* Now I felt like I needed to scrub my brain.

"What's the *matter*, Mason *Alexander*?" She attempted to rhyme in singsong.

"Cute." Okay, good. Back in schoolyard territory.

"You coming? Or do I need to ramp up the torture…"

On a heavy sigh, I leaned forward, bracing my arms on my thighs. "*Going* is more heinous torture."

"Gee, thanks."

"Not you. You know I love you guys. It's my parents. Five civilized minutes in a room with them is like lying flat for five blistering hours on thousand-degree coals."

"That bad?"

"Then rolling in salt."

"Ah, so worse."

"Then being covered in pissed-off fire ants."

"As opposed to delighted fire ants?"

"Sure." Somehow, ridiculous banter with her calmed me. Kristen, and all the Michaelsons, were like family to me—the Norman Rockwell picture everone wanted but never had.

"So, how bad" —her head tilted, voice lowering— "guilt and judgment bad?"

"Worse. Shame and resentment."

"Ah. Sorry."

"It's okay. Not your fault."

A quiet sigh sounded over the phone. "You sure you don't want to come? Your mom pulled me aside yesterday to ask me if I'd ask you."

"She did?" Shocked, I sat up, then stared out the window, made sure the sky was still blue. Because my father had been the cold and demanding one to my face, but most of the shit behind the scenes? All her.

"And she seemed nervous about it. Specifically told me not to tell you she asked."

I huffed out a dry laugh. "Said request blatantly disregarded."

"Duh. You're my brother. We don't keep secrets."

Brother in spirit, not blood. But our bonds were tighter than most for all that we'd shared growing up. Kristen knew me even better than Kendall, Kiki, and Cade did. When I'd been only eight and Kristen sixteen, she'd saved me, literally dragged me from a shed into her comforting arms—the first genuine hug in my life that I'd ever experienced—when we'd played hide-and-seek at her parents' country house; the game had ended hours before and darkness had fallen. Hot off an argument with my parents about their favoritism of my older brother over me, I'd hid where no one would ever think to look—in the darkest cobweb-infested rat hole I could find. I'd stewed for the first hour, as if no one had come looking for me, as if no one cared. Through the shed walls, I'd heard their laughter as they walked by with my brother, Deacon. But none of my delusional self-pity had been true. None of them had ever spoken a harsh word to me. Not even Deke—especially not him.

But that day had been hard. It was the first time I'd realized I was the second son. Second in everything... including my parents' love.

Love.

On a deep breath, I began to smile.

Something incredible had changed between then and now, life-altering and bone deep. I wasn't the kid in the shed anymore. I no longer defined myself as second in anything.

I'd put myself first, chased my dream, searched for a place where I felt most at home.

And at the moment I'd found me? So had the most amazing girl.

Her love? More than I'd ever hoped for. All I ever needed.

Plus, I had my real family in the Michaelsons, the one that mattered: my 'ohana. "Kristen?"

"Yeah?" Understanding eyes stared back at me.

"Count me in."

Because with Leilani by my side? How bad could it be?

Leilani bounded through the front door ten minutes after my video-chat with Kristen ended.

Two tickets to Philadelphia had been selected on the previous screen, and the cursor now hovered over the Date of Birth dropdown bars for Passenger 2.

But my attention zeroed in on Leilani: silken black hair spilling over her shoulders, dark eyes with thick, long lashes under slender arching brows, cheeks pinked from plenty of sun.

They plumped when she smiled wider. "Watcha doin' there?"

"Hoping you'll say yes."

Smile vanishing, she dropped the sandwiches on the plywood-covered counter. Weight shifting to her right, she moved into her trademark hip-pop, hand lowering to rest at the waist of her green sundress. Her face tilted downward as she leveled an intense gaze at me. "Yes. After all the *mind-blowing* things you've done to me? The answer will *always* be yes."

Images of all the things we'd done to one another flashed into my head, heated my blood. "Great. Now you're addicted."

"Definitely." She crossed her arms. "Gonna need a daily hit. You up for that?"

"Only daily? And I'm *always* up for you."

Her head tilted, eyes narrowing. "Got proof of that, surfer boy?" Unfolding her arms, she took measured steps across the ten-foot distance between us. "Twice a day."

I patted my right thigh. "*Getting closer...*"

Instead of taking my offer, she wrapped her arms around my shoulders, slid her hands down my chest, then brushed her lips over the top of my ear. "Should I just sit on your lap all day?"

"Yes. Please." I gripped her forearms, spun her around, and tumbled her sideways onto my lap. The metal folding chair groaned under our weight, teetering. I instantly spread my legs out for stability, holding her tight in my arms as her eyes widened and lips fell open with surprise.

A beat passed. Then another. We both exhaled and sat more upright, reasonably confident we weren't under imminent threat of collapsing to the floor.

She wrapped her arms around my neck, pressing a gentle kiss to my jaw. "Well, maybe not in *this* chair." Sliding her cheekbone along mine as she turned her face toward my computer, she wriggled her ass over my lap.

I groaned, then planted my hands on her hips to still her.

"*Sooo*...what were you hoping I'd say yes to?"

"Well, if you don't stop moving over my *always*-up dick...destroying this chair."

"Oh." Her voice quieted. "Sorry."

"No you're not."

"No" —she angled her face toward mine, gave me a soft kiss— "I'm not."

"Wild island girl," I murmured, kissing her gently back.

"You know it." She pulled slightly away, then stared into my eyes.

Yeah, I do. "Lucky me."

"*Sooo…*" She nodded toward the laptop, where the screen displayed passenger data fields. "A *non*business trip?"

"Yeah." I took a deep breath. "How do you feel about meeting my parents?"

She blinked, then pulled away, scrutinizing me for a couple of beats. "Uhhh…how do *you* feel about it?"

"Near-violently ill."

"*Sounds* awesome."

I raised my brows a little. "I'll be there…"

Wild island girl shimmied her hips. "Sounding *better…*"

Holding her hips, I thrust up against her, proving exactly how *always*-up she'd driven me.

"I'm there." She turned and clicked into the Date of Birth dropdowns, completing the info.

"Thank God." My shoulders relaxed. Hadn't realized they'd ratcheted up toward my ears. When a creak groaned out under us, I smiled. "And we're bringing the chair."

On a deep breath, she turned. Her expression grew serious. "On that note: Want to come to my father's house tonight?"

The weight of her tone told me *near-violently ill* didn't

begin to describe her dread about the flip-side event. But the demons of our pasts were necessary evils we had to bravely face at some point.

"Yeah." I gave her a gentle kiss, then rested my forehead to hers. We exchanged breath: *ha*. And her body began to relax in my hold. "I do."

After our meeting-the-parents plans had been made and the airline tickets purchased, Leilani had gone back to her place for the afternoon. I'd put in some facetime with the chicks, letting them explore their new run while I spent a couple of hours working in the garden.

By the time I picked Leilani up, the sun had begun to set. "You go to your dad's often?"

"No." She picked at the hem of her sundress. "We don't get along."

"As bad as your other two brothers?" Besides Makani. "Koa and…

"Holokai," she provided. "And…no. Worse." She pointed at a dirt driveway. "Turn in there."

"Ah." We'd only driven a couple blocks *makai* of Leilani's house. We could've walked. I parked behind a line of three Tacomas, right behind Makani's.

The decades old single-level structure sprawled across its third-acre lot, original house connecting to one addition after another, the only telltale sign of add-ons being the varying pitches of its rusted metal corrugated roof. The exterior paint had been dark green at one point, but some sections had weathered to a drab brown, others had peeled off entirely, exposing rotting wood. The window casings, once white, were coated with a layer of Maui's reddish dirt.

An older large Hawaiian stepped out the back door, scanning the backyard as he walked. He paused midstep, gaze landing on me. Bright white hair and scraggly beard framed eyes that narrowed in harsh scrutiny. Dressed casually in a faded blue T-shirt, loose cotton shorts, and brown canvas *slippahs*, nothing about his stance gave any sign that he was friendly: hunched shoulders, tensed thighs, clenched jaw. Faded tribal tattoos circled his biceps under the tight cuff of each sleeve. A gleaming ivory shark's tooth, two-inches wide, hung from a short, black leather necklace.

Leilani's three brothers stood a few yards away, gathered around an imu pit. They all held beers and stared our way. None made any attempt to approach.

I got the sense they followed their patriarch's lead. Even Makani, who wore a resigned expression.

"*Makuakane*, this is Mase. My boyfriend."

Instant shock registered on her father's face as the same shock hit me—hard.

She hadn't gone the easing-in route with *Dad, this is the windsurfer Makani has sponsored* or even gentled the blow with *Dad, this is my new boss*. Nope. She'd made an unambiguous statement and had gone for the kill: *Hey, Dad. Meet the* white *guy who's fucking your daughter.*

Pride swelled in my chest that she felt I was worth the risk—even as fear spiked in warning.

Her father didn't say much, simply stared at me with contempt.

I offered him my hand. "Nice to meet you, Mr. Kealoha."

His gaze dropped to my hand. He made no move to take it. I left it there, hanging in the air. Didn't feel one ounce of embarrassment about it. Because if Leilani could make a bold statement, standing up for ourselves and making an effort? So could I, right by her side.

Eventually the staring-at-my-hand thing ended when he cut a critical glare toward her. "No, he's not."

Lani took a deep breath, tightened her lips, then pressed them together. "*Makuakane.*"

When her father walked off, showing us his clear rejection, she squared her shoulders, rose taller, and took a rigid step toward him.

I put a gentle hand on her shoulder to stop her. "It's okay, Lani. He doesn't want me here. *They* don't want me here."

"*I* want you here."

"Is that enough?"

She blinked in shock, as if I'd slapped her. "For me or for them?"

"For you." All I cared about.

"Of course it is. And me wanting you here is enough for them too." She glared toward her brothers. Makani gave a helpless shrug.

"You sure about that?"

"No." She turned her back toward them, huffing out a frustrated sigh. "But it will be. It *has* to be."

"Why is their approval so important to you?" I stared down into eyes that began to sparkle with tears. I wanted to reach out, hold her, wipe her tears away along with every fear she had. But I didn't. Not in the hostile territory we stood in.

"Because you're important to me." She took my hand in hers.

I gave her hand a gentle squeeze. "And they are too."

"Yes," she whispered.

Didn't see how it could happen, their approval. Inborn prejudice didn't suddenly evaporate.

Her stubbornness about not wanting to get involved with me? Suddenly made perfect sense.

And I'd pushed the issue.

So, clearly, I needed to fix it.

31
WHEN MONSTERS ROAR

Leilani...

As I sat on the low lava rock wall, a cramp burned at the base of my throat, making it difficult to breathe, swallow...talk. I stared at my stubborn, hateful *makuakane* and my two boneheaded oldest brothers. At least Makani had come around and kicked it with Mase, the two of them in beach chairs, out front, out of sight and out of the way of all the aggressive testosterone.

"Why do they have to be so stupid, Tutu? Why can't they let me be?"

My grandmother's wrinkled hand cupped my cheek, then brushed strands of hair that had been flying across my face behind my ear. Brown bony fingers reached up to an overhanging plumeria branch and plucked a bloom that had peachy petals trimmed in dark pink. She tucked it into my pinned-back hair. "There."

Wise eyes stared into mine. Then she counseled me as she always did, in her native Hawaiian tongue, "Men have things to prove. Battles to fight. Wars to wage. *Hawaiian* men have more to prove. Our lands mean everything to us and the white man desecrates it. Our glorious koa trees were felled. Their nasty invasive species were brought. Greedy builders contaminate our pristine waters. Business commands us, as if their money gives them the right to."

I sighed. She was right on all counts. "But what about *me*?"

"You are one of us, *mo'opuna i ke alo*. And a *haole* is threatening to take you." She'd called me beloved grandchild.

"He's not taking me, Tutu."

"Isn't he?"

"No."

"When your mind goes quiet, do you think of Ke'eaumoku?" The beer-can-throwing beach bully my father approved of and had been pushing me toward. "Or is Mase the one on your mind?"

I didn't answer.

"It's okay, *mo'opuna i ke alo*. We cannot control who our heart embraces. You are wild and free like the wind yet calm and unmoving like…Haleakala."

Tutu's pause had been deliberate.

Because there'd been another like me. One I'd loved more than anything in the world.

And lost.

I said aloud what my *makuakane* and brothers hated to hear. "I'm like *Makuahine*."

Tutu's eyes welled with tears. Because she believed what all the rest of them did: She'd lost her daughter to the poisons spread by *haoles*.

A week after doing my best to introduce Mase to my family, we stepped onto the petrifying beach as if it was just another routine day at work. Competition had been scheduled to start yesterday, but had been delayed due to negligible wind. Today? Whole other story.

A lawn chair flew by, tumbling in midair only inches from my face.

Shouts sounded, muffled in the distance, as grains of sand pelted my skin.

Mase didn't even turn his head. Only stared straight ahead at the coiling fearsome waves: thirty-foot roaring monsters.

According to the surf report, near-hurricane-force winds gusted through the arena. Scattered across the sand from the dark rocky cliffs to the high tide line, dozens of boards lay in wait, their colorful sails quivering so hard, many looked ready to leap into the sky. In twenty-second intervals, wave after wave crashed onto the rocky points bracketing the bay, each booming an echo out like cannon fire.

Damn. After a hard swallow, I found my breath again. "People sail in that?" It made Hoʻokipa Beach look like the *keiki* pool.

"Windsurfers break bones in this." His solemn tone pinged an ache into the pit of my stomach.

"Ever broken anything?" My legs bounced, anxiety firing nervous energy through me.

"Not while windsurfing."

"Really?" I glanced at him. "What did you break?"

"Collarbone. Third-grade soccer. My shoulder tried to take on the ground. Shoulder lost."

I smiled at his humor, fascinated by the morsel of personal information he'd just shared. Were it any other time, I'd have asked him more.

But he said nothing further.

Focus absolute, gaze trained on cresting angry giants that surged up, darkening the sky, he seemed to have entered a kind of meditative state as he methodically stretched his muscles.

He vibrated with an intensity I'd never seen in him before.

Tension rippled through the air all around us: from the camera crews, from the judges and officials, from a growing crowd of spectators. And from our three-by-three square of sand.

I tried to stamp out my anxiety. Had to suck in a deep lungful of air when I'd forgotten how to breathe. Broken bones? The least of my worries.

Mase was about to go out there—face the wrath of an unforgiving planet.

Pulse accelerating at the insanity unfolding around us, I turned his way. He didn't budge, even when I crossed my arms and stared at him. He'd entered a calm place where none of the environment penetrated his brain, not the hazardous conditions nor the people.

You could die in this.

I didn't say it. Felt sick in my gut that I'd even thought it.

Not wanting to jinx our first real competition day any further, I followed his lead, staying focused on my tasks by giving him the rundown on the day. "You're in the second heat. With two others."

"Who?"

I scanned down my clipboard, holding down the corners of the paper that tried to whip around in the wind. "Royce and Mateo."

He gave a nod. "They ride clean."

The first rounds in the three-day competition were dedicated to wave riding. After that, came freestyle. The last was racing.

The next hour flew by. Before I knew it, Mase sailed out there in the middle of an oceanic grinder. I stood on the beach, gripping my hands together, hoping Mase would step back onto the beach in one piece.

His first ride? Incredible: clean lines, no crazy tricks. Just surviving that beast earned him a great score.

On his second drop in, he caught air. *Big* air. I gasped as the gust ripped him up into the sky. A camera-crew helicopter swung out then up and angled away to avoid hitting him with their rotor wash.

For several death-defying beats he sailed through the air like a kite on a broken string. Then gravity took over, tumbling him down. He spun out of control—and dropped like a rock.

I yanked my hand from my mouth and raced to the shoreline, staring up at the sky. "Pull up, Mase!" I shouted, doubtful about how he'd recover…but hoping all the same.

A million horrible things crashed into my mind at once. Him landing on the board perpendicular to the water, breaking multiple bones on impact. The board hitting the water at an angle and impaling him. And assuming he survived the four-story fall he was about to take, him getting knocked unconscious or his gear tangling around him, causing him to drown.

The next minutes passed by in a blur. Rescue watercraft towing a yellow Lifesled raced into the maelstrom. Tense eternal seconds later, the watercraft reappeared from the undulating surf, one of the two lifeguards who'd ridden out on it holding Mase's lifeless form up on the sled. They angled at high speed toward the far end of the beach, where the medic tent had been located.

Dozens of people rushed to surround them before I even made it over there, medics, race officials, spectators…I couldn't tell. All I remembered was pushing my way through, trying to breathe, praying he was still alive.

By the time I made it over there, his eyes had half opened. Blood streamed down his face.

"Mase!"

His gaze seemed unfocused, but he turned toward me. Then his lips twisted into a lopsided smile. "Hey, island girl."

Then he passed out.

Over an hour later, with a stitched gash on his forehead and deep purple bruising on his shoulder, he glanced up when I walked into the tent.

"Damn, Mase. You look like you've been gang jumped."

He bobbed a nod with low grunt, then a winced as his hand shot up to his head. "Feel like it."

"Here, drink this. Only slow sips. They want to make sure you don't have a concussion."

"When can I bail?"

"Anytime you're ready to stand."

He swung his upper body up and twisted, then wobbled backward until his shoulders hit the towel-covered cushioned table. "Maybe not just yet," he muttered. "How'd I do?"

"Decent. Your first ride scored high enough to advance into tomorrow's round."

"Good." He shut his eyes, dropping his head back to the pillow.

My hands began to shake, tears welling in my eyes. "Mase?"

"Yeah…"

When I didn't answer, he cracked open an eye. Then both opened wide and he sat up with a low groan, but he crushed me against him in a strong embrace in spite of his injuries.

"Please don't die out there," I whispered.

I can't lose you.

He tightened his hold on me. "I won't."

I clung to him, holding on to that promise. But I sighed, terrified, knowing firsthand that forces greater than ourselves sometimes took that decision out of our hands.

32
IN PURSUIT OF HAPPINESS

Mase...

Nine days after I'd won my first competition under Makani's sponsorship, Leilani stared at The Liberty Bell, a piece of American history that I'd seen a million times: as a boy on fieldtrips, with Deke and my father when good ole pops got philosophical and wanted to impart wisdom on his preordained eldest son.

Her eyes narrowed at the bell.

"Don't like it?"

"It's not my liberty."

"No, I guess not." The United States had fought, bled, and died to break free of the tyranny and oppression of the British. Hawai'i had been a sovereign nation then, a kingdom unto its own. Until a hundred years later, when we decided they were too wild, needed to be tamed…civilized. Governed.

Her gaze remained locked on the crack in the bronze bell.

"Why did you insist on coming here, then?" We'd already been to Constitution Hall and the Benjamin Franklin Museum.

"I wanted to understand you, where you come from."

I nodded at the bell. "This isn't me."

"Isn't it? Your beliefs are shaped by the things you're taught. Just like mine are."

"Are they so different? Your beliefs? Mine?"

"How could they be the same? The political system is broken, rigged to line the pockets of the powerful. The ones who get elected are those who lie the best, shout the loudest, shock the most. Those same types of greedy businessmen stole our land from us."

"So make a difference."

She scoffed. "I'm no politician."

"Lead by example, then. What I'm doing."

"Surfing?"

I shook my head. "Living humbly. Being kind and giving."

"But how does that change anything?"

"That's the thing." I'd been giving the topic a lot of thought lately. "Everyone thinks their mark to change the world has to be big, heard it all my life: 'Make a splash,' 'Hit 'em with a game changer.' People in power want one gigantic atomic bomb whose blast vibrates the whole world. But they've got it all wrong. It's *too* big."

Her gaze drifted toward the skyscrapers dominating the Philadelphia skyline, toward a spot on the globe where enormous radical ideas had altered the course of our world. She turned and gripped the handrail, letting out a heavy sigh.

I stepped behind her, wrapping my arms around her to warm her chilled skin.

She nestled back into my hold. "All the steel and concrete feels foreign; it's dead."

"*On* the earth," I agreed. "Not *of* it."

"Yeah."

"When I left here, when all I wanted was to be surrounded by nature and those who valued it, I went back home." To a time when two boys found their hearts in the simple gifts the earth offered. "Untouched beach. Wild jungles. Pure water. But accepting the beliefs of those around me, blending into what already exists and contributing what I can is important to me. If we keep that spirit alive one act at a time—with every act we make—we make the world better."

"Are you happy you came?"

I gently rested my chin on her head. "Ask me again tonight."

"Will it be that bad?"

"The party? No. Stick with me and my friends and you'll be fine. My parents? Yeah. It's always bad."

"Do you want to skip it?"

"No. I need this closure. Like you said, I come from here. It shaped me. But instead of molding me into its cold steel and unforgiving concrete, I broke free. Because one of the true things that mattered to me...the person who mattered the most...died."

She turned in my arms. Black eyes stared up at me, glittering with emotion. "Is it hard being here without him?"

"Some. He karate-kicked that bell once in front of my father. Broke his big toe."

"No!" Her hand flew over her mouth. "Did he not like it either?"

"Nah. Just didn't like being trotted around and lectured about his future."

"I get that. Remember when I said I felt like I was living someone else's life? My *makuakane* has heavy expectations of me too. The boys can be as wild as they want, but the girl in the family? Needs to be proper, follow all the rules. Even though all of us were taught to fight for Hawaiian sovereignty above all else. And my desire to travel? Not something he approves of. Who I want to date? Not *my* choice in his eyes. Why I moved in with Makani when I turned eighteen—to give me breathing room."

"Yeah. I get parents and their unreasonable expectations. The pre-med thing? Mostly them. Took me giving it a try, though, to realize it wasn't for me."

Her voice softened. "Doesn't it bother you that your friends are still here?"

"No. They have their own lives. Are passionate about things they have here. And their ties to family are stronger."

"What are you passionate about? What about your parents?" Her brow wrinkled. "Much as some of my family angers me, I can't imagine living without mine."

"*You.* I'm passionate about *you.*" I tugged her into my arms, hoping we'd survive the coming storm. "Family?" The word had been redefined for me. "You'll…see."

33
A WHOLE NEW WORLD

Leilani...

A mong the couples waiting in line ahead of us, and those dripping one by one from stately limousines and low-profile sports cars at the curb, the men wore black tuxedos like Mase. The women? Flowing ankle-length gowns made of soft silks and rippling chiffons in solid but muted hues of silver, buttercream, peach, or lilac.

"You sure I look all right?"

I smoothed nervous hands over Tutu's vintage 1950's dress that I'd admired ever since I was a little *keiki*. Tonight had seemed the perfect first occasion to wear the flirty dress. But I began to doubt myself with its knee-length flaring hemline and tropical dark-green pattern that was brightened by canary-yellow on both its petticoats and gathered low-cut neckline.

Mase slid his hand along my lower back, possessively gripped my hip, then gave a gentle tug, tucking me up against his side. His lips brushed over the top of my ear, his warm breath over my skin dancing goose bumps down my side. "You look good enough to eat."

I blew out a shaky breath, heat tinging my cheeks as I blushed.

Okay, then. Good enough for Mase? All that mattered.

"Mr. Price?" An auburn-haired woman checking the guest list at the door glanced up for a second confirmation from Mase. At his nod, she raised up a hand and waved her fingers in a beckoning motion to a security guard in a black suit just inside the building who gave her a chin-up signal in reply. After leaning toward a similarly dressed companion, he abandoned his inner post to stand beside us.

"This is Senator Price's son."

"And guest," Mase reminded her.

"Yes." She gave me a cursory glance. "And guest. Please escort them in."

Leaning in toward Mase, I whispered, "We need escorts?"

"Depends on who you ask."

"I'm asking you."

"No. We don't need escorts."

Another security member fell in line on the other side of us. We followed the increasing sounds of ragtime music as they led us down the hall and into the entry of a massive ballroom.

I paused at the entrance, taken aback by the opulence of the grand space.

A wall-to-wall sea of crisp white tablecloths held sparkling crystal and gleaming china. Chairs were draped in matching white, with black satin that pinched tight at their waists then curved behind into a big bow. Each table's centerpiece featured tea light candles flickering in glass as they encircled a regal vase; within, a floral arrangement held ivory roses blushed with a hint of pink, arching Phalaenopsis orchids, white with a spattering of coral specks on their petals, and, surrounded by rich emerald leaves, two King White proteas, one spread wide open, the other a snowy bud about to bloom.

Without thinking, I released Mase's hand and drifted over to the bud, stroking the soft protective petals with a sigh, then a wistful smile. A piece of home had traveled almost five thousand miles to say hello.

Hello, I thought back to the beautiful flower.

In the middle of a hectic political scene, with jostling people uttering sweet platitudes meant to disguise caustic ulterior motives that even an islander could detect, a lone flower stood pure, unaffected by it all.

I straightened my shoulders back, tipping my head high. On a steady inhale, I surveyed the room again, filled with a sense of pride and purpose. The bright tropical silk of my vintage dress stood out among the sleek, sedate gowns for a reason. Those women were vipers in disguise. I would be what the proteas represented: purity, grace, a child of 'āina—Hawaiian.

The aloha spirit vibrated through me and I would share that love of earth and family with those around me, regardless of their attire, beliefs, or breeding. Because if Mase and I expected the world to accept us, to invite unity among race, then we needed to accept them as well.

A gentle touch on my forearm made me turn to face a pretty girl with a widening smile. "*Oh. My. God.* You're dress! Where did you get it?"

Shining cherry gloss covered perfect lips. Thick black eyeliner and long lashes framed striking green eyes. Dark red hair had been sleeked back into an impeccable high chignon, even though a few wisps of hair had been teased loose at the crown and nape.

And she wore a vintage halter dress in the same silhouette as mine. Only instead of tropical green with bright yellow accents, hers shimmered a deep satin red with black.

"My grandmother." I grinned, happy to find a kindred spirit, in fashion if nothing else. "She wore it to her high school prom."

"It's to die for." She cocked her head, reaching for the hem. "May I?"

I glanced at Mase, who wore a huge grin. "Sure."

With care, she pulled the hem up a few inches, revealing more of the yellow petticoats. "I *knew* we should've gone louder."

"You're the one who wanted to dress conservative for 'business' respectability. I had to give, you had to give." A tall man appeared beside her. And although he wore a black tuxedo, the lapels were a shinier satin and trimmed entirely in silver-braided piping.

I couldn't tear my gaze from his head. Shaved clean on

both sides up to the top of his head, inky black hair stood on end, two inches out from his scalp.

The man caught my stare and smirked as he ran his fingers over the top, brushing the ends. "Taming down the clothes, yes. The Mohawk? No."

When he shook his head, metal piercings in his eyebrow, ears, and nose glinted even in the dim candlelight.

Mase wrapped an arm around my shoulder, then tilted his head down toward mine. "Don't let these two scare you. They're good friends of mine. Chloe and Daniel own and run a sinful bakery. I'm guessing Sweet Dreams is supplying this shindig?"

"You bet your ass, we are." Daniel gave a Mohawk-bouncing nod. "Figure we can get everyone high on sugar, hook 'em into booking more events with Invitation Only, and keeping everyone in the black."

"Guys, this is my girlfriend, Leilani."

"Girlfriend?" Chloe stretched out her arms, then gave me a gentle hip-bump. I shot Mase an amused look but grinned and hip-bumped her back as Mase fought a smile.

"Girlfriend!" A brunette with bright blue eyes whirled in beside Chloe, then gave me a gentle hug. "Mase, you holding out on us?"

Mase laughed. "Never from you, Kiki. Leilani, this is one of Cade's three sisters."

Kiki wrapped an arm around Chloe's waist and her other around mine. "C'mon, new girlfriend. We've got primping going on in the bathroom with Kendall, Kristen, and Hannah; we'll introduce you."

Panicked, because I'd never run off with girls I'd just met, I usually hung out with guys, and I'd never primped in my life, I blinked and stared over my shoulder as Kiki and Chloe dragged me away.

Mase waved me on with his fingers and mouthed, *"Go. You'll be fine."*

Says him.

I'd also never been thrust into a mostly *white* world.

Who was the haole *now?*

34
WHEN NOTHING AND EVERYTHING CHANGES

Mase...

On a hard breath, I prayed Leilani would relax and enjoy herself.

With Chloe and Kiki? She was in good hands.

But my island girl had looked very fish-out-of-water in the shark-infested crowd. Not all those from my old world saw beyond a person's skin. Most in tonight's country-club crowd had preconceived notions of class. But in the end, only a few in attendance mattered to me.

And Leilani could take care of herself.

Me? Well, the night was young and I hadn't bumped into my parents yet...

Without giving another thought down that catastrophic memory lane, I veered toward the packed bar at the far end of the room.

"Well, what do ya' know?" I murmured, lips kicking up in a grin as I closed the last few feet. My two best friends in the world were manning the drinks, Ben behind the bar, Cade warming a stool on the end; each held a half-full beer.

"Hey, fuckers." I knuckle bumped them. "How's Philly hangin'?"

"Same ole, same ole." Cade gave a one-shoulder shrug, like life was no big deal.

Ben almost choked out a mouthful of beer, swallowed, then snorted. "Fucking liar."

He turned around, grabbed another beer from the bar fridge, then popped the cap before sliding it over.

I caught it with a nod in thanks, before staring at Cade. He glared at Ben.

"He's sleep deprived." Ben gave a knuckle-bump to a third bartender who stepped in behind the bar before she began hustling to handle orders.

I frowned, confused. "Doesn't that come *after* the baby?"

"Not when his wife's up puking all hours of the night."

"Isn't it called *morning* sickness?" Cade grumbled, before taking a long pull off his beer. "Apparently Hannah didn't get the memo."

I thought about restless nights of my own. "You know what else doesn't only happen in the morning? Roosters crowing. Damn birds screech twice as much at night."

Cade stared at me. "Dude. You moved to the beach, but you sound like a farmer."

"Damn straight." I gave a short nod. "I live in Mediterranean-climate Upcountry; got a ten-by-twenty garden and second one I'm clearing. And my twelve girls will give me fresh eggs every morning."

"Sounds awesome," Ben said.

"So when are you heathens going to come visit?"

Ben nodded toward the lucrative bar, what his business provided to Invitation Only events. "Hey, I'm just a workin' Joe. Don't have the money to be flyin' halfway around the world."

"What about you?" I glanced at Cade who downed the last of his beer. "You're obscenely rich."

"Not anytime soon."

"Another beer?" Ben asked.

"Make it a scotch." Cade sighed, then glanced at me. "No way I'm making Hannah suffer through travel like that. And doc says could be a good couple of months before the queasiness dies down."

Ben arched his brows. "By then she'll be what? Eight months? She may not want to get into a swimsuit at all."

"Maybe..." Cade's expression went unfocused. He was either deep in thought or sleeping with his eyes open. Then he glanced toward the doors at the front of the hall, as if looking for the subject of our discussion.

No one stood in the vicinity but a dozen or so constituents, smiling their fake smiles, whispering, and nodding. Wielding power and bartering favors, no doubt.

Seconds later, my parents walked in.

My pulse kicked up.

I took a slow, deep breath, narrowed my eyes, and forced myself not to react.

"Catch you guys later?" I stood from the stool, downing the rest of my beer.

Cade turned, stared in the direction that held my attention, then gave a nod. "Yeah, man. We'll be here." *Translation: We've got your back.*

They always did. None of us fit into the typical country-club mold. We'd chafed at the rules, the entitlement of those who belonged. From kids, we'd always yearned to break away from the gilded paths our parents had intended for us. Was never meant for us. Had always fit wrong from the start. Restless independent souls, we needed to blaze our own trails.

Cade had. A couple years older than me, he'd graduated business school with honors. Before he had graduated, he'd already created a successful bar, Loading Zone, then had sold it to run one of the largest companies in the world. He'd also formed the wildly successful event-planning company, Invitation Only, with his sisters. But when his future with Hannah had been on the line, he'd traded in the corporate world to start a boutique restaurant and bar.

Ben was well on his way; He'd bought out Cade's interest in Loading Zone, planned to expand into other locations.

Then there was me.

Figuring out what road to travel.

I stared hard at the one obstacle that had tried to bar my way to discovering my own destiny. Two people who'd only had kids to further their cause, to carry on their legacy. They'd tried to direct me, reason with me, bribe me, and ultimately threaten me. But I would've had to care about what they were offering…or taking away…for it to control me.

All it did was push me closer to the edge of leaping off the cliff without a parachute.

Why the hell am I here again?

Oh, right. Supporting friends. The Michaelson's, Cade, Kristen, Kendall, and Kiki. Plus Ben, Chloe, and Daniel. They were throwing the bash. And it meant something to them to please their client: Senator and Mrs. Price. The couple of the hour.

I sized them up as I crossed the room.

"Perfectly coifed," My mother would say and used the phrase often enough when getting ready for parties for me to know she'd achieved her goal. Not a platinum-blond hair out of place, upswept and pinned with a sparkling clip. A flowing white gown portrayed the appearance of innocence. It was also cold, devoid of life.

My father wore his standard conservative tuxedo. Black tie. Crisp white shirt. The stiff attire suited him; I'd never seen him fidget or tug his tie. Not once.

They wore their uniforms like the soldiers of fortune they were.

Me? I'd caved and wore a white dress shirt, gray silk tie, and cashmere pants. I slid my hand into the pockets as I approached, counting the minutes until I could put on a T-shirt and jeans again.

Anxiety welled up from deep within my gut. The kind that churned to life when a kid trudged a grim march toward the principal's office. Same kind of situation. Appearing before the authority to be judged. Ready to be deemed unworthy.

On a hard sigh, I shook my head and blew off all the mental anguish.

I don't care what they think. What I kept telling myself. If only my self-lecture would stick. Because it clearly hadn't. Not all the way. I wouldn't be here if it had.

"Mason." My father refused to call me Mase.

"Father." Civil and cold right back at ya.

"Couldn't be bothered to wear a tux?" My mother's perfect manicured left eyebrow arched in judgment. "You know we're being watched."

"You're being judged, you mean." Donors only supported those who had great election odds. "Be lucky I'm not wearing a Tommy Bahama tropical shirt and flip-flops."

"Watch your tone, son."

"*Son*? What a joke," I muttered.

My father got up in my grill. At six-foot-three, he had a couple of inches on me.

I rolled my eyes up to meet his gaze.

"I'm not above having security escort you out."

"Oh, really?" I snorted at the image in my head. "Sure you've thought that through? Me shouting about how abusive you are. How racist. Hmmm..." I turned and scrubbed a hand over my mouth in thought as I assessed the hundred plus donors carrying on conversations but casting curious glances our way. Because we looked like a family dressed for the cover of any magazine, yet anyone with eyes could see the tension between us. "I wonder if your bigotry will garner you more votes, not less. Discussed it with your campaign manager?"

"*Enough.*" My mother's cutting word broke through our pissing match.

We both turned to stare at her.

"We're here for your father. I wanted you to be here."

"For *him.*" I wanted to clarify the private plea she'd made to Kristen, not to me.

"Of course." She sniffed and raised her nose. Then she wielded a practiced smile at their adoring crowd.

Right. Not because she missed her son. Or wanted to make amends.

Thank God Leilani hadn't been with me to witness my parents' cruelty.

Done with our charade of the "good family," nervous energy made my legs bounce. Cade had left the bar, probably to find Hannah. Ben worked double-time with the other two bartenders to handle the throng of thirsty patrons wanting to get drunk on an open bar.

They weren't who I really wanted to be with right at that moment, anyway.

I took a step to the side and glanced down the hall toward the restrooms.

And there she was. Surrounded by people who loved me, the *real* me. One arm looped in Kiki's and the other in Chloe's. Behind them, Kristen and Kendall flanked Hannah. Daniel, Cade, and Kristen's husband, Jason, brought up the rear, guarding the flock of beauties.

The women wore bright dresses and glowing smiles.

But my breath caught as Leilani's gaze locked on to mine.

Her smile widened. And I swear my heart stuttered.

In two quick strides, I closed the distance.

Chloe and Kiki released her, right as I spun her into my arms. I nodded at Hannah, Kristen, and Kendall as they passed. "Ladies. Great to see you. Looking beautiful, as always."

When the gang walked out of earshot, I tucked Leilani against the wall behind a potted spiral of greenery. "*Fuck*, I missed you," I murmured against her mouth. After a relieved sigh, I kissed her more thoroughly.

"*Mase*," she whispered fiercely, eyes glittering. "I've got that word echoing in my head while you're doing scandalous things to my mouth."

"*What* word?"

"The *f*-word."

"You've said the word before." I turned my chin, narrowing my eyes at her with a skeptical look.

"No, I haven't." Her expression grew somber.

"Yeah, ya have." I specifically remember her mouthing *What the fuck?* and saying various other random profanities.

"Well, I try not to. It's something I've been working on this past year."

"Really?"

"For sure. My *makuahine* didn't like profanity. She taught me to carry my words with care and grace, for pride of self, love of language, and sharing the aloha spirit."

In that instant, all anger at my parents and their failings faded away.

At least she'd had someone love her. And I would endure everything all over again for her to always have that.

"You know, I would've liked your mom."

Happiness instantly beamed on her face, in the sparkle in her eyes, her wide easy smile.

"She would've loved you."

"Really?" I held up my hand to hers. "I don' *knowww…*" I teased. "He be lookin' like one pale *haole.*"

"*Ahhh*, but dat sexayyy boy's my *haole.*"

Speaking of parents who cared, the glare of the narcissistic quieted all conversation in the hall. Leilani even glanced up and shivered, as if my kind permeated the air with a level of frost.

And they kinda did.

"C'mon. That's my parents. Let's get this over with," I grumbled.

With a nod, she clasped her hand in mine, then tugged me forward. "It'll be okay."

But she said the reassuring words on a stiff exhale, as if mustering her courage. And when she glanced at me, jaw set with determination, her brow wrinkled slightly with worry.

I didn't like her doubting herself. Or her being concerned about anything. She was out of her element because of me. And it was up to me to make it right, make her feel safe.

I squeezed her hand. "Yeah, it will."

It had to be.

35
IF YOU LOVE SOMEONE...

Leilani...

No wonder Mase's parents got to him. They looked chiseled in stone.

Nothing about them was approachable. They shined like packaged merchandise and neither one smiled. When they managed to tear their scrutinizing gazes from me, they glared at their son.

On a deep breath, I pulled my shoulders back, lifted my chin to meet their hard stares, and held my head high, unafraid to own who I was the way *Makuahine* taught me.

"Mother, Father, this is Leilani, my girlfriend."

His father sighed heavily, then swept a second obligatory glance at me, scanning my body from head to toe, pure contempt in his expression. His mother only bothered with a split-second look at my face, lifting one corner of her upper lip, before she shot Mase a harsh glare.

"Mase." His mother nodded, pursing her lips tightly. "We'll see you inside." They turned, offering us their backs as they walked into a sparkling ballroom filled with energy.

"I'm not invisible, right?"

"No." He wrapped his arm around me, pressing a kiss to my temple.

"And I don't stink?"

He snorted, then gave me an incredulous look. "You do *not* stink."

"Could've fooled me the way your mom curled her lip."

"Do *not* care what they think. I've spent my whole life trying to ignore them."

Trying. Not flat-out ignoring. Which meant they got to him; he cared what they thought. Just like no matter how unjustified *Makuakane's* and Koa's and Holokai's hateful actions and beliefs were, I cared what my father and brothers thought.

"N'kay."

"And I happen to think you smell amazing." He buried his nose into my hair as he slid his arm around me, guiding us forward into the room. "Like flowers."

"Plumeria."

"Fucking *love* plumeria," he growled low, over my ear.

I fought a smile, nudging closer into his side. "There you go with the swearing again."

"Does it make you blush?" He pulled back a few inches, never releasing his hold, and dropped a provocative stare at my cleavage, causing my breaths to quicken. Then he drifted his gaze up my neck, pausing at my lips before his eyes met mine. His lips curved with a smug smile.

"Yes." Face heating, I hid it against his neck, inhaled his masculine scent, then pressed a gentle kiss there. "You know it does."

"Then prepare yourself, Lani." He turned, touched a finger under my chin until I glanced up at him, then gave me a sensual kiss. "I plan to swear up a storm just to see your cheeks pink up."

For those brief seconds, the rest of the world vanished. Only he and I existed, warm skin, shallow breaths, rapid heartbeats, and his protective arms wrapped around me.

But the moment our kiss broke apart, Kiki, Chloe, and Daniel rushed in around us, guiding us toward a table on the far side of the room. "Break it up, lovebirds." Kiki shot Mase a pointed look, raising one brow. "No R-rated activities in the main room."

Mase coughed out a laugh, glancing around. "Kristen put you up to that?"

"I'm only protecting you. Mama Hen has her hands full keeping Cade behaved at parties. Kristen will skin you alive if you step out of line too."

Chloe tugged on Kiki's hair, then stepped between Mase and me. "What Kiki meant was there are designated R-rated zones. Behind potted plants, in supply closets…"

Daniel roped an arm around Mase's shoulder. "In the coatroom: down the hallway, third door on the left…even has a lock."

Chloe rolled her eyes. "Not that you've checked it out."

"Hey." Daniel waggled his brows, his silver piercings glinting in the light. "You never know."

We all gathered around then took seats at a table set for ten. Mase and me, Cade and Hannah, Jason and Kristen, Kendall, Kiki, Daniel and Chloe.

"Where's Darren?" Mase asked, then he leaned close, murmuring, "Kiki's new boyfriend."

"In New York with Logan," Kiki replied with a wistful smile, then she glanced at me. "Logan is Darren's younger sister. They're at a string quartet performance at Carnegie Hall."

"What?" Mase dramatically thumped a hand on the table. "And I missed that scintillating entertainment?"

"Hey." Kendall tapped a knife on the side of her water glass, ringing a chime out. "Entertainment's at this table, buddy. The balloons? They're all Kiki."

"Hey!" Kiki discretly tossed an herbed roll at her sister. But it tumbled short, landing with a wobble on the edge of Kendall's salad plate. "I'll have you know a lot of thought went into those balloons. Republican red."

Kendall rolled her eyes. "Real imaginative."

"I pushed for white and blue. *Hellooo*, patriotic."

"Or at least some silver." Chloe chimed in. "Jazz it up."

"Let me guess." Mase leveled a stare toward his parents who'd taken their seats on a raised dais at the front of the room.

"Yep." Kiki gave a nod. "Team Price vetoed it."

"Along with a stellar cake." Hannah shook her head. "Chloe and Daniel went to a lot of trouble making those Capital Hill sketches."

"No sweat." Daniel shrugged. "They want a basic sheet cake for four thousand dollars? Basic sheet cake it is."

"Psshhh." Chloe waved a dismissive hand, settling back in her chair. "Nothing about that cake is basic."

"Flat, then." Daniel gave one of his hard Mohawk-bobbing nods. "It's definitely flat."

Kiki nudged my arm. "Hannah started a bakery that Chloe and Daniel took over. They're genius artisans with cake."

"My Maestro designed and made an eleven-foot dragon cake once." Cade lifted Hannah's hand and kissed her knuckles. She brightened at the loving touch.

On instinct, I leaned further into Mase's side, nestling under the arm he'd loosely draped over my chair. His fingers had been absently drawing small circles over my shoulder, but he stopped just then and gave my shoulder a possessive squeeze.

In those short minutes after the coldness of his parents had faded away, my heart warmed. The people present at the table were Mase's real family. The ones who mattered to him most.

Quick banter continued to fire back and forth across the table all through dinner. Mase, Cade, and Jason talked baseball for a while. Hannah squealed when the baby gave a sound kick, and Kiki, Kristen, and Kendall all surrounded her.

I smiled at Hannah's coddling friends.

'Ohana.

In the East-coast home Mase had left, even at a function

meant for parents who didn't give him the affection or respect he deserved, he was still surrounded by loving family.

"Okay, boys and girls." Kristen stood from beside Hannah's chair, then glanced at her watch. "Duty calls. The best events don't run themselves."

Folding my napkin on the table, I stood, then leaned toward Mase, whispering, "I gotta make *shishi.*"

"What-she?" Confusion wrinkled his brow a split second before a glint sparked in his eye.

"*Shishi.* I have to pee."

"Oh." His expression fell. "I thought it was code for coatroom."

I shook my head on a soft laugh, then kissed his cheek. "Be right back."

After spending time with the girls in there earlier, I knew exactly where to go: down the corridor and off to the right. Even though no one sat on the beige couch or chairs in the sitting room, my thoughts buzzed with fondness of the few minutes earlier when I'd met the girls, laughter echoing off the walls.

While I was in the stall, a distant low thump sounded: the main bathroom door closing. When I came out, all five bathroom stalls were angled slightly open, empty.

Only my reflection appeared in the mirror above the three white marble sinks, and I smiled. Tutu's dress made me feel beautiful and loved, as if I'd brought her there with me. My hair fell straight to my shoulders, and the only makeup I wore was mascara on my lashes and clear gloss on my lips. *Makuahine, I wish you could see me now.* Her little orchid, had blossomed into a woman.

"It won't matter."

I gasped and spun around. Mase's mom stood in the waiting area.

"Mrs. Price?"

"Nothing you do will make a difference. You are not the kind of girl we approve of." Glaring at me, she crossed her arms. "You will *never* be good enough for him."

I winced at her cutting words. A tight band constricted around my chest. Unable to breathe, I pushed past her. Mase's father stood right outside the door. When I spun around, his wife joined him. They stood side by side, united against me... the girl not from their world.

Mr. Price's chin raised. "You need to end things with our son."

The same judgment had come from my family toward Mase. Yet his parents didn't know me, didn't understand my heart. They didn't even care enough about their child to want to try. Just like my father with Mase and me.

I hesitated, wanted to say something—anything to stand up for myself, for Mase, for our love. My lips parted, an explanation about Mase's true passion hovering on the tip of my tongue.

Mr. Price's eyes narrowed. "If you don't end it now, he *will* be cut off." Steel edged every word. "He'll have no choice but to drag his ass back here."

My heart shot up into my throat at the dire warning. Until that point, I hadn't realized they had that kind of control over Mase. But now the reason why Mase had said that he hadn't needed my brother's sponsorship money made sense.

Tears sprang to my eyes, then I whirled away from his parents.

I rushed down the carpeted hall, unable to breathe. The suffocating hold of Mase's city, too many calculating people, and his cruel and ruthless parents choked the air from my lungs.

Gasping for breath, almost about to pass out, I paused and gripped the doorframe that led into the ballroom. With great concentration, I focused to suck air in, expel it out.

*In…Out…*None of it fresh and pure, the perfumed air was tainted with lies and motives.

Desperate to find something to ground me, give me balance before I collapsed to be trampled under the crushing weight of the place, I scanned the tables, searching for him.

Mase, where are you?

On the far side of the room, he sat at the table, right where I'd left him.

At that moment, his head tipped back in laughter, raw happiness emanating from him. All his friends had gathered closer to him. Even Ben, who'd swung by the table to introduce himself while we'd been eating dinner earlier, had abandoned the bar and grabbed a seat beside him. Mase clapped his shoulder, leaned in, then said something that made Ben nod.

Panicked, I took a closer look around the ballroom. All the men wore suits or tuxes. The women, extravagant dresses, glittering diamonds. The tables were adorned with flash. The carpets, ornate and plush. The walls, pristine.

And in the middle of the opulence sat Mase, relaxed back in his chair—genuinely happy. He was surrounded by those who loved him. No matter what he'd said, he belonged in the world around him.

He fit.

I didn't.

He'd said he didn't want to be there, believed himself destined for a more simple life. But it didn't look it. And he needed the money his world provided. Would he be happy with *none* of it? Without it, could he be free?

His parents had implied that he wouldn't survive if they cut him off.

I'd thought they'd meant money.

But what had they really threatened to cut him off from? From his friends? The only family he'd ever known? Would his parents turn them against him? Did they have that kind of power?

Or had *they meant money?*

I'd witnessed much on Maui. Hawaiians hated big-business *haoles* stealing their way of life. Yet many succumbed, working for those same corporations to be able to eat and clothe themselves.

The lure of money was great when you had none.

Take away friends and money and what did anyone have left?

No matter what Mase said about not needing money, I'd never seen him without. And even though he'd begun to fit into my world…nothing compared to the wealth in front of me.

The family surrounding Mase at the table were filled with love for him. They'd grown up with him, been there for him in good and bad times from grade school on. I had that 'ohana in Tutu and Makani...but also with *Makuakane* and Koa and Holokai. No matter how bad things got, my own blood would always be there for me. I knew that in my heart.

"Champagne, miss?"

A waiter stepped into my view. He held up a crystal glass with white-gloved hands.

Barring my way into the room, into Mase's world, stood centuries of privilege, generations of societal expectation... decades of strong friendship. His parents had no right to take that away.

But I began to think they could—that his choosing me over them would make them try.

I have no right take your 'ohana *away from you either.*

But oh, how I wanted to. No better than the rest of them, I wanted to steal Mase away from them, keep him as my own. Tears welling in my eyes, I shut them, and drew in a shaky breath.

"Mase, I need you." But the whisper never made it into the room. My needs were secondary. My wants? Inconsequential.

"Let him go, little one..." As I stood there fighting for breath, *Makuahine's* advice shimmered into my mind, along with a distant memory:

I opened my hand, let the beautiful gecko back into the garden from which he'd come.

"He only knows his home. Wouldn't do well cooped up in our house. He will find others of his own kind. That's where he'll be happiest."

"He wouldn't be happy with me?"

"Let him go, Lani..."

Makuahine hadn't answered my question back then. Because there hadn't been a good one to give.

When I opened my eyes, tears formed anew, blurring my view of Mase.

Swallowing past the choking cramp in my throat, I blinked and took one last clear look. Then I whispered out what I'd known on some level all along. "I have to let you go."

36
TAKING A STAND

Mase…

"What did you do?" My roar echoed from the front of the ballroom. And I didn't care who overheard.

"Not a thing." My mother sniffed with disdain.

My father gave me a stern look. "She's not right for you, son."

In other words: They'd told her so. At some point, behind my back, they'd decided to take matters into their own blackened hands. Leilani had never returned from the bathroom. After a twenty-five minute search by the troops, we'd confirmed with the door security that she'd left.

My gut churned. Them even speaking to her and thoughts of how she would've reacted, sickened me. "*Don't* call me 'son.' Neither of you have earned the right. You can't just slap a label on me. Family is earned from the heart, not

338

entitled by blood. And the woman you so coldheartedly dismissed is righter for me than you've ever been."

"You *are* my son," my father snarled, harsh tone more possessionary than loving. "And you need to give up this ridiculous 'journey' you're on. You belong here. With us."

"Why do I belong here? Because it's good for your campaign? Perfect optics for the media? Bet it'll poll well with all your cherished white middle-class voters. Obedient 'son' standing by his father's side. Said son going to medical school to be a world-class surgeon."

His lips curled into a smug smile. "Works for me."

"Not for me. News flash, *Father*: You don't get to play God with my life."

"I wish to fucking God Deacon was still alive," he grumbled, scrubbing a hand over his face.

"Yeah, well me too. Deke knew me, better than anyone. Better than you ever will."

He glared at me. "Deacon knew his place."

"Deke knew his heart. Big difference. Lucky for you, he had a natural gift for politics. But you didn't bother getting to know him well enough to see he excelled in *everything* he did. And enjoyed it because he thrived on charming others by simply being himself—generous and kindhearted. Not manipulative and controlling."

My father crossed his arms. "You'll stay here."

"Or what?"

"Or we'll cut you off."

I coughed out a laugh. "Where's the machete? I'll save you the trouble and do it myself."

"Machete?" My mother frowned. "You've been stuck in the jungle too long. It's affected your brain."

"No. I haven't. I've never understood things more clearly in my life."

My mother began to breathe heavily, worry flashing over her face. She clasped her hand into my father's.

His jaw clenched. "You'll never survive on your own."

They knew they were losing the battle. But not one ounce of me gave a damn for their pitiful feelings. I spread my arms wide. "Take a good hard look, folks. *Already have been.*"

Twenty hours later, I flew over the Pacific.

I hadn't slept. Couldn't eat.

Everything had changed.

Life had deadened.

And the world wouldn't come alive for me again until Leilani brightened it.

My phone calls had gone to her voicemail, with no reply from her. Countless texts had gone unanswered. She hadn't left a note. She'd simply vanished, had fled to where she felt safe.

Eventually, I'd called Makani. He'd heard from her. She'd already caught the first flight available to LAX with a connecting flight to Maui.

Determined to right the wrong, to win her back, I'd caught the next flight out.

And on the plane, I'd wrestled with what I'd done…or

hadn't done. Should I have foreseen her being confronted? Had I left her alone for too long? Why hadn't I escorted her?

In the end, the glaring mistake finally hit me: I'd gone there in the first place.

My parents, and others like them, ruled the world I'd come from. Always had.

Did I have ties there beyond my parents? Friends who I considered family? Sure.

But even those closest to me played by society's rules. They accepted the social classes, the hierarchy, the structure meant to protect those that "have" from the "have nots"—at all costs.

I didn't. Simple as that.

Not like I flew a democratic flag either. Nor socialist. I flew my own flag of independence.

And no matter how pale my skin was, I had more in common with Leilani and Hawaiians than I did with anyone else. All I wanted? To live a simple life, live off the land.

No political games. No manipulation.

What kind of world would we have if instead of putting a priority on *taking*, everyone decided to *give*? *A great one.*

I stared out the tiny window of the plane. Stuck in a metal tube. Thousands of miles above the surface. The higher you go, the greater perspective you have? *Bullshit.*

Life existed with hands and feet covered in dirt and sand. The power of that life? Water.

Only those who revered all of that, who lived in it, touching it, efficiently using while protecting it, had discovered the true meaning of life. And I wanted to be among them.

Leilani wanted that. She wanted to wander the globe, but to connect with others like her. Not those who valued only the dollar and whose passions were fueled by greed.

Like me, she wanted to be of and for our earth. And more than that, more than anything on the planet, I wanted her.

How do I get her to see that? Believe it?

I had to show her that we fit together—we belonged together.

And although no other place on earth connected with me like her island did—with its generous people, the vibrant land, waves carved from my dreams—Maui hadn't become my home...*she* had.

The jet touched down with an uneventful vibration, then taxied to the gate. My truck stood in the space I'd left it, up front near the crosswalks. A too-slow drive to Upcountry to grab what I needed cleared my head but buzzed nervous energy through my veins.

On the way back down the mountain, during what felt like the longest drive of my life, doubt crept in...

Would she listen to me?

Had her father and brothers gotten too deep in her head? Had my parents?

Couldn't we tell the whole world to go fuck itself and only focus on each other?

Does she love me enough to? My lungs froze, then I forced out a slow exhale.

Yeah, she does—all I would allow myself to believe.

And as I drove with undeterred purpose, along a winding road through towering eucalyptus and vine-covered signs,

I forced my fears out of my head and focused on the only thing in my control.

I loved *her* enough.

We couldn't care what anyone else thought. No matter the risks, we had to give it a try with all we had. Nothing else would do.

Screw racial prejudice on both sides. All of it—every last biased thought, cutting word, and violent action—had been born of ignorance and fear.

No more fear.

I'd had enough. Had begun my journey away from that concrete jungle, sickened by the shallow-mindedness of greed and hatred. The rest of my life began with my next step. And with every breath, I grew more determined never to look back.

"It wasn't a mistake," I whispered, suddenly less angered and more relieved that Philly had played out the way it had. Leilani had helped me learn a valuable lesson: Where I'd come from had played a vital role in shaping who I'd already become. And facing my past hadn't only been cathartic, it had helped me grow, had solidified in my heart and mind what—and who—I wanted most in the world.

But the eye-opening trip had greatly upset the one person who I wanted most, the one meant for me, the only person on earth who got me on an elemental level.

I needed to right that inadvertent wrong. Hoped I hadn't fucked it up too badly.

The thought that maybe I'd caused irreparable damage— by not stopping her from leaving, by not protecting her in the first place—constricted my chest. I fought for oxygen as I pulled behind Makani's board shop and shoved the truck into park.

Trying to steady my breaths as I walked toward the front of the building, I focused on the only other thing that calmed me: waves. Over and over they tumbled in, coming home, fulfilling their destiny.

I imagined Leilani on an eight-footer. An instant later, all I could picture was me riding a perfect glassy wall beside her—with her—connected to the waves, to the earth. That oneness with ʻāina resided in our bones; it defined us.

But for two lost souls, our rare connectedness hadn't just grounded us, it had made us a part of each other. Which was why I hurt so badly—because she hurt.

Choking cramp in my throat, heavy weight on my chest, I pushed the door open to her brother's shop. "It isn't too late," I bit out under my breath. It couldn't be. My hopeful words were drowned out by the deafening buzz of a board sander.

When I pressed the buzzer on the front counter, the sander powered down. Makani appeared from the back room, pulling his mask down and goggles up. "*Howzit*?"

"Shitty." But he knew that; I could see it in his eyes. "Where is she?"

"Not wantin' to see you, *brah*."

"I know." I forced out a breath. "Gotta straighten things out with her."

He gave a nod of solid agreement. But instead of answering my question, he pulled his mask and goggles back

344

on. He powered up the sander again, blocking me out.

Defeated, I turned around and stood in the doorway. Staring at the ocean, I wondered where she'd go. Her favorite spot at La Pérouse? No. She wouldn't want to torture herself with memories of our first date.

Ahead, to the left and right, stretched crowded north shore beaches. She wouldn't be there.

All of a sudden, the sander shut off, right when it hit me: where she'd go.

He reappeared in the doorway. "She's where you're not welcome."

Of course. Under the protection of her people. Where she wouldn't have to see me, face what we'd done—handle what we'd become.

"You know I'm going there, right?"

"Yeah." His tone sounded grim. "You got a death wish."

"Maybe."

But the time had come to put every *maybe* to rest. I had to take a stand in a big way, prove what I was made of.

Leilani needed to know what I believed: *Her people are my people.* If not on the outside, to the bone on the inside. No piece of dirt or anything on it belonged to *any*one. It all belonged to *every*one.

And if she wanted—if I was lucky enough—she would want to belong to me. Seemed only fair. She already had me, heart and soul.

Took a torturous hour to get there. The sun had already clocked into midafternoon, steaming the earth. Windows down with my vintage A/C on the fritz, the wind brought in both much-needed breeze and biting mosquitos; little fuckers chewed my ankles like corn-on-the-cob.

But I didn't care what it took. Would drag my ass for days in a hellish swamp if I had to.

A hundred feet after I drove past the mile-marker I remembered, I pulled in behind a dozen cars. Which likely meant couple dozen locals. Or more.

Common-sense alarm bells fired off at the danger. But I did a gut check: took note of it, then ignored every instinct screaming to turn back. Adrenaline's flight-or-fight drug fired through my veins. But I ignored the flight, embraced the fight. On her turf. My way.

I grabbed my board from the back.

A few paces down the dirt shoulder, I ducked under the overgrown vines that hid the only access. Negotiating down the slippery slope, I worked my way along the narrow path well-worn by the locals who watched over their secret bay.

And then it opened up, revealing what I stood up against.

Ten guys sat in chairs on the sand. Two manned a makeshift barbeque. A dozen surfers sat on boards in the lineup. Only one woman floated among them.

"Fucking *haole*!" The alarm sounded out from a beach-chair guy.

The rest stood as a unit as I stepped onto the sand. Aggression curled their shoulders. Hate etched into their deepening scowls. Leilani's other two brothers, Koa and Holokai, were there, stink-eyeing me with the rest.

"*Boddah you, haole!* Go home!" Ke'eaumoku, her wanna-be boyfriend, led the pack.

"I *am* home."

Battle not with the Hawaiian gauntlet blocking my way, I shouted out. "Lani!"

Her head snapped my direction. I couldn't make out her expression, only her forceful headshake. She didn't want me there. Because she didn't want me? Or because of the danger?

I planted my board in the sand, taking a stand. But with her brothers—by blood and race—about to pummel me, I needed to step up the program. Ignoring the threat of meaty fists quickly closing the remaining few yards of distance, I abandoned my board and veered straight toward the shoreline. "I'm here! I am here—for you. And I'm not going anywhere."

"How you *figgah*?" A shove at my shoulder had me stumble into a retreating wave. "You goin' six feet undah."

The lineup had come to rapid life, all speed-stroking toward shore to catch the fight.

Lani rode an incoming wave, along with two of her brethren. The pair gave her space for safety, but all her attention zeroed in on me.

A sudden blow to my right kidney knocked the wind out of my lungs. But I refused to react. I wasn't there to fight them. And I wouldn't throw even one punch.

I sucked in a determined breath. "Lani!" She needed to know. In the next seconds of my life, before it was over, she needed to know how I felt. Even if I died trying to tell her.

"I love you!" The wave crashed, collapsing in on itself, but I made sure my words rose above the chaos. A punch hit my head from the side. Black dots fuzzed in, but I fought to stay standing, stumbling between two Samoan-built bodies that partially blocked my view of her.

She leapt from her board the moment the nose skidded over sand.

"I am here. For you," I repeated.

A hard punch landed into my ribs. Bone cracked, fiery pain flared.

"Stop!" she screamed as she ran toward me.

Our eyes locked as I fell to my knees. Hers were filled with terror. Mine teared up with love. "Not going anywhere," I bit out through the pain as my vision began to fuzz.

When she got within reach, a muscled arm clotheslined her, sweeping her off her feet. *Koa.* She slapped and scratched at her brother, kicking and flailing in his arms. "Don't kill him! Please! *Leave him alone!*"

A kick to my back. Pain exploded up my spine.

Her form blurred as sobs racked her body. "I love you too, Mase. I love you too!"

Struggling for breath, as my awareness faded, I clung to her words, to what I'd hoped for—what I'd known.

I know you do, Lani.

37
WHAT DO YOU BELIEVE IN?

Mase...

An incessant beep droned rhythmically.

My head throbbed.

Every muscle ached.

Throat bone dry, I tried to swallow. Then I choked out a ragged cough.

Excruciating pain exploded up both sides of my ribs.

"*Fuck*," I bit out. Then coughed. Then winced in more pain.

When I tried to open my eyes, tightness burned across swollen skin on my eyelids. I managed to lift one a crack, nothing more. Monitors glowed green on a contraption over my shoulder. When I lifted an aching arm, a prick of pain pinched the back of my hand. IV lines stuck out from my skin, led to a bag hung from a metal stand.

Hazy memories hovered on the fringes of my mind. A sharp punch to my kidney. A punishing kick to my ribs. Again. And again.

"Finally. You're awake." *Father.* His terse words were laced with judgment, as if I'd been sleeping in too late—instead of recovering from a near-fatal beating.

"What are you doing here?" I rasped. More agonizing coughing followed.

"Trying to make sure you're not dead."

"Not dead." Could've fooled me, though—clearly I'd woken up in hell.

"Got water?" *And a few minutes to catch up?*

"Ice chips." *Mother.* A low clinking sounded to my right.

With my good hand I reached out, a rigid plastic cup pressed into my palm a second later. Trying to ignore why they would be in my room…in a hospital—thousands of miles away from everything they held sacred, dead center in a world they sneered at with contempt—I tipped the cup to my face. Wet coldness hit my lips, my chin. A few chips made it into my mouth. Half of it fell onto my chest.

I sucked on the bits of ice, trying to get some moisture into my throat. "Why are you here?" I hoped to God *here* still meant Maui, that they hadn't kidnapped me.

"We're taking you back with us," my mother replied, tone matter-of-fact.

Good. Still on the island. Somewhere near Leilani. "No, you're not."

"We'll see about that, son." Father's voice held its usual layer of threat.

"No, you won't. And don't call me 'son,'" I insisted again. "*Son* is someone you love, not a pawn in your political game."

My brain started screaming inside of my skull, every heartbeat a lancing stab. "Where's the nurse's button?" I huffed out through shortened breaths.

"What do you need?" My mother's voice drew near, hovering over my face.

"The nurse."

Seconds later, I heard a door open. "What can I do for ya, Mr. Price?" Lyrical tones held a distinctive Southern accent.

"My son needs you," my mother replied.

"I was *addressin'* yer son."

Stern. *Good.* "Need them to…leave," I bit out through gritted teeth. "Head…killing me. Got…meds?"

"Out." The nurse's warning tone came from near the foot of my bed.

"But," my mother argued, "we have a right to—"

"You heard the man. Out! He's the boss."

After a silent pause, my father's leather-soled shoes shuffled while my mother's heels clicked. "We'll be back to finish this," he ground out. Had to get the last word in, veiled as a threat: the Senator's MO.

Moments later, the hum of a motor sounded as my shoulders began to slant upward, the top of the bed raising. "Here ya go, Mr. Price."

"Mase," I corrected. The other sounded too much like my old man.

"Mase." She placed a cup in my hand and gently lifted. Through my slitted eye, I made out a bendy straw. She lifted a small paper cup containing two white tablets and tipped it to my lips. I cracked my mouth open enough to let the meds tumble inside. "These are Vicodin. Should knock yer pain right out."

aka: knock me out.

But with the level of pain screaming through every cell in my body, I didn't argue.

I sucked in a mouthful of water, downing the wide tablets on a forceful swallow. Then I took another swig to coat my throat before she stole the cup away.

"Anyone else been by?" I asked before she left.

Her voice came from farther away, near the door. "Pretty young thang, volcano of attitude?"

I huffed out a laugh. Then I winced as pain exploded up one side of my face, across my ribs. Holding my breath for a few beats, I tried to ignore the pain, then blew out a slow breath. "Yeah, that's her. Leilani."

"Oh, she's been by our station. More'n once. Yer parents sent her away."

"Any way we can bring her back?"

"Sure thang, sweet cheeks." The door whooshed.

I waited as the rhythmic beeping continued, the only sound remaining.

Beep...

So weird my parents had flown out. They never came for anything, not anything good.

Beep...

And Leilani had come.

Beep...

Through the fog of painkillers taking hold, I wondered how long I'd been unconscious. How bad it had to be that family who'd never bothered to show an ounce of support or care in my life had dropped every carefully scheduled political and social event to come to my aid.

Beep…

My head grew too heavy to hold upright, and I tipped it back onto the pillow. An odd crinkle sounded, like paper getting crunched in the pillow or maybe it was the sleeve of a hospital gown. But when I turned my cheek, cotton. I rubbed my fingers on the bed: cotton. Maybe the sound came from a crushed tag. The drugs had to be affecting my brain already.

"*Mase…*"

My one eye could barely crack open. It shut a split second later. But I felt the warmth of her fingers on my arm.

"Lani, I…" *love you.*

In the far reaches of my mind, I heard her soothing voice. But I couldn't make out the words.

When I awoke again, the beeping continued.

My eyes opened easier this time.

Annnd my parents sat on a couch on the other side of the room.

I sighed. "I want you both to leave. Not just this room. Hawai'i. Go back home."

My father arched a brow at me. "And you're staying?"

"Yes."

He snorted. "Why? So they can beat you to a pulp again?"

"You're no different."

"Watch your tone." He tilted his head an inch downward in the way he often did, glaring at me from under his brows.

"You mean my words? Truth hurts, doesn't it?"

"What truth?" Even in my mother's whispered tone, I heard her confusion, the denial.

They truly had no idea what they'd done: narcissists to the core.

"I took harder blows from you—only yours were verbal. They cut far deeper."

His nostrils flared, but he didn't argue. Hard to dispute fact.

"At least Leilani's brothers are fighting *for* something, protecting what they believe in. I just got in the way. What are you fighting for? What do you believe in? Sure as hell isn't me."

Shock registered on his face. "*That girl's* brothers did this?"

Some of them. Not all. And none in their right mind. The reason was greater than me. I got that. But the man in the room with me was worse. He couldn't see the problem— even though I practically held up a mirror and it stared him in the face.

"Her brothers didn't do this," I finally replied. "No *person* did this. Oppression did."

On a deep breath, pain speared into my chest. I winced, but gritted my teeth, worked my way through a full inhale, a slow exhale, then kept going. Because I had to get it all out.

"And 'that girl' is my *girlfriend*. And her name is Leilani." I kept my tone low and calm. But my words held the weight of an entire lifetime of frustration of being viewed as unworthy.

Father crossed his arms, staring at me, incredulous.

Mother sat down, but still looked at me. Tears began to glitter in her eyes. *Good.* About time one of them felt the gravity of the situation.

I grabbed the cup from my table, then swallowed a sip of water from melted ice chips before I glanced back at them. "And until you take a hard look at who you are and what you do, you'll never be any different than any other angry bully. In fact, you're not only the problem, you're worse."

"I've heard enough." He leveled that glare at me again. "Too much sun has fried your brain. You're coming home with us."

I snorted. Pain flared, in my ribs, up my face. But I still smiled through it. Damn shit was all kinds of funny. "Why? To live a lie? So you can pretend to your constituents that you have a whole family? Well, got news for you, Dear Ole Dad. Your family is broken. And you swung the sledgehammer."

Rage widened his eyes, clenched his jaw. "*Claire.*"

My mother stood, blinked away burgeoning tears, then pressed to his side. *Like a dog heeling to its master.*

I'd never realized until that moment that she might've had a different point of view once.

But then she spoke with steel hardening her tone, with no one forcing her. "If you don't come home, we're cutting you off."

I almost laughed. They thought they could control me with money.

"I don't need my trust fund."

"Since when?" He rolled his eyes, actually had the balls to disrespect me at the exact moment they thought they had me.

"Since always."

Disbelief washed the harshness from their expressions. She shook her head. "From the moment you turned eighteen, you've been withdrawing money from the account."

I shrugged with my one good shoulder. "Automatic transfers to an account in my name alone, money I've never touched. Money you can never control."

"But how have you supported yourself?"

"With jobs. Two and three, to begin with. But you never bothered to ask what I did with my time before I moved out. You probably didn't even notice I'd been gone before I moved in with Cade." Even then, I'd made sure the construction jobs I took more than covered my expenses.

"So leave," I repeated. "You have no hold on me. You began to lose your grip when you gave all your love to your other son. Was it even love, then? Did you even love Deke? Or was it simply that he was cursed enough to be the first son. And he fit into your definition of the ideal family perfectly."

Both of them visibly changed, features hardening in outrage at my cold accusations, faces reddening, chests rising and falling with shorter breaths.

"Did you think I wouldn't notice? The son you forgot? The one you never wanted."

"Enough!" A barked order from the patriarch.

"Is it? I guess it is. You only want to hear what gets you

elected. All you care about is power and praise from all the minions gullible enough to believe your lies."

"*Enough.*" The snarled whisper made it through peeled-back lips. A vein on his forehead pulsed, threatening to explode.

"Yeah. We're done." Satisfied I'd made my point, I pressed the nurse's button.

When the nurse entered the room, I stared for a beat at my parents' outraged expressions, then nodded toward the door. "Out."

The nurse glanced at me. "They causin' you grief, honey?"

"No." The absence of emotion surprised me, but then, my parents had sucked that well dry long ago. The glaring void crystalized my thoughts on the matter, though. "Not anymore."

In a way, the beating I'd taken on the outside had dealt the final death blow to the suffering I'd endured on the inside. Because all of their anger was temporary and none of it had really been about me—it had been about them.

What mattered to me? An island girl I wanted to share my love with.

"I've got just the thang for ya." The nurse disappeared before I could stop her; I didn't want my mind numbed with drugs again.

Dropping my head back, my eyes drifted shut as my thoughts shifted to Leilani. The sweet scent of plumeria soon followed.

"Mase?"

My eyes blinked open to the most beautiful sight: Lani's

smile. I reached my hand toward her. "*Heyyy…*"

"I just saw your parents leave."

"They tip over any medical equipment on the way out?"

"No. Your dad had a tight grip on your mom's arm. And they stormed down the hall. Punched the elevator button three times so hard all the nurses popped their heads up to watch."

"C'mere." She stood too far away. "I need to touch you."

Hesitation washed over her face, but she took slow steps toward me until she reached the middle of the bed. Standing her ground there, she squared her shoulders, then rested her hand on the edge of the bed, inches from mine. "Why were they so upset?"

I pulled in a slow breath, then reached my fingers out. Inches became a hairsbreadth. Without lifting my hand, I could reach her. But her shortened breaths stopped me.

My heart ached to make things right with her, but I could wait. As long as it took, for her to be okay with us, I *would* wait. "Because they couldn't herd their black sheep home."

"They wanted you home?" Her dark slender brows furrowed deeply. "Isn't that what you've always wanted from them?"

"No." Not even close. "All my life, I wanted them to accept me for who I am. Love me. Funny thing about love; it has to come from a place of selflessness. My parents? Not a chance. And all they care about is themselves."

Her head tilted a little. "But didn't they come out here? Doesn't that say something?"

"Yeah. They cared about themselves *a lot*. My near-death experience looks bad to their campaign. Me out here 'cavorting with the natives' is bad enough. But to get the shit kicked out of me in front of national media?" —I nodded toward the stack on the end of the couch, front-page news articles the nurses had brought at my request— "Smudges their pristine family name. Their empire is at stake."

"Oh," she glanced over her shoulder at the stack, understanding washing over her features.

The more I shared, the hotter the anger boiled in my gut. Families weren't supposed to use their kids as pawns in political chess games. "They cut me off," I grumped.

Her attention snapped back toward me. "Cut you off?"

"My inheritance. The trust fund."

"Can they do that?" Her breaths grew choppy. "Isn't the money yours?"

"My grandparents put the money there, but since they've died, my parents control it. In a few minutes, I'm sure they'll transfer the money out and leave nothing."

"But…" Worry creased her brow. "Will you be okay?"

"Hey, I'm a scrapper. Nothing beats me down."

"No, seriously. Makani offered you that sponsorship money. I don't need it."

"Yeah, you do."

"No, really, I don'—" Her protest faltered as she stared at the hand I'd just put over hers. Turned out my patience had a limit when it came to her.

"That's your money, Leilani. I want you to have it. And I want you to keep working with me." *Because I want you. I need you.*

She pulled her hand out from under mine, gripped the white blanket draping over the edge. "But you can't afford it."

"I'll be okay."

"How?"

Her concern made me smile. "You my accountant now?"

"Somebody has to be."

Fine. No biggie. She wanted to know my financial status? I wanted her on my team. Disclosure wouldn't be the end of the world. Maybe it needed to happen to start my new one. "When I turned eighteen, I was able to withdraw monthly amounts. I stashed it all away into a bank account."

"Enough to live off of?"

I considered the obscene cost of living on Maui. Then I estimated the amount of bank I'd collected. "For a little while. Couple years, three maybe." Then what would I do? Better to try and make it on my own before I drained it dry. "But I don't think I'm gonna touch it."

"What will you do?"

"After I finish remodeling my house, I'll see if anyone else needs any construction work for decent pay. But…I'm thinking about learning more about herbs and studying to practice alternative medicine, like I've always wanted to do. Keep the chickens healthy with it…maybe work my way up to people."

"Mase, I'm sorry. I'm so sorry I left you back in Philadelphia. You looked so happy with your friends and…your parents threatened to hurt you. I thought I was protecting you by stepping away." Her eyes welled up with tears. "I didn't want you to get hurt."

Her gaze traveled over my battered body, and she pulled in a shaky breath.

"You can't fight my battles for me. And I don't want you to."

"Mase…I…" Her fingers stretched out as if to touch me, but then she clenched her hand into a fist. "I can't see you get hurt again. You could've died out there. What were you thinking?"

"That I'd rather die with you knowing that I loved you than pull in another breath with that ever in doubt."

"How 'bout you don't die at all?"

"You know there're no guarantees." I thought of Deke, of her mom. "We both know that. But if we're not living life for the incredible moments, what are we living it for?"

"You can't go back out there. My brothers, those *kanaks*, they'll do the same thing…or worse."

"We can't live in fear of hate, Lani. We have to rise above it. If we don't, how can they?"

"You're starting to sound like Makani."

"Wise man." I stared hard at her. "Will you? Will you rise above it *with* me?"

"I want to. I just…I can't lose you. I cannot love you with all my heart" —her breath caught— "then lose you."

"I'm not going anywhere. I'm here with you—for us. All you have to decide is where you want to be with it all."

Through all the fear she had, she gave me a nod. It wasn't an agreement; I got that. From the moment I met her, she'd been struggling with all of it.

I only hoped that after she took whatever time she needed, that where she wanted to be—was with me.

38
THE TRUTH ABOUT BLOODLINES

Leilani...

Two weeks had passed since Mase had lain there all beat to hell in that hospital bed.

Two weeks more than I needed to know what I wanted.

But there were other things that had to be figured out. And arrangements had to be made before I could move forward—before I'd ever feel comfortable taking the risk.

When we pulled up to Hoʻokipa, I spotted Mase's truck, Halia, backed into a space in the lower lot. We parked a few spaces down and walked up the sidewalk.

Mase had the tailgate down, was chillin' in the back, watching the surfers in the lineup.

"Hey, *howzit*," I called out to him, giving him fair warning as we approached.

He glanced our way, surprise registering on his face. His eyes widened when he looked over my shoulder, at the rest of the crew I'd brought.

"Hey." Mase gave a chin-up, expression wary. "*Howzit.*"

"My guys have something they want to say to you."

"Hey, *brah.*" Koa started. When he hesitated, I nudged him. "Leilani say she like you. An' is gonna be wit' choo. An' say if we don' like dat, we not her bruddahs no mo'. So...I guess, if yo' good 'nuff fo' her, yo' good 'nuff fo' me."

Mase just stared at him.

"You guess?" I asked Koa, crossing my arms.

"Nah. Yo' good 'nuff." Koa sighed. "Sorry, *brah.* I nevah shoulda hit you. It'll nevah happen again."

I nodded. Damn right it wouldn't.

Holokai stepped forward, offering Mase his hand. "Sorry, *brah.* Shit got outta hand. We got yo' back now."

Mase took a deep breath, then reached his left arm out, taking Holokai's hand. I noticed his right arm tucked close to his side. His eyes still had dark purple bruising toward the outer bones but all the swelling had disappeared.

"Mahalo, guys. That means a lot."

Proud of my brothers, how far they'd come, I nodded. "*Makuakane* would've been here, but he's still coming around to the idea of you."

Koa laughed. "He hate you, *brah.*"

Holokai punched Koa so hard, he stumbled sideways into the metal railing. "He hate what we did ta ya mo'."

"Hey," I nudged through my brothers. "My turn. You *kanaks* go. I'm fine." I pushed them back down the sidewalk.

I glanced at Mase.

He had the oddest expression on his face. "You did that…for me?"

"Yeah." I toed the back tire, then glanced back up at him. "For us. I need to protect you. Only way I can be with you."

"I'm proud of you."

The wind whipped my hair across my face, and I glanced down toward the beach. "Wanna go for a walk?"

"Sure." He leaned his good hand on the tailgate, then stood, stepping onto the sidewalk.

I slipped my hand into his as we walked. He gave it a light squeeze, but said nothing.

When we hit the sand, I kicked off my *slippahs*, feeling the sand between my toes as the wind sprayed ocean mist over our faces. I took a deep breath, both excited and a little terrified. "Offer still open to work with you?"

He shot me a deadpan look. "I can't believe you just asked that."

"Right. *Sooo*…I definitely want to keep working with you."

"Good."

We walked ten more steps before I found my voice again. "I'm still scared to death that I'm going to lose you."

He tugged at my hand, stopping.

Still holding tight to him, I turned to face him.

A gorgeous man stared back at me: messy blond hair, ice-blue eyes, rugged stubble covering a strong jawline. "In order to lose me, you have to *have* me first."

"Yeah. I guess I do."

His lips quirked up into a smirk. "So will you have me, Leilani Kealoha?"

"Ummm…right." I took another deep breath. "Could we get everything out in the open before you decide?"

"Before *I* decide?"

"Yeah. On whether or not *you'll* have *me*."

"*Okaaay*…" He tilted his head, narrowing his eyes a little.

"Stop trying to figure me out. I'm telling you already."

"*All* your secrets?"

"Two. Don't push it, surfer boy. I've decided on two."

He laughed. "Okay. I'm listening."

"Remember how I owed Makani a favor? Why I had to go and recruit you in the first place?"

"Why do I feel like I owe Makani big for that?"

"You listenin' or talkin'?"

"Sorry. Listening."

"Yeah. So, after I went grad, we had a big beach party. The police came out. While they were busy keeping the peace, I kinda…went for a joy ride."

"With one of their cars?"

"No…with one of their ATVs. Got it stuck down in a gulch and had to abandon it there."

Mase fought a smile. "You *are* a little criminal."

"Yeah. Not exactly. I called Makani. He knew *Makuakane* would kill me if he found out I'd done that. Then kill me all over again when he'd found out I'd done it drunk. So Makani came out and rescued me."

"Wait. That police officer that came out to my house…"

I nodded. "Kanaloa."

"Was he there?"

"Yeah. He drove up right as Makani was helping me hike up the steepest part, back onto the road. Makani immediately took the blame for it. But Kanaloa had been on the beach earlier and accused me, even though he had no proof. With Makani's confession, he had no choice but to accept his statement and charge him for the theft and damage."

"Ahhh…" Mase pulled me into his arms, wincing a little when I collided into his side. "You did owe him big. I was wondering what could possibly be enough to send you chasing me across the Pacific."

"Yeah. But he'd have taken it to his grave anyway. He's protective like that."

"So that's one secret. What's the other?"

I tugged out of his hold, pulling him forward, walking down the beach again. "Remember when you were guessing on fishing lodges?"

"Yeah. Inuit…Viking…"

"Australian…"

He laughed. "I think that's my favorite. I want an Australian fishing lodge."

"So did I. When you said that, it made me not want to have the one I already own. I like your dreams. Never really fit in with the reality I've been born into."

"I'm not following. What lodge do you already own?"

"The house in the jungle on the Big Island? That's my house."

"Your house." His voice flattened.

"Yeah. The paces I counted off at the door to find the

key? I'd done once with Tutu, when I was twelve. The only time I'd been there. Tutu's my *makuahine's makuahine*. But Tutu's *makuakane*? Was British—the only *haole* blood in our family. And he was a lord with a vast amount of wealth. Other than Tutu, I'm his only remaining female descendant."

"Sooo…what are you saying, Lani?"

"That I have a little *haole* blood too. And…that Tutu has lived a very good life off of her inheritance. But she's already given me all she owns."

"So you've got money?"

"Yeah."

"Sooo…enough to live off of?"

I smiled. He'd thrown my question back at me. "Couple years, three maybe. Times a hundred…give or take."

His eyes widened. "And you took my sponsorship money?"

I shrugged. "You insisted."

"So I guess we only have one more obstacle."

My gut clenched. Because making light of everything was easy. Reality was the hard part. "Right. Do we want to fight for us? Do we want to take on the challenges of your family, of mine, of everyone else who doesn't approve of my skin color—"

He nodded. "—or mine."

I stared out at the ocean, finding courage in the unknown, in the unexpected possibilities out there. "A very wise surfing magazine once said 'Life begins at the end of your comfort zone'—"

"Which magazine?"

"*SurfGirl*, why?"

"I'm sending them a personal thank you note."

"Why?"

"Because, that's actually awesome." He released my hand, then walked to the smooth hardened sand just inside of the high tide mark. He bent down, sank a finger into the sand, then dragged out a three-foot line toward the ocean. Standing back up, he dusted his hand over his thigh twice, knocking off damp clumps of grit. "I've heard that before. That's where adventure lies too."

I nodded toward his line. "What's that?"

"The end of your comfort zone."

The rugged mark, etched only an inch deep, would be washed away with the very first wave of the next high tide. Even now, the wind caught the tiny individual grains, eroding it.

"It's all that stands between us." Expression stone-cold serious, a hint of excitement sparked in his eyes. A dare, even.

Step across the line. The voice in my head wasn't *Makuahine's.* It was my own.

Without doubt, willing to fight for him, for us, no matter the risk, I took the step.

The last time he'd walked onto a beach, for me, he'd risked his life. And had almost lost it. To simply tell me he loved me.

I could do no less. Would forever do more. I gently slid my arms around his waist, gazing into his eyes with no more fear. "*You* are my adventure."

He enfolded me in his embrace, happiness sparkling in his eyes. "Good. Because *you* are my life."

EPILOGUE
THE NEXT ADVENTURE...

Mase...

"**B**rrrr..." Leilani shivered. "Explain to me why I'm here again."

The Columbia River Gorge sprawled below us, a wide waterway snaking through a pine-covered canyon that had been formed by millions of years of erosion through the Cascades in the northwestern United States. "You booked the trip. You tell me."

"Adventure."

"Exactly." I pressed a soft kiss to her temple and stared toward the east as the breaking sunrise splashed gold across clouds that edged the horizon. "Where the whole world is waiting for us. Right outside of our comfort zone." *My new favorite place.*

"Forty-five degrees is *not* my comfort zone." With a

belabored sigh, she curved her fingers around a steaming mug of coffee, huddling over it as if it were a campfire.

"Pffft. Try fifty-five."

"No way. Not with that fifteen-mile-an-hour windchill," she grumped.

"We've only been out here ten minutes." Standing on the deck of a Craftsman-style bed-and-breakfast, we'd been the first guests to come down.

"Still." She glared at me over the rim of her mug.

"Mmm-hmm." Wrapping my arms around her, I pulled her away from the wood railing. "But are you having a good time?"

She nestled back against me. "Yeah...this place is *pono*."

"Maybe we should get some sleep." Because we hadn't yet.

After flying into Redmond's municipal airport early yesterday, then enjoying a picturesque breakfast on historic Mirror Pond, we'd wandered along Bend's cobblestone sidewalks, exploring quaint shops and galleries. After a late lunch, we'd driven north, curving around a slightly snow-veined Mount Hood before winding our way down through the lush pastoral hills of the Hood River Valley. Both of us had had trouble keeping our eyes on the road ahead of us, amazed by endless rolling acres of apples and pears hanging from trees.

Darkness had fallen by the time we'd checked into the B-and-B for our first night, but we'd been too excited to sleep. So we'd stripped down, soaped up, rinsed off...then tumbled under the sheets, earning the room's DO NOT DISTURB sign all through the night.

Blowing out a measured breath, I grew lightheaded as images of Lani naked in various positions rushed too much blood southward again. "Sleep. C'mon." I tugged her toward the french doors.

"No." She spun free, put her mug on the railing with a clunk, then stepped back, eyes narrowing. "You're just trying to get into my pants."

"*What* did you just say?" She'd spoken identical words months ago, the afternoon we'd first met. And she'd been just as feisty then—what had drawn me to her in the first place.

A devious smirk curled one corner of her mouth up.

"No."

"Say it again." The moment hit me hard, feeling righter than I'd ever imagined, and I slipped my hand into the pocket of my sweatpants.

Amusement sparking in her eyes, she stared at me like I'd gone nuts. "No."

"*Say it again*," I teased, tone dropping soft and low as I pulled out a black velvet box.

"*No*," she whispered with a heavy blink while I opened its lid.

A shaft of sunlight hit the one-and-a-half-carat round diamond, refracting brilliant rainbows onto the decking around us. Watching her eyes widen and her breaths quicken, I dropped to one knee, offering her the platinum solitaire... along with my heart and soul.

"I sure as hell hope that's with a capital *Y* and a shitload of exclamation points."

On a deep breath, she smiled. "There you go swearing again."

"I'm willing to be reformed."

Her expression fell into a confused frown. "You are?"

Tilting my head in thought, I gave a half-shrug. "Maybe a little."

"No." Brows furrowing, her voice developed a stern bite. "Don't you change one *damn* thing about you, surfer boy."

Relieved at her instant opinion on the matter, I let out a dramatic sigh and pulled the ring from the box. "I'm getting mixed signals down here. Do you want me for the rest of your life, or don't you?" With a pointed look, I arched my brows at her.

"*Yes!*" She extended a trembling left hand.

Rising up, I slid the ring onto her finger, then pulled her in close. Gratitude flowed through me, warming my heart. Then I kissed her with all the passion I felt for her.

When I bent down, crooked an elbow under her knees, and swept her up into my arms, she squealed. After hoisting her higher, I fumbled with the door latch. Then I strode through the small dining room and up the staircase.

She clasped her hands behind my neck. "I *knew* you wanted to get into my pants."

"Actually, you *out* of them."

When we reached the landing, she pressed her face into my neck, then let out a deep breath. "You know this won't ever be easy." Doubt edged her tone.

I paused at our door, then lowered her down. Her hesitant gaze met mine.

Over the summer, everywhere we'd gone, either she'd caught stares or I had. Each time, I'd explained that people couldn't take their eyes off her because of her breathtaking beauty, and when they bothered to look at me, it was because they couldn't figure out how a scruffy guy like me ended up the lucky bastard who got to be with her.

But the occasional heated altercations at the beaches had still happened, even with her brothers' approval—they hadn't gone everywhere with us and we didn't want bodyguards anyway. And with my parents' ambitions, we'd still made headlines: Senator's Son Courts Hawaiian Beauty.

We did our best to ignore it all. Every heckler. Every label. We fought for our happiness by living each day right in that moment—all we could do.

But the doubt in her voice, in her eyes right there in the hallway? Proved we were still human.

With unwavering conviction, I stared into her incredible dark eyes and locked on the clear hope radiating in their depths. "Since when has life every come easy for you or me? To us? *We* will always be worth every bit of the struggle if we keep true to our hearts."

"But my...father?" That she'd changed what she called him—distanced herself with one simple word—hadn't escaped me.

"Your *makuakane* already knows."

She straightened in surprise. "He does?"

"Well, duh. I do things right. I asked him for your hand."

Shocked eyes blinked at me. "What did he say?"

"No."

"And you defied him." She huffed out a laugh.

"Absolutely." I fought a smile. "He followed up his refusal

with all the ways he planned to torture me if any harm ever came to you. In excruciating detail. He mentioned my skin melting off over molten lava and my heart being extracted through my throat by ghostly night marchers."

"Wow." Her expression turned horrified. "That's...*really* bad."

"Nah." I gave her a soft kiss. "Like daughter like father. All I heard in the subtext of his list of threats? His permission." She had proprietary rights to the capital *Y* and exclamation points, but her father's lowercase agreement with a conditional triple dots would work for me.

"Now." I unlocked the door, then crowded her inside the dark entryway before kicking the door shut behind me. "Let's see about getting you out of those pants."

Almost an hour later, we relaxed back under a pile of bedding, plenty warm.

Leilani snuggled up against me. "I *dunnooo*...this feels a lot like my comfort zone."

I draped an arm around her shoulders, hugging her close. Her enchanting scent, plumeria mixed with wild island girl, wafted around me. "Huh." She had a very good point. "We'll have to find our adventure *elsewhere, then...*" My tone turned teasing; it wasn't as if we couldn't find plenty of adventure on our private mattress-playground.

"Out there, somewhere." Her voice slowed, developing a dreamy quality.

I closed my eyes, imagining us on a random beach, staring up at a starry midnight sky. Neither one of us afraid of what the future might hold. In fact, exhilarated by it.

"Across the ocean?" I kissed the top of her head, pulling her tighter against me.

"With you," she murmured.

"*Only way* it's happening." Where I belonged—my home. No matter where our adventures took us.

The barest nod moved against me. She pressed a gentle kiss to my chest, then whispered, "Riding the next wave..."

Want to read more of your favorite characters from
***Rule Breaker*?**

In the **Unbreakable** series, Kiki and Darren's
romance ignites in…
Heartbreaker

Cade and Hannah fall in love in the **No Weddings** series…
No Weddings
One Funeral
Two Bar Mitzvahs
Three Christmases
For Valentine's
(a steamy nightcap novella)

Coming Summer of 2017 in the Unbreakable series…
Lawbreaker

AND

Coming soon in the Highland Legends series…
Born of Mist and Legend

Want a pre-order alert for upcoming books?
Keep informed of new releases by joining their Email
Subscription list:
www.katbastion.com/email-subscription/

One lucky subscriber will win an eBook of their choice
from the backlist AND a $10 gift card each time a pre-order
or new-release announcement is sent.

We promise to email only a handful of times a year to
announce pre-orders and new releases.

Author's Note & Glossary
Hawaiian, Pidgin & Surfing

The Hawaiian and Pidgin languages are beautiful, poetic, and complex. There are also differing opinions on correct spelling and use of the ʻokina (like a backwards apostrophe) and kahakō (line above a vowel) in some Hawaiian words and names. The world of surfing also has its own terminology. We've done our best throughout *Rule Breaker* with words and terms, using artistic license where we felt necessary to be more digestible for smooth reading. Any deviations or errors appearing within the book, including terminology and ʻokina and kahakō use, are ours and ours alone. Below please find a glossary of the Hawaiian, Pidgin, and surfing words and phrases used in *Rule Breaker*:

> **aʻa** (ah-ah): rough, jagged, sharp lava (versus smooth *pahoehoe*, like a parking-lot surface)
> **ʻāina** (EYE-nah): land, earth
> **aloha** (ah-LO-ha): spirit of love, affection, kindness – often used as hello or good-bye
> **ʻass right:** Pidgin for "that's right"
> **auntie** (ANT-tee): an older female, not necessarily related, is a term of respect
> **barrel**: surfing term for the tube, curl of the wave
> **brah**: Pidgin for friend, brother (also bruddah) even if not by blood
> **boddah you**: Pidgin for "Get lost!" or "Wot, you

like start somet'ing?"

bure (bur-AY): a Fijian word for a hut, typically made of wood with a thatched roof

corduroy: surfing term for the image of a line of swells flowing endlessly from the horizon

da kine (da-KYN): noun or verb that can mean anything…like whatchamacallit

drop in, dropping in: surfing term used in *Rule Breaker* to mean the first descent into a wave, a drop-in can also mean when one surfer cuts off another surfer

figgah, figga (FEE-gah): Pidgin for figure, typically used as "How you figgah?", meaning "That makes no sense."

grindz, grinds: Pidgin for food

grom: surfing term for a young surfer

hā (hah): Hawaiian for the breath of life

haole (HOW-lee): white person, non-Hawaiian, foreigner, outsider

honi (HOH-nee): a Polynesian kiss where two people touch foreheads and noses, inhaling simultaneously

howzit (HOW-zit): Pidgin greeting for "How's it hangin'?", "How goes it?", "Hello"…etc.

imu (EE-moo): Hawaiian cooking pit where stones are used to bake food, typically pig

kai (KIE): the ocean, the sea

kanak (kah-NAHK): Hawaiian man typically referred to by a Hawaiian, strong macho man

keiki (KAY-key): child, children

lanai (lah-NIE): porch, patio, veranda

lineup: surfing term for the area in the ocean where surfers wait to catch waves, behind the breaking zone

local: someone born in Hawaii but not of Hawaiian descent

lolo (LOH-loh): crazy, feeble-minded, stupid

mahalo (mah-HAH-low): thank you

makai (mah-KIE): toward the ocean

mana (MAH-nah): spiritual force or power, in *honi*, between two people

mauka (MAU-kah): toward the mountain, inland

makuahine (mah-KOO-a-HEE-nay): mother

makuakane (mah-KOO-a-KAH-nay): father

moʻopuna i ke alo (MOH-oh-POON-ah ee kay AH-low): Hawaiian for beloved grandchild

ʻohana (oh-HAH-nah): family

ʻono (OH-noh): delicious, tasty

paniolo (PA-nee-OH-lo): Hawaiian cowboy

poi (poy): Hawaiian starchy food from the taro root, fermented, baked, and mashed

point break: surfing term for a wave that break perpendicular to a point of land jutting out into the ocean

pono (POH-noh): goodness, righteous, moral, excellence, fitting, proper…and the list of meanings goes on

quiver: surfing term for a group or collection of surfboards

rail: surfing term for the edge of a surfboard

rash guard: surfing term for a tight-fitting polyester shirt to prevent skin irritation from the board

reef break: surfing term for a wave that breaks over seafloor rock or coral

rocker: surfing term for the curve of a surfboard bottom from nose to tail in profile

sailboard: surfing term for a board used in windsurfing

shaka (SHAH-kah): common hand signal with closed hand but raised pinky and thumb, used for many things, as a greeting, "What's up?", "It's cool."…etc.

shishi (SHEE-shee): to pee, urinate

sick: surfing term for wicked cool

slippahs (SLIP-ahs): flip-flops, sandals

stoked: surfing term for exhilarated, excited, buzzing with energy

swell: surfing term for the energy-driven oceanic ripples powered by localized winds or distant storms

talk story, talking story: Pidgin phrase meaning to chitchat or gossip

uncle (un-KOH): an older male, not necessarily related, is a term of respect

went grad: Pidgin for graduated

wot: Pidgin interjection used like "what", typically before a question

ABOUT THE AUTHORS

Kat Bastion won several awards for her bestselling debut novel *Forged in Dreams and Magick*.

Kat and Stone Bastion's bestselling first novel *No Weddings* and the No Weddings series were named Best of 2014 by multiple romance review blogs.

When not defining love and redemption through scribed words, they enjoy spending their time mountain biking and hiking in the beautiful Sonoran Desert of Arizona.

Stay in touch with them on their social media pages:

t @KatBastion
t @StoneBastion
f Kat & Stone Bastion
www.talktotheshoe.com
www.katbastion.com

Keep informed of new releases by joining their Email Subscription list:
www.katbastion.com/email-subscription/
One lucky subscriber will win an eBook of their choice from the backlist AND a $10 gift card each time a pre-order or new-release announcement is sent.

We promise to email only a handful of times a year to announce pre-orders and new releases.

CHARITY SUPPORT AND AWARENESS

Your purchase of *Rule Breaker* helps the victims of human trafficking because a portion of the net proceeds of all Kat and Stone Bastion's books are donated to charities who support them. These charities are creating legislation and prosecuting criminals, rescuing and restoring victims, and raising awareness in the effort to eradicate the tragedy of human trafficking.

Please visit the Charity Support and Awareness page on their website www.katbastion.com and blog www.talktotheshoe.com to learn about some of the organizations they donate to and to find out how you can further support them.

"A single act of kindness is the foundation of many miracles."
~ Kat Bastion, *Utterly Loved*.